VIOLETS ARE BLUE

MIRANDA RIJKS

INKUBATOR
BOOKS

Published by Inkubator Books
www.inkubatorbooks.com

Copyright © 2025 by Miranda Rijks

ISBN (eBook): 978-1-83756-520-7
ISBN (Paperback): 978-1-83756-521-4
ISBN (Hardback): 978-1-83756-522-1

Miranda Rijks has asserted her right to be identified as the author of this work.

CONTENT WARNING

This novel contains sexually explicit scenes.

Please visit Miranda's website for further content warnings.

https://mirandarijks.com/trigger-warnings/

PROLOGUE

What would you do if something really bad happened to you? Would you confront it head-on or bury your head in the sand? Perhaps you'd live in a fog of confusion before working out your next steps. Maybe you'd turn to confidants for help. Or perhaps you're one of those people who takes things in your stride. Honestly, until a few weeks ago, I'd never thought about it. My life has been good, on the whole. Besides, I reckoned I was the resilient type, able to deal with anything.

The truth is, until something dreadful happens to you, you don't know how you'll react. I'm ashamed to say that I froze. I was like the proverbial deer in the headlights. I just let the bad things happen to me, and I didn't fight back. And then I didn't tell anyone. I simply shoved the terrible memory deep down inside myself and pretended everything was normal. I'm no psychologist, but oh my goodness, repression isn't healthy. You might get absorbed in your normal day-to-day life and forget about it for a few hours, except the nightmares haunt you, and tiny little things create triggers that reverberate like shock waves. A song playing in a shop, a woody scent, or the date. In my case, the 7th of every month.

Last night, after about twenty minutes of sleep, I realised I can't go on. I am so, so tired. I need to talk about it. For my own sanity.

It's easier to talk about bad things in a neutral place, so I've chosen my favourite spot in nature. There's a footpath that meanders along the side of the river, with views across the plain to the town beyond, and the hills behind. It's got really overgrown recently, with tall weeds and brambles, probably because most dog walkers avoid coming here. The path gets flooded when the river rises, and in the winter months it's impossibly muddy. There's a bench, one of those 'in memoriam' benches, with the words *Remembering Marjorie Jones, 1932–2005*. I've no idea who Marjorie Jones was, but I like sitting on her bench.

We sit down, side by side, and I explain everything. The only sounds are the quacking of a duck, out of sight, and my hesitant voice.

When I finish talking, I turn to look, to gauge the reaction. And that's when I see it. A glint of metal.

'What's that?' I ask.

This doesn't make sense. Who carries a knife in their jacket pocket? We're in the bucolic countryside, not some perilous urban jungle caught up with rival gangs. We just went for a quiet walk and are having a little heart-to-heart, trying to put things into perspective. But I can't take my eyes off the knife. This isn't a pocketknife used to cut back branches. It's a carving knife with a terrifyingly sharp edge.

With a sickening sense of foreboding, I rise from the bench.

Some moments stretch like elastic. That's what

happened the last time something bad happened to me. Time morphed and spun out so that some seconds felt like hours and others simply disappeared.

'What are you doing?' I edge backwards. My heart begins hammering because I don't recognise the expression. The focus, the piercing hardness of the eyes, the shallowness of breath. And the determination. Something is horribly wrong.

Sunlight glints off the metal, beautiful little bouncing beams. Yet I know that evil can lie behind great beauty.

I stumble, my left wellington boot catching on the root of a tree. I put out my hands, but I fall, my jean-clad knees sinking into the squelching mud. I try to get up, but I'm not quick enough.

'No!' I scream.

For a moment, I don't feel the pain. I just look down and see the redness pumping out of my torso. But then it comes again, and I know that this is no practice run. I have made a terrible mistake, so much greater than the one I thought I'd made. I realise then that I'm going to pay for this mistake. With my life.

CHAPTER ONE

I stand in the doorway of my new house and watch the removal lorry reverse slowly and laboriously back down Violet Lane, its beeps echoing across the old buildings. The narrow road is not designed for modern trucks.

This is it.

I'm finally free and on the cusp of my new life. I stand in the front doorway and place my right palm on the dark wooden beam that runs vertically down the side of the wall. How many hands have touched this, I wonder, noticing for the first time all the tiny crevasses and holes left by ancient creatures and the ravages of time. My new house was built in 1752 or thereabouts. No one can be sure exactly, but the estate agent told me I should visit the town's museum, where they'll be able to tell me more. I haven't had time to do that yet.

A young woman exits an ancient and crooked cottage to the left of the house opposite mine. There's a baby in a sling on her chest, and she smiles at me. 'Welcome to Violet Lane!' she shouts. 'Sorry, I'm in a hurry.' And then her infant starts wailing, and she waves at me distractedly before striding away. I try to dismiss a pang of jealousy and turn quickly to close the door behind me.

There's a small window above my front door, divided into three panels, that throws some light into the narrow hallway. The walls are painted a cherry red, and I'm undecided if I'll keep the colour or change it to something a little less lurid. A single bare bulb hangs down from the centre of the ceiling where the previous owners displayed an ornate glass chandelier. It's just one of the numerous things on my list that I need to sort out.

I'm alone in here, yet I don't feel alone. Perhaps it's the history oozing out of the walls, or the quaintness of a property that is devoid of harsh, modern straight lines. The staircase zigzags up to the first floor, the camber of the steps all wrong; the floorboards creak with age. I walk through to the narrow, galley-type kitchen and switch on the kettle. I've been feeding the removal men with tea and biscuits for the past couple of hours but have forgotten to look after myself. It's time to sit down and take stock. I glance through the open door at the mantelpiece above the working fireplace in the living room. There are several *Welcome To Your New Home* cards, a couple from new neighbours I haven't yet met, the others from friends and family. Nothing from Jacob, though.

My lovely best friend, Jazmin – spelled with a *z* and without an *e* because her mother didn't want her to have an ordinary name – was eager to help with the move. Gently, I turned down her offer. This is the first time I will be living alone for more than a decade, and I reckoned jumping in at the deep end would be best.

Having said that, I couldn't have done the past few years

without Jazmin. When the only conversations I had with my husband, Jacob, turned into screaming matches, and when I found him having sex with his assistant in our marital bed and he told me not to make such a big deal out of it, I grabbed a suitcase and left, heading straight for Jazmin's house. With hindsight, that was a bad idea. It was deemed that I had left the marital home, and by the time I sought the advice of a family law solicitor, I was already on the back foot in the negotiations for our divorce. And being a lawyer myself, I should have known better. But that's the trouble with the law. Emotions get in the way.

It's taken just under three long years to finalise our divorce, for me to get the money I am entitled to, to find and buy a new home. To start again. In the meantime, I've been living in Jazmin and Yves' little annexe, the garden room they built for Yves' elderly mother, who passed away before she could enjoy it. In return, I babysat their two young children, cooked the odd meal, and kept Jazmin company when Yves was away on business. I owe them so much.

As I wait for the kettle to boil, I unpack a box of utensils. I don't have much. Jacob kept our four-bedroom barn conversion along with pretty much everything inside it. I'd lost the energy to fight towards the end, and frankly, all I needed was a fresh start. He paid me off, and I was happy to go. The only things I insisted on keeping were the painting given to me by my artist godmother and the battered leather chair Dad sat on every day.

I pour myself a cup of tea, using the last tea bag in the box. When I was married, using up the last of a foodstuff evoked stress and required planning for restocking. But unlike the isolated country house that Jacob and I shared, I'm now living in a little town with an upmarket grocery store a hundred metres down the road and all the amenities within walking distance. Even my new place of work is just two streets away.

I carry my mug into the living room and sink onto Dad's leather chair, which squeaks with age. There's a pretty little garden at the back of the house, full of mature plants that are overgrown, flower heads drooping and branches curling around each other. I'll have to get into gardening because the cost of a gardener will be an unnecessary expense. That's another thing I've had to accept. A lower salary; the need to keep a careful eye on my money.

The back door that leads out of the house into the garden is open, and I can hear the sounds of my neighbours. The mowing of a lawn, the yells of young children. The scent of a barbecue makes my stomach growl, but I don't move. I luxuriate in the hope of being part of a community and being free to make my own choices. I try not to think about what I have lost: all of those years, and most distressingly of all, the chance to have a family, children of my own.

The doorbell rings, and it startles me. Placing my mug on the ground, I hurry to the door, where a young woman stands holding a large bouquet of flowers.

'You Laila Bowden?' she asks. I've started using my maiden name again, but it's still a jolt to be called that.

'Yes,' I confirm.

'These are for you, then.' She shoves the bouquet towards me.

She's gone before I can thank her. I assume the flowers are from Jazmin, but they're not. They're from Mum. I thought long and hard whether I should move back to the Midlands to be closer to her, but in the end she made the decision for me. 'Your friends and your work are down south,

Laila. It's bad enough having to start again, but doing it where you know no one is completely bonkers. I'll be fine. Your stepdad is a good man, and you don't need to worry about me.'

I followed Mum's advice, which is why I'm living just twelve miles away from my previous home. It also means that I can look after Ludwig, the black Labrador that I fought Jacob for custody. The court awarded me two days per fortnight and two weeks in the summer. It's extremely unfair, especially since I was the one who mostly looked after our dog. But Jacob's new wife, Rosa, is installed in our old house, and she works from home drawing pictures for children's books and apparently loves Ludwig as if he is her own. Consequently it was deemed better for the dog to remain in the familiar. I can't wait until next week when he'll be with me again.

By the time it's dark outside, I have unpacked most of my belongings, and I'm exhausted. After a quick shower in a surprisingly modern bathroom, I collapse onto my bed. The room is small, with just enough space for two narrow bedside tables either side of the bed. At least there's a built-in wardrobe running the full length of one wall. I purchased a slim chest of drawers, which sits opposite the bed, but even so, there's barely room to open them. I don't care. This is all mine, and mine alone. If I want to paint the walls a lurid pink, I can do. I can play whatever music I like at full blast and order take-ins every night if I wish, although on my lower salary, I'll need to be more careful with my money. The freedom brings tears to my eyes. As I drift off to sleep, I hear the delicate notes of a piano somewhere in the distance.

MORNING COMES TOO SOON, and now I'm getting ready for my first day at my new job. I can't be sure if it was a recording that I heard last night or whether someone was actually playing the piano, or perhaps it was fragments of a dream, but either way, the simple melody has earwigged in my brain, and I hum it repeatedly as I get dressed. My smart navy-blue trouser suit may be too formal, but I see my clothes as an external armour, and I need that today.

Ten minutes before 9 a.m. I leave the house. Once again, it's all quiet on Violet Lane, although I notice a large motorbike parked outside number 32, which I don't recall seeing last night.

It's a fine morning, and my shoes clip-clop along the pavement as I make my way to South Gridgley's high street and then turn right, walking past the newsagent's, an upmarket dress shop and a wine bar. Cassel, Everett and Parker is a solicitor's firm situated above an estate agent. I hesitate before ringing the gold buzzer on the door. This is it. My new life.

I press the buzzer, announce my name through the intercom and am immediately let in. My heart is pounding as I walk up the stairs. I didn't think I'd be so scared starting this new job, but now I'm here, I realise how much depends on it. If I lose my job, I won't be able to pay my mortgage. I'm completely alone, financially and every other way. I have to make this work.

'Laila!' William Parker is standing at the top of the stairs, and as soon as I'm level with him, he extends his hand and then grabs mine with both of his, squeezing tightly. 'So good to see you.'

I smile awkwardly. William Parker is my new boss and the sole partner of Cassel, Everett and Parker. Quite who

Everett and Cassel were, I haven't yet found out. He's seventy-two years of age, and if he'd been working in a larger firm such as May, Maclachlan and Thacker, the firm I just left, he likely would have been pushed out at sixty-six. Wearing a grey suit and a pale yellow tie that's seen better days, his mannerisms are spritely, although with a bald head and a wrinkled, leathery face, he looks older than his age.

'Come and meet the team,' he says, striding briskly along a narrow, carpeted corridor towards an open-plan office. I don't have a chance to tell him that I've already met the team. A team that consists of two other solicitors and three support staff, whom he introduced me to when I accepted the job offer. The interior of the office is about as far removed as can be from the shiny, new glass and steel block where I used to work. Here the ceilings are low and beamed, the floor as crooked and creaky as mine at home. There's a slight musty scent, and the air feels warm despite the early hour.

'So, everyone, this is our new hotshot criminal solicitor, Laila Bowden, who has left the heady heights of May, Maclachlan and Thacker. Quite why she's chosen to join us remains a mystery, but we welcome her nevertheless.'

It isn't a mystery. In my interview, I explained to William Parker that I had to leave May, Maclachlan and Thacker due to my divorce and the difficult relationship I have with my ex and senior partner, Jacob May. Perhaps he's forgotten, or perhaps he's just being polite. I smile awkwardly as a couple of the women clap half-heartedly.

'Perhaps you can introduce yourselves individually once Ms Bowden is settled in her office,' he instructs his staff.

'Please call me Laila,' I add.

'Laila it is, then,' William Parker says with a flourish.

One of the other solicitors, Kaitlyn, who wears a bobbly

sweater and looks as if she's in her mid-forties, throws me an awkward smile. She showed me around the offices after my second interview and warned me that William Parker was, as she described it, a little eccentric. She's worked here for a decade as a property specialist and says that the hours suit her, as she can leave to collect her kids from school. I, on the other hand, will be working a full day. If only I were in her position with children.

I stop myself from becoming wistful as I follow William Parker into a small room kitted out with a faux-wood desk, chair and bookshelf across the back wall. There's a sash window that looks out onto the street below. Although the office is small, there's an intimacy to it, and it reminds me of my new home. I think I'll be happy here.

'Debbie is our secretary and manages all the admin, keeping us solicitors on the straight and narrow. If you need anything at all, she's your first port of call. There are a couple of cases that have come in over the weekend that I thought you might get your teeth into. I've left the files on your desk.'

'Perfect,' I say, fingering the pale blue paper folders.

'Jolly good, I'll leave you to it. And welcome to the firm, Laila.'

William Parker closes my door on his way out, which feels strange. I'm used to the hustle and bustle of a busy solicitors practice, and here, it's so quiet. Perhaps it's what I need. A job without too much stress.

THE NEXT FEW days pass quietly. My work is easy, simple criminal cases that require me to attend interviews at the police station, advising individuals caught drunk driving or shoplifting, women brave enough to report domestic abuse or people involved in affray or grievous bodily harm. I knew by moving to this smaller, provincial practice, I wouldn't be exposed to the high-profile murders or criminal investigations that I was assigned to at May, Maclachlan and Thacker, but that's okay. I'm happy at the prospect of an easy life, for now at least. At 4 p.m. on Friday, William Parker gathers up his staff and insists on taking us all out for a drink, to welcome me to 'the gang', as he describes it. It's an awkward affair with a disparate group of people. But he tries hard.

Back at home, there's a small envelope with my name handwritten on the front of it lying on the doormat in the hallway. I pick it up, open it and remove a stiff, white card. It's a handwritten invitation to 'A Violet Lane BBQ' for the following day at 5 p.m. The RSVP is to Phyllis Hallett at number 41 along with her phone number. She's scribbled a PS. 'Please come! Bring a plus one if you have one.' And a PPS. 'Organising this for you so you can meet us all!'

I don't have a plus one. And I don't want to go. And who sends out an invite with so little notice? I consider my response. *Apologies, but I've already got commitments for the weekend.* Except it's a lie. I could go and see Jazmin tomorrow night, but it's really time I give her and Yves a break. I've been in their lives much too long. Perhaps I could go to the cinema or shopping. I'm prevaricating as to what excuse I should use when the doorbell rings. I open the front door to a woman who I'm guessing is in her early seventies, with short grey curly hair, wearing elasticated trousers and a floral, loose-fitting top.

'Laila, isn't it?' She peers at me and extends her hand for me to shake. 'Such a lovely name. I'm Phyllis, and I posted the invitation for the BBQ through your door earlier today.

You will come, won't you? I just wanted to check if you have any special dietary requirements.'

'Oh, thank you,' I say, taken aback to be put on the spot. 'It's very kind of you.'

'Gluten, dairy, vegan?'

'No, no. I eat everything.'

She claps her hands together. 'Marvellous. See you at five tomorrow. Oh, and welcome to Violet Lane.'

And before I can come up with some excuse as to why I can't make it, Phyllis has turned on her heel and is striding across the street to the large house opposite mine.

CHAPTER TWO

On Saturday morning, I wake up late, luxuriating in my new bed. The weather is fine, which is rather annoying because perhaps the barbecue would have been cancelled if it were raining. The day passes quickly as I unpack the remaining boxes, hang up a few pictures and make a start on weeding the overgrown borders in my courtyard garden. By mid-afternoon, I'm weary. I hurry to the local delicatessen and buy a bottle of white wine and box of chocolates to give to Phyllis and then wonder if I should have offered to make some food. Too late for that.

Scurrying back home, I shower and then dither about what to wear, eventually choosing a flowy white and blue summery dress paired with sandals. It's 5 p.m. and time to go, but my feet feel leaden. I should be used to this by now, attending events by myself, except I'm not. Jacob's betrayal hit me so hard, and although some of the wounds are superficially healed, I haven't tested the scars to see whether they'll pop back open. I haven't gone on a single date; I haven't socialised beyond my small familiar group of friends. And even with them, I've been taken aback at the number of times I've been shunned as the singleton divorcee, as if I'm a pariah with the sole motive of stealing other women's husbands. So this afternoon is a big deal, and as this is my new home and I intend to be here for some time, I want to leave a good impression on my neighbours.

I open my front door, balancing the wine and chocolates, and see another couple arrive at Phyllis' house. They're in their forties, I assume, two men, smartly dressed in matching dark jeans and starched shirts.

Phyllis opens her door, and I watch her embrace both men warmly. And then she sees me and beckons me over. There's no going back now. I hurry across the road.

'Laila, let me introduce you to Jamie and Rico. They live at number 33, but they're only here at weekends and holidays.'

I give Phyllis the wine and chocolates and shake the hands of the two men.

'Come in, come in.' Phyllis ushers us into her hallway. Her house is the biggest on Violet Lane. A handsome Georgian property with large, symmetrical windows and a proud, black front door set in walls constructed from grey flint and faded red bricks. The hallway is wide and smells of furniture polish and lilies.

'Go straight through,' she tells us. I follow the two men into a beautifully proportioned living room and through open patio doors into a fabulous garden. It's not overly large, but it's brimming with colour and mature shrubs, with stone paths meandering through the vegetation.

'This is stunning,' I murmur.

'Indeed it is,' Jamie says. 'Rico here did the garden design for Phyllis a couple of years ago. My husband is very talent-ed.' He puts his arm around the waist of the smaller man.

'Hello.'

I turn to see a young woman and then recognise her from the day I moved in. She was leaving her house with a baby strapped to her front.

'I'm Jackie, and I live with my husband, Finn, and our baby, Melanie, in number 43. That's Finn over there.' She points to two men standing by the barbecue, their backs to us. 'Finn's the blond one, and Melanie is asleep in her pram.' There's a tightness to her, in the way she's holding her shoul-ders and how she twiddles her wedding band around and around her ring finger. She's wearing cut-off jean shorts and a bandeau top, which shows off her trim figure. Her black hair falls to her shoulders, and her eyes are covered in dark glasses too big for her small face.

'What can I get you to drink, Laila?' Phyllis interrupts us. 'A glass of bubbly to welcome you to our little part of heaven, perhaps?'

Rico appears at her elbow, holding a bottle of Prosecco and a couple of empty champagne flutes.

'Look how the boys care for me.' She giggles, and I realise that she's already a bit tipsy.

I accept a glass of Prosecco and follow Phyllis further into her garden. It's about three times the size of mine and has views towards the foot of the South Downs, framed by a willow tree on one side and a silver birch on the other.

'I gather from dear William that you're a solicitor and have joined his firm. It's lovely to have a neighbour with both looks and brains.' She peers at me, and I feel ridiculously self-conscious. 'So tell us a little more about yourself, Laila.'

She points to a couple of sun loungers. Phyllis climbs onto one, and I perch on the end of the other.

'Um, I'm living alone now. I'm divorced. I'm originally from the Midlands but have been in Sussex for over ten years. And you? How long have you been here?'

'Goodness. Roy and I have lived here for thirty-one years. He passed away four years ago, and these lovely people couldn't have been kinder to me in my time of need. These days, I spend my time gardening, playing bridge and helping out at various local charities. It's a simple life but a good one.'

A shadow falls over me, and I glance upwards, putting my hand over my eyes to shield them from the sun.

'I hope you're not interrogating our new neighbour too much, Phyllis,' the man says.

As my eyes focus on him, I go very still. He is staring at me with irises the colour of rock pools, biceps straining through his pale blue cotton shirt, dark hair curling at his neckline. He extends his hand towards me, and instinctively I take it. His cool, firm grasp sends a violent electric current up my wrist and arm, shooting straight down to my core. I think he feels it too, because he holds my hand for too long and raises a dark eyebrow.

'I'm Max,' he says eventually, his voice deep and mellow.

Phyllis breaks the magnetic tension by clearing her throat, and Max removes his hand from mine, but his eyes are still fixed to my face, as if they're boring a hole deep into my skull.

'Max is our local hero,' Phyllis says. 'He's a paramedic and swoops to the rescue of any poor damsel in distress, normally on the back of his motorbike.'

At last he looks away, and I realise that my cheeks are

ablaze whilst I'm gripping the stem of my champagne glass so tightly, I might crack it.

'Hardly.' Max laughs, his straight teeth sparkling white. 'I'm only doing my job. It's lovely to meet you, Laila.' He turns then, and I watch him stride back to the barbecue, throwing a tea towel over his shoulder, the muscles in his back rippling through his thin shirt. What a cliché, a voice murmurs in my head.

'Good-looking chap, isn't he?' Phyllis says in too loud a whisper. 'And he's single.'

I cringe inwardly and am relieved when Jamie and Rico stroll over and start chatting about the upcoming village fete and their recent holiday to Thailand.

Finn steps away from the barbecue and walks towards me. 'Hello, Laila. I'm Finn, married to Jackie.' He's holding a plate piled high with a selection of barbecued chicken thighs, burgers and mushrooms. 'Will you have a bit of everything?' He proffers it for Phyllis and me to view.

'It looks delicious,' I say. 'But I'll just have a chicken thigh, thank you.'

'And you, Phyllis?'

'A bit of everything for me, sweetheart.'

Finn turns towards me. 'Welcome to Violet Lane, where you've got the best neighbours in South Gridgley!' His laugh is deep and infectious. With his brush of golden curly hair and wide, smiling eyes, he's also good looking but not quite in Max's league. 'And by the way, if you need any odd jobs doing, I'm your man.'

'Finn is a carpenter by trade,' Phyllis adds. 'Very good with his hands.' She winks at me, and I cringe.

'Do you make furniture?' I ask.

'No, I've got my own business building wood-framed

garden rooms.' He glances over towards Jackie. 'If you'll excuse me, I need to check on Melanie, and then the food will be on its way.'

'Another attractive chap, isn't he?' Phyllis says in much too loud a voice again. 'Jackie is a lucky girl.'

Jamie catches my eye and throws me a wink. I watch Finn walk over to Jackie, who is rocking the pram. I notice him whisper something in her ear, and she turns away from him, her shoulders even tenser than before. It's clearly not a good day for her.

The next hour passes with pleasant chat and delicious food, the salads and accoutrements provided by Phyllis and the barbecued foods by Max. I feel deeply self-conscious. Every time I glance up, Max's eyes are on me, a hint of a smile playing at his lips whenever our eyes meet. Yes, he's a startlingly good-looking man, but there's something more. A deep sexual attraction that I haven't felt in years, perhaps never. It's quite ridiculous, but it feels like he's ripping my clothes off with his gaze, as if there's a shimmering energy between us, yet I can't be sure if it's just me who feels that way.

Occasionally the others also look at Max with expressions of adoration. Even Rico, who spends most of the time with his arm around Jamie, stares at Max with his lips open. It's strange, because Max might be good looking, but I can't imagine him in the pages of a magazine. His forehead is a little too wide, his smile slightly lopsided, and his nose has definitely been broken in the past. Yet he is beautiful, perhaps even more so because of his imperfections. I want to stare at him, drink him in like a stunning picture in a museum, but I don't. In fact, I spend most of the time consciously avoiding looking at him.

The conversation flows around me, stories about people I don't know, tales of holidays and house renovation disasters. These people are comfortable in each other's company, and I feel a total outsider. Jackie is sweet and tries to include me in the conversation while Phyllis continues to interrogate me. Yet I feel awkward. And after ninety minutes or so, we've finished eating, and I stand up.

'Thank you so very much for inviting me,' I say, careful not to look in Max's direction, although I feel the heat of him despite him standing a few feet away. 'I'm very grateful to have landed in such a lovely neighbourhood, and thank you for accepting me.'

'You're not going so soon, are you?' Phyllis' words are slurred now.

'I'm afraid I still have so much unpacking to do, and as I'm working full time, I've only got the weekends to sort the house. I hope next time, when I'm a bit more sorted, you'll all come over to mine.'

'We'd love to,' Finn says.

I say my goodbyes and thank yous, and Phyllis, who is distinctly unsteady on her feet now, sees me out.

Back at home, it's a relief to shut the front door and be met by silence. I walk slowly up my creaking staircase into the bedroom and sit on the side of the bed. They seem a lovely bunch of neighbours, but it's Max's face that I can't banish from my thoughts. My phone pings with a message from Jazmin asking how my weekend has gone, and I spend the next twenty minutes chatting with her.

After a while, I decide to do some food preparation for the week ahead. The freezer is empty, and I've promised myself I'll cook at the weekends so I don't have to do so much when I return from work mid-week. I've got music blaring in the background and quickly lose myself chopping and stirring. When the doorbell rings, I jolt. Wiping my hands on a tea towel, I hurry to the front door and swing it open. Max is standing there, holding a bottle of champagne by its neck.

'Hello, next-door neighbour,' he says, his head tilted to one side, a cheeky grin on his face.

Immediately I feel the blood rush to my head whilst my legs feel weak. I lean against the doorframe. This is ridiculous. I've never felt such an awkward physical reaction to anyone, not even Jacob in our early days.

'I was wondering if you'd like to...' He lets the words peter out as he holds up the bottle.

'Um, I'm sorry. I'm not feeling so well,' I mumble, hoping he can't smell the scent of cooking drifting from the kitchen into the hallway.

'Ah, yes, of course,' he says, taking a step backwards. 'Rather presumptuous of me,' he mutters, and now I wonder whether I see him flush underneath the designer stubble. 'Another time, perhaps?' he asks.

'Another time would be lovely,' I say. But the moment is broken; awkwardness as thick as a black fog of smoke envelops us both.

He nods before turning on his heel and striding down the steps. I shut the door hurriedly, a wave of self-loathing stabbing me. Why am I so awkward? Why did I say no? I groan as I return to the kitchen. No. It was the right call. I can't start a relationship with my next-door neighbour. And then I chastise myself. Who says he wants a relationship? Maybe he's just being nice.

CHAPTER THREE

When you haven't lived alone for more than a decade, the solitude can be daunting. I was worried that every little creak in the night would awaken me, that I'd be fearful of being by myself. Strangely, I haven't felt that way. It's probably because subconsciously I know that if I scream, someone might hear me. At the converted barn where I lived for all those years with Jacob, our only neighbours were sheep. As our marriage broke down, the isolation was devastating. Even when we were together, I felt utterly alone.

It's Sunday morning, and I lounge around drinking tea and reading newspapers on my iPad. I'm aiming to do some more work in the garden, but for now, I'm sitting in my pyjamas on the window seat of my bedroom, the window flung wide open, letting the warm sunshine bathe my face.

There's the sound of a lawnmower starting up, and I glance across my garden into the garden next door. That's when I see him. Max is mowing his lawn. He's topless, wearing jogging bottoms, and the muscles in his back ripple as he pushes the mower. I redden at the thought of my awkwardness last night. Will I ever be able to talk to the man again? As I'm looking at him, noting the dark hairy chest and the broadness of his biceps, he turns. Glancing across towards my house, his eyes lift up and meet my gaze. Oh, the embarrassment. Here I am, my hair tousled, no make-up on, and he's caught me staring at him. He lifts his hand up and waves. I give an awkward wave back, and the moment he turns away, I slip off the window seat into the room. What is it about this man?

As I take a shower, I can't stop myself from imagining his hands on my body, his lips crushing mine, and I have to pinch myself to stop the ridiculous thoughts. I groan. It's been way too long since I had sex, and I have to recognise what this is. A visceral need for physical affection prompted by laying eyes on a good-looking man. 'Ridiculous woman,' I mutter to myself as I scrub myself dry with a scratchy towel, wondering whether I should hunt for my old vibrator. And yet, when I stand in front of the sink, I stare at my face, and although it's the weekend and I normally don't bother with make-up on Sundays, I run mascara over my lashes and dab a little blusher on my cheeks.

I'M in my small garden. A fence set behind mature shrubs conceals me from the neighbours on either side – Max on the right and a kitchen shop with a small concrete car park on the left, which Phyllis told me was empty at the weekends. I spend a couple of hours on my knees, weeding and cutting back overgrown plants whilst listening to an audiobook, blocking out any noise that might come from the neighbours.

When the garden is looking reasonably tidy, I make myself a light lunch and then drag my sole sun lounger into the garden and read a book. It feels good to be in my own pretty space, answerable to no one. I must have dozed off because I'm awoken by a man's voice. It takes a moment for me to realise where I am, to recognise the eyes that are peering over the garden fence.

'Oh,' I say, hurriedly pulling my sundress down over my knees, running my fingers through my hair.

'I'm so sorry if I woke you,' Max says.

I wonder if he's standing on a ladder, because only his head is visible. 'I didn't mean to disturb you. I just wanted to check that you're feeling better.'

'Um, yes, I am. Thank you.' Well, this is embarrassing.

'I was wondering if you'd like to...' A bottle of champagne appears up in the air. 'I really don't want to drink it by myself, and you are my neighbour.' He grins at me, and something about his smile makes my stomach flip.

I hesitate for so many reasons. I don't know this man. Firstly, he's my neighbour, and the last thing I want is things to get any more uncomfortable than they already are. Secondly, I have to work tomorrow. And thirdly, just by looking at me, he sends electric charges through my body.

'Pretty please?' He tilts his head to one side.

I groan. 'Alright then. One glass because I've got to be up early tomorrow.'

'One glass it is. Come over to mine. There's no way through the gardens unless you want to climb over the fence, so would you mind coming in through the front door?'

'Sure. Give me five minutes,' I say, jumping up and hurrying into the house.

Why did I say five minutes? It's not long enough to take another shower or to sort out my hair and make-up. But then I chastise myself. This is not a date, I don't want to impress him, and I certainly don't want anything to happen other than a neighbourly chat. After a quick brush of my hair and swiping on some berry-coloured lipstick, I grab my keys and phone and walk out my front door. It's all quiet on Violet Lane, so I walk down my steps and up the steps of number 32. Before I can ring the bell, the door swings open.

'Come in, come in,' Max says, ushering me inside quickly as if we were on some clandestine mission. He is wearing pale beige chinos and a white shirt with the sleeves rolled up to reveal bronzed arms covered in dark hair. He sports a gold watch that catches the light.

His house is similar to mine, the same age, but the ceilings are a little higher, and the place seems more neutral somehow. I notice that there aren't any pictures hanging on the walls or knickknacks on sideboards. I wonder how long he's been living here.

'Let's go through to the garden. It seems a shame not to take advantage of the late afternoon sunshine.'

He leads me through his living room, which is dominated by a black lacquer baby grand piano, the lid up and sheet music on the stand.

'So it's you who plays?' I ask.

'Guilty as charged. I hope I haven't disturbed you.' He gives me a bashful look.

'Not at all.' I run my fingers lightly over the smooth black wood. 'You play beautifully.'

'My mother wanted me to become a professional musician, but it's too competitive, and honestly I never thought I'd be good enough.'

'It sounded pretty good to me,' I say.

He laughs. I like the timbre of it, the rich baritone sound, and an involuntary shiver runs through me. God, I hope he hasn't noticed.

'You can't just be *good enough* to make it as a professional pianist. You have to be the best, and there were too many other things I enjoyed in life to make the ultimate sacrifice of practising eight hours a day. It's my way of relaxing, particularly after a gruesome day at work. Do you play an instrument?'

'No.' I would have liked to learn the cello, but my parents couldn't afford to buy me an instrument let alone have lessons. 'I'm a good listener though.'

'If you get a couple of glasses of champagne in me, I might play you a few tunes,' he says. That cheeky grin appears again, a dimple in his right cheek, his eyes glistening. I have to look away because I feel a stab of desire, and it's just embarrassing. I'm a grown woman, nearly forty years old. This doesn't happen to me.

I'm grateful when he leads me out into the garden, with its small lawn mowed in straight stripes and neat borders filled with white and mauve bedding plants. It's all meticulous, not a weed in sight. On the narrow patio there is a wrought-iron table and two chairs, both with white seat pads. A champagne bottle stands in an ice cooler next to two champagne flutes and a couple of bowls of crisps. The whole scene looks like it could be a photograph from a house and gardens magazine.

'Sorry, this was all a bit impromptu, so I can't offer you anything more exciting.' He waves his hands at the crisps. 'Please have a seat.'

He pops open the bottle and pours me a glass. When he hands it to me, our fingers touch, and a spark of electricity fires up my arm. I think he feels it too because he hesitates for a second, his right eyebrow rising. But he doesn't say anything and sits down in the chair opposite me, his long legs jutting forwards, his ankles just millimetres away from mine, so close I can almost feel the heat of him.

'So, neighbour, tell me about yourself. How did you end up on Violet Lane?'

'I fell in love with the house, particularly the history of it, and I've always liked this town. And it helps that my new job is just two streets away. What about you?'

'It's the nicest place I've ever lived in. I'm sure you'll be really happy here, as I am.'

I smile, unsure where to look, overly conscious of Max's soft gaze. 'Tell me about your work,' I say.

He groans. 'I'm a paramedic and spend my days dealing with horrors. That's why I need to come back here to my little sanctuary, where everything is in its place and I can decompress in front of the piano. Don't get me wrong, I love my job, but it can be overwhelming and exhausting.'

'I can imagine.' Although I can't really because I'm horribly squeamish. It does explain why Max's house and garden look so very perfect.

'I guess we both have jobs where we help people. It can't be easy being a criminal lawyer.'

We chat for a little while about our work, and then Max asks the question I always dread. 'So, are you in a relationship?'

I shake my head. 'A messy divorce that took nearly three years to resolve.'

'Ah, poor you. I hope you've been enjoying your newfound freedom.'

I redden. 'I haven't dated. And you?' I need to twist the conversation back to him.

'I'm also a singleton. Never been married although I've had a few serious relationships. I work such long and unsociable hours, it's hard to sustain a relationship. At some point I might have to think about changing careers.' He gazes wistfully into his garden.

'I also have to work unsociable hours,' I explain. 'Particularly when I'm the duty solicitor.' Except I haven't been doing much of that recently.

'It's tough, isn't it, balancing jobs we love with a normal home life,' Max muses. 'I also spend a lot of time caring for my mother, who has mobility problems.'

'Do you have siblings?' I ask.

'No. I'm an only child, so Mum is my responsibility.'

After finishing a second glass of champagne, I'm feeling a little light-headed. Max makes as if to pour me another glass, but I put my hand over the top of it. His wrist grazes mine, and that jolt comes again. Max's Adam's apple bobs up and down, and his dark eyes bore into mine. The tension is almost unbearable.

'Would you play me something on the piano?' I ask, desperate to bring levity to our conversation.

He lets out a slight sigh as he places the bottle back into the cooler. 'Of course,' he says, unfolding himself from the chair. 'What would you like me to play you?'

I'm stumped and reply, 'You choose. Whatever you enjoy the most.' I follow Max into the living room and perch on a cream armchair.

Max removes some sheet music from the stand and lifts his hands so they're positioned over the keyboard. He closes his eyes, and his fingers start moving, playing a heart-wrenchingly romantic tune that I think I recognise but can't name. There's such a lightness to his music, but then it builds and builds into something utterly passionate. He keeps his eyes closed as he plays, his body moving backwards and forwards, his face contorting with pleasure. I can't keep my gaze away from his face as I'm drawn into the exquisite and painful intimacy of his performance. His lips are parted, and it's as if I'm watching something so very personal, I'm embarrassed to be here. And then after some crashing chords, the tune gives way to a simple, haunting melody before fading to silence. Only then does Max open his eyes, lean back and smile at me. It feels as if my heart has just been smashed to smithereens and put back together again. I'm almost breathless.

'Wow,' I say quietly. 'Just wow. I've never heard anyone play like that.'

'I'm glad you liked it,' he murmurs, gently closing the piano lid.

I find it difficult to match together all the parts of this man. The breathtaking sensitivity of his piano playing, the strong muscles that suggest he regularly works out, and his job, which must require resilience, quick thinking and compassion. It's as if someone has created a tick list for the perfect man, and Max is its embodiment. The only question is, why is someone of his age still single?

'Can I get you another glass?' he asks.

My body is tingling and begging to stay, to feel those delicate but strong fingers on my skin, but I force myself out of the pathetic dream. 'No, it's kind of you, but I really need to be getting back. I've got to get ready for the new week. You know what it's like starting a new job. I have to be on my A game.'

'I'm sure you're always on your A game, Laila,' he says, but this time his gaze is intense, and there's no smile.

I giggle awkwardly and walk towards the hallway, Max following just behind me. He places a hand on my arm and gently edges in front of me, putting another hand on the door handle. We are so close now, his breath is warm on my cheek, his eyes boring into mine and his hand burning through the thin cotton of my blouse. The moment seems to stretch and morph, and he moves his head ever so slightly as if he's going to kiss me. I hold my breath, and we're both completely still, my nerve endings on fire. And then he lifts his hand from my arm and gently wipes a lock of hair off my face.

'It's so lovely to get to know you,' he says, looking away from me and turning the handle on the front door. 'I'm a lucky man to have you as my next-door neighbour. We should do this again sometime.'

I float down the steps and think I can feel his eyes on my back, except when I turn around and walk towards my house, Max's front door is closed, and he's no longer there. It isn't until I'm getting ready for bed that I realise he didn't ask for my phone number, and I didn't ask for his.

THE NEXT DAY I find it hard to concentrate at work. I'm called to the police station, the local one, which is within walking distance. This is a relief because mostly I have to attend the stations in towns much further afield, with hours wasted travelling. The client is a friend of one of William Parker's previous clients, and the suspect has specifically requested representation from our firm.

I've attended this police station a few times previously, but it generally was outside my regular patch. It's almost quaint, housed in a historic building on the end of a residential street. I'm ushered in by the duty sergeant and taken to one of the two meeting rooms, where my client is waiting. The CPS disclosure pack was already emailed to me, and I flicked through the many pages, so I'm aware that the man has been charged with Driving with Excess Alcohol.

He's well-spoken, wearing a smart suit, but the air in the interview room is rancid with the fumes of stale alcohol and sweat. I should be used to it by now, but I'm not sure it's something you can ever become immune to. The client reminds me a little of Max, with his dark hair and suave manner. But everything and anyone is reminding me of Max this morning. I can't get him out of my head.

It's only as the police questioning progresses that I realise I've missed something utterly critical. This man has a previous conviction for driving while intoxicated. It must have been in the paperwork, yet I missed it. I manage to rectify the situation, but my client is furious. Having told him he'll probably get off with a fine and a six-month ban, I now have to tell him that he faces a mandatory minimum three-year disqualification. He's livid, puce in the face, ranting and raving, telling me how useless I am, and on this occasion, he's right. I slipped up, and I hope word doesn't get back to William Parker.

Following a difficult afternoon, I'm relieved to be walking home, the fresh air going some length to calm me down.

I'm completely torn over Max. I want to see him again, yet I don't. The last thing I want is a relationship, especially with my next-door neighbour, yet his magnetic allure – I mean, how do I describe it without sounding clichéd? – is overwhelming. Or perhaps I'm imagining the attraction; after all, I'm completely out of practice. He might just be being nice to me because I'm his new neighbour. Perhaps I need to follow Jazmin's advice and join a dating app. Or maybe I'm only feeling this way because I'm in need of sex. Perhaps. Perhaps. Perhaps.

As I turn into Violet Lane, I'm disappointed that Max's bike isn't parked in front of his house. The street is so quiet, as if no one is living there.

I make myself a quick supper and get changed into jeans and a shirt. It's book club night, and Jazmin has been badgering me to carry on attending even though I've moved a few miles away. I don't feel like going out tonight, and I've only flicked through the novel that I should have read, but I know I'll enjoy the evening when I'm there. It's more of an excuse for a girls' gossip than any deep analysis of a book.

As I'm shovelling lasagne into my mouth, I take out my phone and search Facebook and Instagram for Max Critchley. I find a Max Critchley in Alabama, USA, and another one who is a student at Edinburgh University. But my Max Critchley doesn't seem to exist on social media. That's weird. Then I do a Google search, and a few people with the same name pop up, except none of them are him.

I scroll through several pages until I find an old newspaper report in *The London Standard*. Max was one of the paramedics attending the scene of a fatal accident in south London just under two years ago, and he's quoted as giving evidence at the inquest. It's a distressing story about the death of a young mother. I wonder how Max copes with seeing such horrors on a daily basis. Even though the story is sad, I'm relieved. Max really is a paramedic; he really is an accomplished pianist. He really is rather special. And he isn't obsessed with social media.

I DRIVE to Jazmin's house, and it's strange to be here as a visitor when this was my home for close on three years. It's also strange to be ringing the doorbell. It appears that I'm the last one to arrive, as the others' cars are already in the drive.

'Laila, we've missed you!' Jazmin says as I walk through the door of her house. She leans towards me and gives me a kiss on both cheeks. As I walk into their large, airy living room, I receive similar greetings from the four other women, who have become close friends during the past few years.

Jazmin hands me a glass of wine and peers at me. 'There's something different about you.'

I wish my best friend weren't quite so observant.

'You're glowing. Have you met someone?'

I can't believe she can read me that easily.

'She's been out of my clutches for two weeks, and she's already flying!' Jazmin exclaims, throwing her arms up into the air.

'Spill the beans,' Sophie says, edging closer to me.

I'm the only one of my friends who is divorced, and for a while I felt different and ostracised. To be fair to them, they never made me feel bad; I do enough of that for myself. It's the people I don't know so well who seem to be threatened by me.

'I haven't met anyone,' I say, laughing and trying to bat them away.

'Yes, you have,' Jazmin says. 'You're a bloody awful liar. Not the best trait for a solicitor.'

They all laugh.

'There's a very hunky neighbour living next door to me on Violet Lane, and we had a drink last night, but nothing has happened, and nothing will.'

Jazmin tilts her head at me and raises an eyebrow. 'Tell us more.'

'There's nothing to tell,' I say. 'Let's talk about the book.'

WHEN I GET HOME, Max's bike is parked in front of his house. I can't help but smile, and I linger at my front door, slowly retrieving the keys from my bag. As I pretend to struggle to put them in the lock, I hope that he might just pop out of his house. Except he doesn't. There are lights on in the windows of several houses, including in Max's, but otherwise it's completely quiet, just the occasional sound of a distant car passing by and the faint music drifting from an open window farther down the street.

I head upstairs and throw open the bedroom window. That's when I hear it. The gentle sounds of a piano being played, a romantic tune with a melody that I'm sure I've heard on Classic FM. As I climb into bed, I leave the window open and lie on my soft mattress, listening to Max's performance, wondering if he's thinking of me.

CHAPTER FOUR

I'm awoken by my window creaking. The fine weather has given way to a storm, thunder echoing through the darkness, lightning flashing and torrential rain, which has puddled on my windowsill. I wipe it dry, close the window and, after what seems like forever, drift back to sleep.

When I next awake, my alarm clock is chiming, and I realise I'm going to be late. I have to be at the county court in Brighton this morning, and I'm cutting it fine. Dressing hurriedly, I eat a piece of toast whilst I'm putting on my make-up, gather my soft leather satchel stuffed with papers, and hurry out to the car. The day is grey, overcast, and it makes for a miserable Tuesday morning. There are puddles on the road, but at least it's not still raining.

To my dismay, my normally trusty Mini Cooper doesn't start. I try over and over to start it, but the engine is completely dead. Why does this have to happen today when I have a deadline? I try not to panic, but how the hell am I going to get to Brighton on time? I search for the telephone numbers of local taxi firms, calling one after the other. Most can't get to me until mid-morning, citing rush hour, school runs and the like, and Uber doesn't exist in this small West Sussex town.

There's a knock on my window, and I jump, dropping my phone into the footwell.

'Everything alright?' Max asks as I open the door because even the window isn't opening. He's dressed in his dark green paramedic's uniform, which gives him an air of authority and, despite its utilitarian unattractiveness, makes him appear like a hero.

'Um, not really,' I garble. 'My car won't start, I can't find a taxi, and I have to be in court in Brighton in forty-five minutes.'

'In which case you'd better hop on the back of the bike,' he says with his trademark grin.

'What? No, I can't. I'm dressed for court, and it's probably completely out of your way.'

'Nope. It's in exactly the right direction. Give me two ticks, and I'll find you some leathers to wear over the top of your clothes.'

'It's kind of you, but no,' I mutter, except Max is already striding back to his house.

I've never been on a motorbike. Does that make me pathetic? And I've never been rescued like this. I glance at my watch and realise I really don't have any choice if I'm going to make it to court in time. A moment later, Max is standing in his open front door. He beckons to me, so I get out of my car, grabbing my bags, lock the car and hurry towards him. He's holding up a pair of leather trousers and a jacket.

'They should fit you,' he says. 'Tug them on over your clothes. At least you're wearing trousers and not a skirt.'

I feel anxious and self-conscious as I put the leathers on, the faintest hint of perfume coming from them, and I wonder whether they belonged to an ex-girlfriend of Max's. He produces another helmet and holds it out. I fumble putting it on, and he gently helps me fix the strap. Once again, he's so close to me I can smell his musky aftershave, and I have to concentrate to remember to breathe.

'What about my bags?' I ask, holding them up.

He takes them from me, helps me onto the back of the bike and pushes my satchel and handbag into the pannier.

'Have you done this before?' he asks, and for a moment I feel embarrassed, as if I haven't lived. A motorbike virgin.

I shake my head.

'You'll be fine.' He pats my arm reassuringly. 'Just put your arms around my waist and hold on tight. I'm a trained rider, so you'll be quite safe.'

This is not how I imagined my Tuesday morning would go.

As it turns out, the ride is exhilarating. I feel like whooping with joy, clutching onto Max, feeling his taut body, the air racing past my face, the throbbing vibrations of the machine between my legs; the countryside that I normally barely glance at when I'm in the car is within touching distance. By the time we arrive in Brighton, I'm a motorbike convert, invigorated and ready to start the day.

Max slows the bike to a stop outside the courtroom and helps me dismount. I fumble with undoing the helmet, so once again he removes it, carefully lifting it off my head and placing it on the seat I've just vacated. He hands me my satchel and handbag.

'How do you feel?' he asks, biting the side of his mouth, his eyes sparkling.

'Alive,' I say.

'It's magical, isn't it?'

'A bit scary, but yes, I really enjoyed that. Thank you for making me feel safe.'

'That's my job,' he replies. 'What time do you finish in court?'

'I expect to be here all day, finishing around 4.30 p.m., but don't worry, I'll organise a taxi to get me home.' I look down at myself and remember I'm wearing his leathers, wondering if I can find a locker in the courthouse to store them in. 'I can drop these off later, if that's okay?'

'Have a good day, Laila.' He turns and mounts the bike, and then with a single roar, he's gone.

AND I DO HAVE a good day. My client's trial goes well, followed by productive meetings with counsel. At 4.20 p.m. I book a taxi to take me home, and with Max's leathers over my arm and my bags slung across my body, I walk down the stairs and out of the courthouse.

'Hello!'

I glance up at the now familiar voice. Max is leaning against his motorbike, his helmet in one hand and that insouciant grin that gives me butterflies.

'What are you doing here?' I ask as I hurry across the road towards him. 'You really didn't need to pick me up.'

'I was passing.'

'I hope you haven't been waiting long,' I say, unable to swipe the smile from my face. Yes, it really is a good day.

'About forty seconds. Can I help you slip back into the leathers?'

There is something inherently sexy about the way he

said that, and I blush, fiercely. I cancel the taxi via an app on my phone and let Max help me into the leathers.

'Are you in a hurry to get home?' he asks.

'No.'

'In which case I thought we could go for a ride. What do you think?'

I glance up at the sky, which has morphed from grey and threatening to clear blue over the course of the day.

'That would be lovely,' I say.

Max rides his bike to a spot high up on the South Downs with far-reaching views to the glistening sea and the wind turbines that stand proud on the sea's horizon. In front of us are rolling hills and chalky paths and the occasional tree bent from the prevailing winds, a faint hint of salt in the fresh air.

'Fancy a walk?' he asks as we dismount the bike.

It's a completely silent late afternoon with no one else in sight, and we walk close together along a path that wends between two large fields. Our conversation is easy, talking partly about our respective jobs, and then Max asks where in the world I'd most like to visit.

'The Galapagos Islands are top of my list,' I say.

'Really?' he exclaims. 'Me too. I love nature and animals, and I'm saving up to go on a horse-riding safari in Botswana.'

'You ride as well?'

'I used to, but it's been a few years. Hopefully it's like riding a bike and will all come back.' He laughs. 'Have you ever ridden?'

The way he's looking at me is so intense, my mind is flooded with inappropriate thoughts. And then, as if he can read my mind, he stops still and reaches out to me, cupping his hand gently over the left side of my jaw. With his other arm, he pulls me towards him, his eyes gazing into mine, his lips parted. My heart feels like it's going to jump out of my chest.

'May I?' he asks huskily as he lowers his mouth towards mine. I don't answer.

And then he's kissing me, and for possibly the first time in my life, I feel like my legs might buckle underneath me. My brain is empty, and my whole body is clinging to Max's as if I might melt into him. The moment seems like it goes on forever, and I don't want it to end.

'Wow,' he says softly as we part. 'You're quite something.'

I laugh as he holds my face in his hands and stares deeply into my eyes. 'I want to go home,' he says huskily. 'Do you?'

I nod, the laughter fading, a deep longing in my core making me wonder how I'm going to restrain myself. We're almost running as we hurry back towards the bike, hand in hand. This might be an ordinary Tuesday, but it's about as magical as it could possibly be.

'I'VE GOT some food in the fridge,' I say as we dismount outside our houses on Violet Lane. 'Would you like to come in?'

'You don't need to ask,' he replies with a grin. I expect him to grab my hand or put his arm around me, but he doesn't. He follows at a distance as I open the front door, and we walk inside. As I'm peeling off the leathers and balancing on one foot, Max grabs me. Before I fully realise what's happening, it's not just the leathers that are tumbling to the ground. There's a desperate urgency for both of us as he tugs at my clothes and kisses me. Our hands are everywhere.

'Is this okay?' he asks breathlessly.

I nod, and before I realise what he's doing, he has lifted me up, and he's kissing me whilst carrying me up the crooked stairs.

'First door on the left,' I whisper against his neck, breathing in his delicious scent.

And then we're on my bed, ripping each other's remaining clothes off until I'm lying there completely naked. For a moment, embarrassment courses through me, and I try to cover myself up.

'Don't,' Max says, grabbing both my hands and holding them against the mattress either side of my body. 'You're beautiful. Absolutely stunning.' His eyes run up and down my body, and then very slowly, holding my gaze with his eyes, he lowers his face and kisses me on the lips, his tongue probing and nipping my lips. Then he's moving downwards, running kisses down my neck, between my breasts, before taking each nipple into his mouth in turn, licking, teasing. By the time his mouth reaches my clit, I'm breathless, my body writhing. I want this man so badly, but he plays with me until I'm literally begging. I'm dripping by the time he enters me, gently edging me open and then plunging deep inside.

No one has made love to me like Max. Not Jacob. Not the boyfriends before him. I have never been made to scream, never felt such a deep, delicious desire and never made to come in synchronicity with my partner. As he sinks back down on top of me, groaning with satisfaction, I realise I have spent the whole of my life having mediocre sex. Max is a caring, accomplished lover, and I think he's ruined me for ever.

'God, you're gorgeous,' he says as he rolls to one side and runs his fingers slowly down my torso. We're both glistening with sweat, panting, relaxed. 'I want to make love to you all night long.'

He's nibbling at my earlobe, and I'm reaching down to feel for him again when a mobile phone rings. Its ringtone isn't mine. Max pauses and groans loudly.

'What is it?' I ask.

'My work phone. I'm so sorry, darling, but I'm going to have to answer it.' He rolls off me and slides his feet to the floor, standing up and then searching for his trousers, which are discarded on the carpet near the door. I watch the ripples of his muscles as he moves, his tight, neat buttocks, his large semi-erect manhood. When he answers the phone, he turns to look at me and mouths, 'Sorry.' Max is beautiful. But then he turns again and walks out the door into the hallway.

I listen. 'Yes, of course. Yes, I can be there in fifteen minutes. Sure.'

He's back in my bedroom again, scooping up his discarded clothes, tugging them on, hiding that stunning body.

'There's been a multi-car accident on the A24. I'm afraid I've got to go.'

'It's okay,' I say, although it really isn't. My body is burning for him all over again.

We swap phone numbers.

He blows me a kiss, and then I hear him running down the stairs, and my old house shivers as he slams the front door closed. I jump up and hurry to the window in the spare room that looks out onto the street. Standing just behind the curtains, to hide my nudity, I open the window a little and watch as he flings himself onto his motorbike. I hope that he'll look up at me, perhaps see me here, throw me a wave.

He doesn't. The motorbike starts up with a roar, and two seconds later, he's gone.

Every part of me is aching, sore from our passion but ready for more. I take a long shower and then heat up some food. I have a smile on my face, humming under my breath, a feeling of happiness shimmering through my veins.

But then I stop myself.

For heaven's sake. It was sex. I had sex with my neighbour. Undeniably good sex, but that's all it was. I cannot allow myself to fall for this man. I made myself promise that I would tread so gently, protect my heart, never allow myself to be hurt in the way that Jacob destroyed me. Not to trust. No, this is just a physical thing, an intense magnetic attraction, but that does not mean it will lead to a relationship. In fact, perhaps it would be better if it was a one-off. We live next door to each other, and surely that in itself is a recipe for disaster. I resolve to keep my distance and protect my heart. Nevertheless, I go to sleep happy and realise this is the first time I've drifted off with a smile on my face for years.

THE NEXT DAY flies by with client meetings and a mountain of paperwork, and although my mind drifts to Max from time to time, I succeed in keeping my focus on the law. When I get home from work, his bike still isn't there, and I haven't heard from him, despite glancing at my phone numerous times to double-check for messages. He's probably been on a long and difficult shift.

I'm not too worried because I have something else to look forward to. Tonight is my first night having my beloved black Labrador, Ludwig, to stay. Last week, I purchased a new bed for him, along with several overpriced soft toys and a feeding station so he doesn't have to bend his neck to eat. And I've ordered in his favourite food.

At 6 p.m. the doorbell rings, and Jacob is standing there, Ludwig attached to a red lead that I don't recognise.

'Oh my boy!' I exclaim as I bend down to hug him. He seems as delighted to see me as I am to see him, his bottom wiggling in that comic way so unique to Labradors.

'You going to show me around?' Jacob asks, peering over my shoulder into the hallway. 'It looks a bit pokey.'

'No, I'm not going to show you around,' I bite back.

'That's a bit petty,' Jacob says. 'If that's how you want to play it, then I'll be off.' Jacob turns on his heel and strides to his gleaming black Range Rover, which he's double-parked, blocking Violet Lane. I no longer care about Jacob. I've got my beautiful boy to stay.

'Come on then, Ludwig. Let me show you your new home.' He trots into the house behind me, sniffing in the corners of rooms and then loping towards his new bed before collapsing into it with a big sigh. I spend the next few minutes sitting on it with him, burying my face into his velvety soft fur, letting him lick my face. I've missed my dog so much.

My worst fight with Jacob was over the dog. I was never convinced that he actually wanted full-time custody of him, but he knew how much Ludwig meant to me and, as such, fought tooth and nail.

After a while, I get up. 'Fancy going for a walk, Ludwig?' I ask.

He leaps from his bed, his tail wagging furiously. I want to show him off, particularly to Max, but as normal, all is quiet on Violet Lane, and the motorbike is still missing.

When we return from our walk, I send Max a text message.

> Hope all's well. Thanks for a great evening! L.

I don't add an X or an emoji. It's polite, and that's all.

Before I switch out the lights for the night, I check my phone again, but it looks like my message hasn't been read. I can't help but hope that Max is alright.

I WAKE WITH A START. It's dark outside, and Ludwig is downstairs barking. My heart is racing, and a fine layer of perspiration coats my chest. Why is he barking? He's not a great guard dog, but perhaps it's because he's in an unfamiliar house? I sit in the dark for a moment, straining my ears, but hear nothing except Ludwig's barks. After switching on my bedside lamp, I let out a little squeal. Something has hit my bedroom window. It happens again. And again. Meanwhile Ludwig's barks are getting more frantic. What the hell?

I tread cautiously towards the window and pull back the curtains just in time to see a little stone hit the glass and bounce off into the darkness. Peering out into the black night, I'm startled by the sensor light above the patio door coming on. I see a figure in the garden, arms waving at me.

'Laila!'

Quickly, I open the window.

'I thought you'd never wake up! Your phone is off, and I didn't know how else to contact you. It's not like I could stand on Violet Lane with my finger on your doorbell buzzer. I'd be worried about waking the neighbours.' It's Max. He's in my garden, chucking little stones up against the window like some modern-day Romeo. The sensor light goes off, but as my eyes adjust to the darkness, I see that he's still in his paramedic's uniform with one arm extended in front of him, his hand clutching a red rose.

'What!' I laugh.

'Aren't you going to let me in?' he asks.

Pulling on a dressing gown, I hurry downstairs, patting Ludwig, telling him he's a good boy. He calms down at the sight of me and trots at my heels as I walk towards the back door. I glance at the clock on the kitchen wall. It's 1.06 a.m. This feels a little bit like a booty call, but nevertheless, I unlock and open the door and beckon Max inside, if only to stop him from waking up any of the neighbours.

He hands me the rose, but there are thorns on the stem, and I prick my thumb. 'Ouch,' I exclaim. Max takes my hand and lifts it up to his lips. I shiver as he licks the blood from my thumb, unable in the moment to work out if that's loving or gross.

'You look gorgeous,' he murmurs. 'All bedroom eyes and tousled hair. So sexy.'

Ludwig growls.

'Hello, who are you?' he asks, pulling away from me and bending down to say hello to the dog. Except Ludwig doesn't walk up to Max as he does to most people. The hair on the back of his neck is standing up, and he bares his teeth.

Max stands up and takes a step backwards. 'I don't think your dog likes me.'

'He'll be fine,' I say. 'It's probably because he's in a strange house, he doesn't know you, and you were chucking stones at us. He's called Ludwig, by the way.'

'I could have named him myself.' Max laughs. 'Although

I'm more of a Brahms than a Beethoven man.' Max doesn't seem worried about Ludwig's reaction. Instead he reaches for me, pulls me tightly up against his hard chest and lowers his lips to mine, kissing me deeply. I'm sinking into his lips, enjoying his probing tongue, when Ludwig barks again, more insistently this time.

'Sorry,' I say, pulling away. 'He probably needs to go out for a pee.'

I open the back door and try to encourage Ludwig to go out, except he doesn't. Instead he throws me a disdainful look and sits down so close to me, he's almost on my feet. 'Come on, boy, don't be jealous,' I say laughingly. I reckon that's what it is. Ludwig has never seen me around anyone except Jacob, so it's understandable that he's feeling unsettled and possessive.

After a little cajoling, I get Ludwig to go back to his bed, and then Max follows me upstairs. Even before we reach the bedroom, Max has undone my gown and is lifting my nightdress over my head.

'I've missed you so much,' he says huskily, his hands running up and down my body, his lips tugging my nipples, his breath heavy.

Somehow we make it to the bed, but this time our lovemaking is urgent and fierce, and I let out a scream that must reverberate around the whole of South Gridgley.

CHAPTER FIVE

A week later and I can't deny that Max and I are in some kind of relationship. Our bodies crave each other, and even though I'm trying not to let that affect my heart, I feel like I'm falling hard. I'm exhausted but happy. Somehow it compensates just a little for being without Ludwig, whom Jacob collected on Sunday evening.

Max works extensive shifts and unsociable hours. He tells me that the thought of making love to me gets him through the difficult times, and that he can't bear to go home to bed alone when he knows I'm just two walls away. And so the idiot I am, I let him in in the middle of the night, although now I leave my phone on, so he calls to let me know he's waiting outside. This is, of course, unsustainable, and I wish I could spend more time with him, time to get to know him as opposed to just making love, but Max works such long hours.

I missed this week's book club, so I haven't seen Jazmin in over a week, and as she's eager to view what I've done to my new house, she's coming over for supper, having left the kids and Yves to themselves for the evening. Of course, I know she has another reason for coming over too; she wants to pump me for the information I've been withholding from her. It's hard to keep secrets from my best friend.

Jazmin and I met at my first job. We were eager young trainee solicitors, desperate to make a good impression on our new employers, but we were just two of an intake of thirty and had been told in no uncertain terms that there were only fifteen jobs available at the end of our training period. Many of the others came from top-notch universities or had been privately educated, and they had an inner confidence that terrified me.

Jazmin, on the other hand, had had no helping hand in life. The daughter of a Black, single mother, she was there on her own merit. She was ballsy and ambitious and, for some reason, decided she and I would become best buddies. I'm not sure I would have been one of the fifteen chosen for a job at the end of our probation period if Jazmin hadn't bolstered my confidence and made me realise that I could be a great lawyer.

In the end, we parted ways career-wise. Jazmin became a fierce commercial solicitor, working in a leading London firm until she married Yves. She still works in the law, but for a smaller, provincial firm that allows her the flexible working hours she wants so she can balance children and work.

When I married Jacob and we found ourselves living just ten miles from each other, our friendship resumed at full throttle. She never much liked Jacob, although she didn't share her misgivings until my marriage had completely broken down.

Jazmin arrives laden with extravagant gifts. An apple tree for the garden, a Le Creuset pan just like the one she has in her kitchen, which I've always coveted but considered too expensive, two bottles of wine and my favourite gift of all: welcome-to-your-new-home drawings made by her two little girls. I particularly love Zara's picture. Jazmin's six-year-old also happens to be my goddaughter. She's made an excellent effort of drawing Ludwig standing outside a crooked house. I tape them to my fridge.

'This is so cute,' Jazmin says, admiring my house. 'And I can't believe how homely it all feels. So tell me about the neighbours.'

Over a simple supper and copious glasses of wine, I tell Jazmin about the barbecue at Phyllis' house, and then I mention Max, and of course, my cheeks redden, and Jazmin knows immediately that he is my secret.

'Come on, spill the beans,' she urges.

'He's gorgeous, and we're having a bit of a fling.'

'You mean you're sleeping with him?'

'Yes.'

'Oh my God!' she says, clapping her hands together. 'I didn't think you'd find someone new that quickly. Tell me everything and don't miss out a single detail.'

'Well, he's a paramedic and works crazy hours, so we've only really spent time together in bed.' I blush again.

'So what you're saying is he's using you for booty calls.'

'No. Well, yes, but that's just because of his working hours. And it's what I want too.'

'I don't want to put a dampener on things, but is it sensible to be having a relationship with your neighbour?'

'It's not a relationship as such. We're just having sex.' Except for me, it isn't just sex. Way too many of my waking hours are spent thinking about Max, wondering what the future might bring.

'Please be careful, Laila. What happens if this all goes belly up? You're living next door to each other.'

'I know,' I say rather petulantly. 'I'm just having a bit of fun, and goodness knows, it's been a long time since I've had fun with a man.' What I don't tell Jazmin is that Max makes me feel amazing; it's as if I've reconnected with my body, and the vigorous, erotic sex is making me feel truly alive, even if I am sleep deprived.

'Just take care,' Jazmin says, reaching across the table and squeezing my hand. 'I don't want you hurt again.'

After supper, we take our glasses and the second bottle of wine and sit outside in the fading light. The garden smells of sweet, scented roses, and as I languish on my chair, I feel a deep sense of gratitude that I'm living here and my life is truly back on track. As we're chatting, the tinkle of piano notes starts drifting from next door, a gentle haunting tune at first, which soon builds to furious chords before fading away.

'That's Max,' I say to Jazmin.

'What? He likes listening to classical music? That's a new one for you.'

'No, that's not a recording,' I explain. 'Max plays the piano. He's got a baby grand in his living room.'

'Bloody hell.' Jazmin lets out a whistle. 'He's a paramedic saving people's lives, and in his spare time he's a concert pianist.'

'Something like that,' I say.

'Well, I need to meet the man.'

Before I can stop her, Jazmin is on her feet and striding to the fence that divides our two gardens, dragging her chair behind her. She's found the lowest shrub, the one that I assume Max must have hopped over to get into my garden the night he woke me throwing stones.

'Stop it!' I exclaim, but I'm laughing so hard, it's difficult to get the words out. This is so typically Jazmin. She stands on the chair, puts two fingers in her mouth and whistles so loudly, I jump.

The music stops for a moment before restarting.

'Jazmin! For goodness' sake!' I rush over to her, grab her hand and try to pull her off the chair, except she's having none of it.

'Oi!' she shouts, completely ignoring me. 'Max!'

'What's his surname?' she whispers down to me. I tell her.

'Max Critchley, this is Jazmin. Laila's best friend. I want to meet you.'

'Jazmin!' I exclaim. I'm cringing with embarrassment. This is not how I imagined the two of them meeting. The piano playing stops, and a couple of moments later, Max's head appears over the top of the fence.

'Laila?' he asks.

'I'm so sorry. This is Jazmin, my best friend, and she's drunk too much. Well, we both have, really.'

'You'd better come and join us,' Jazmin says, wobbling precariously before she jumps down from the chair.

'Alright,' Max says, that slightly lopsided grin making my insides clench with longing.

Max is more elegant and athletic and makes the hopping over the fence seem effortless. He's wearing khaki shorts and a close-fitting T-shirt that shows off his fit body in all its glory. He carries the chair that Jazmin stood on back to the table. Jazmin sits on another chair and indicates to Max to sit too.

'Would you like a drink?' she asks, holding out the nearly empty bottle of wine.

'I won't, thanks. I'm on duty later.'

'And then you'll come back in the middle of the night all horny and slip into Laila's bed.' Jazmin ruins the atmosphere. I look at her in horror.

'It's not like that,' I say.

'Well, it kind of has been the past week,' Max admits, reaching over and holding my hand. He then turns to face Jazmin. 'I'm sorry, but I'm on horrible shifts this week, and frankly, the only thing that has got me through has been your amazing friend. I hope you don't think I've been taking advantage of her.'

'Well–'

'I'm a grown woman, Jaz.' I interrupt her and smile up at Max. 'She's just worried about me because the past couple of years have been challenging.'

'I can assure you both that I only have Laila's best interests at heart, and I can't wait to have the time to take her out to dinner and for us to meet each other's friends. It's just we have rather a strong physical connection, and it's proving hard to deny.'

I suppose that's a way to phrase it. Jazmin rolls her eyes. 'Well, I'm happy for you both. At least someone is having good sex. Enjoy these early stages because it doesn't last.'

I wonder for a moment if things aren't as rosy between Jazmin and Yves as I assumed.

Max stands up, leans over me and places a chaste kiss on my lips. 'I'm afraid you'll have to excuse me. I need to get ready for work. I'll message you, Laila. And, Jazmin, I hope to see you again soon.'

We sit in silence, my cheeks aflame, as Max disappears back into his property.

'In the house,' I whisper, cocking my head towards the

kitchen. I pick up the glasses and bottle, and Jazmin follows me inside. I shut the patio door so we can't be overheard.

'Bloody hell, Jaz!' I exclaim. 'That was excruciating.'

'Nah, it wasn't so bad. But I do understand what you see in him. He looks like an Adonis and can charm the pants off anyone. And added to that he saves people's lives and plays the piano like a romantic. My only question is, why isn't he married or in a long-term relationship?'

'We haven't talked much about our past relationships,' I say.

'Sounds like you haven't talked much at all.'

She's right, of course, and I realise that has to change.

AFTER JAZMIN HAS LEFT (thanks to a taxi because there was no way she was in a fit state to drive home), I sleep well despite the alcohol, and I awake feeling a little disappointed that I'm alone in bed. I glance at my phone and see I have a message from Max saying he got home very late and reckoned we both could do with a full night's sleep. He's probably right. The day races past with a plethora of clients, mostly needing advice on driving offences. It's easy, rather dull work, not as exciting as last week, and I wonder whether I'm going to be sufficiently stretched in this new job. But at least I'm not feeling any undue pressure, and that counts for a lot at the moment.

At the end of the day, I wander home, picking up a few groceries from the local Co-op shop, walking slowly and looking forward to the next time Ludwig comes to stay. But as I round the corner into Violet Lane, I come to a sudden stop.

There are two marked police cars parked at the far end,

wedged between cars outside Phyllis' house and Max's house. My heart thumps as I stride quickly down the lane. Max's bike isn't there, and I have a horrible thought that something terrible might have happened to him. But then I reassure myself that because none of us have assigned parking spaces in front of our houses, these police cars could be here for anyone on Violet Lane. All the same, a nub of dread wedges in my sternum.

I hurry up the street, glancing at all the houses as I do so. There's no one around. I walk slowly up my steps and slide my key into the lock. Leaving the door open, I hurry inside, but everything seems fine in my house. I return to my open doorway just as Phyllis emerges from her house. She waves her arms at me, gesticulating for me to come over the road. I step over the bags that I dumped in the hallway, shut the front door behind me and hurry across the street.

'Come in,' she whispers conspiratorially.

'What's happened?' I ask as she ushers me into her hall and closes the door behind us.

'It's Jackie. She's gone missing, and Finn has called the police.'

'Oh my goodness, that's awful,' I say. 'How long has she been missing for?'

'I'm not sure, but things like this don't happen on Violet Lane. I think we've only had one police car here in the thirty-odd years I've lived here, and that was over some ridiculous argument between a couple of neighbours who have long since passed away.'

'If there's anything I can do,' I say, letting my words fade because as the newcomer here, I can't imagine how I can help.

'I just wanted to let you know,' Phyllis says, 'because the

police officer said they'll be talking to us all. Except not Jamie and Rico because they're not back in South Gridgley until the weekend.'

'Right.'

'Jackie's such a lovely girl. I really hope she's alright, and then there's their little baby she's left behind.'

'I'd better be getting back,' I say. It's evident that Phyllis is the self-appointed matriarch of Violet Lane, and I don't want to be swept up in her cobweb of gossip and speculation. 'Thanks for letting me know. And when I'm a bit more settled, you must come over for a drink.'

'A sherry would be lovely, my dear,' she says as she opens the door for me. 'We must all stick together on Violet Lane.'

HALF AN HOUR LATER, there's a knock on my front door. It's no surprise to see two police officers. They're not in uniform, rather wearing dark, smart clothes, and they both show me their badges.

'Good evening,' the man says. He has a long rectangular face with floppy sandy-coloured hair. His colleague is short and plump with black hair tied back into a severe ponytail. 'We're here regarding a missing person and wondered if we could come in for a quick chat?'

'Of course,' I say, stepping back and gesturing for them to go into my living room. 'My neighbour has already told me that Jackie from number 43 has been reported missing.'

'Yes, that's correct. I'm Detective Sergeant Stefan Kolinsky, and this is Detective Constable Vicky Mortimer.'

'Please have a seat,' I say, gesticulating to the sofa. They sit down next to each other, and DC Mortimer produces her notebook and pen. She asks me for my name and contact details, and I mention that I'm a criminal solicitor.

'Thought you looked vaguely familiar,' DS Kolinsky says. 'How well do you know Jackie Walker?'

'I don't. I only moved into this house a fortnight ago. I met Jackie at a barbecue at Phyllis' house, and I've waved at her a couple of times when she was going out with her daughter, Melanie.'

'When was the last time you saw her?' DS Kolinsky asks.

I pause to recollect. 'I think it was last Thursday. I was coming home from work, and Jackie was pushing Melanie in her pram.'

'Did you talk to her?'

'No. I waved, and she waved back. Melanie was crying, and Jackie looked a bit harassed. Is their little girl alright?'

'Yes, the child is fine. She's with her father. I appreciate you haven't lived here long, but have you noticed anything strange? People or cars you don't recognise, perhaps?'

'No, I can't say I have. It's very quiet on Violet Lane, probably because it's a cul-de-sac.'

'Have you heard any raised voices or fights, perhaps?'

I shake my head again. 'Everyone has been really kind towards me, and I'm not aware that there have been any disagreements or domestics.'

'Right. If you think of anything else that might be relevant, please get in touch.' DC Mortimer hands me a business card.

'What's happened?' I ask. 'How long has she been missing?'

The two police officers stand up. 'I'm afraid we're not able to disclose that information at this stage.'

Of course they won't. I understand how the police work,

and I know that we'll only be drip-fed information that they want us to know about. That is until the media get wind of what's going on, and then we'll be caught up in a tsunami of speculation, inquisition and backstories. I just hope Jackie reappears quickly and it doesn't come to that.

My good mood evaporates once the police have left. Jackie seemed like a nice young woman, a little frazzled perhaps, but that's probably due to having a baby, and I really hope that she hasn't come to any harm. It would be a tragedy. I send Max a message.

> Have you heard the news? What time will you be home, and any chance of seeing you tonight?

The two ticks next to the message turn blue to suggest he's read it. I expect a reply except nothing arrives. After a while, I put the phone on the countertop and leave it there.

Every so often, I glance outside. Violet Lane is still quiet. One of the police cars remains parked in front of Finn and Jackie's house. Even when it's dark and I go to bed, the windows in number 43 remain illuminated, lighting up the pavement and the cars in front of the house. I check my phone periodically and am disappointed that Max hasn't replied. Is that strange?

It takes forever to drift off to sleep, and when I do, my dreams are a confused mash-up of me desperately looking for Max but unable to find him and then running down street after street, footsteps pounding behind me.

CHAPTER SIX

The next morning, a police car is still parked on Violet Lane. That can't be good news, because if Jackie had been found, then surely it would have left. I check my phone yet again, but I still don't have a message from Max. I wonder if he's had a difficult couple of shifts, or perhaps he's still at work. But I refuse to become the needy girlfriend, especially since we're not official yet, or are we? It's been so long since I've been in the dating game, I really haven't got a clue.

I force myself to eat a piece of toast with marmalade and drink a strong cup of coffee, but the thumping heart and unsettled feeling I awoke with barely shifts. I leave the house for my walk to work. Max's bike isn't outside, and I can't help but feel a kernel of concern. It feels a little bit like I'm becoming a stalker, wanting to know what he's up to at the same time as being worried about him. Or perhaps he's seeing someone else as well, and he's with her. I groan. I've already stepped over the mark.

I have to give myself a good talking-to. I do not want a

relationship. I do not want to get hurt. Max can do whatever he wants. Except, in my heart, I know I don't really believe that. I hold on to what Max told Jazmin, how he wanted to take me out for supper, how he wants us to get to know each other's friends. That's indicative of a proper relationship.

As I'm thinking this, a woman opens the door to Finn and Jackie's house and pulls out a pram. Little Melanie is sitting up in it, dressed in a cute bonnet and anorak. The young woman has choppy blonde hair and is wearing sunglasses, which seems strange for this grey early morning. It hits me then that she might have been crying, and I feel a wave of empathy for the pain the family must be feeling. I nod at her, but I'm not sure that she sees me, so I carry on walking down the street.

I spend the day at my desk, completing paperwork, meeting a couple of clients. It's late afternoon when my phone pings. My heart quickens as I see a message from Max.

> Sorry haven't been in touch. My mum isn't doing too well, so I'm staying with her for a couple of days. Are you free to go away this weekend? Or next weekend? I can swap shifts. Let me know.

I fizz with excitement. A weekend away with Max sounds glorious, a chance for us to get to know each other better. I consider not responding straight away but then decide we're grown adults and we're not playing games.

> This weekend is great. Looking forward to it. Hope your mum improves soon.

I copy his style and don't sign the message off. I feel like doing a little jig around the office.

IT'S BOOK CLUB NIGHT, and this evening we're convening at Sophie's house, a smart townhouse in Arundel with impossible parking. I trundle up the hill, a bottle of wine in hand and the book, which once again I haven't read. It's a convivial evening where Jazmin teases me about my budding relationship with the hunk next door. The girls want details, but I'm reluctant to give them.

'Hold on a second,' Sophie says, glancing at the screen of her phone. 'Isn't Violet Lane, South Gridgley, where you're living now?'

'Yes,' I confirm.

'There was a report on the early evening news on Radio Sussex that a woman has gone missing. I'm sure they said it was Violet Lane, South Gridgley.'

'Yes,' I say. 'It's my neighbour. Really worrying.'

'It's always the husband or boyfriend,' Ruby announces.

'I don't think any detail is known yet,' I add.

Jazmin starts scrolling on her phone. 'You're wrong. It's all over social media. She's called Jackie Walker, married to Finn, with a daughter called Melanie. There's a picture of her here.' Jazmin holds her phone up for us all to see.

'Bloody hell, she looks a bit like you,' Sophie exclaims. 'What with her black hair and blue eyes.'

I squint at Jackie's photograph, which looks like it's been lifted off a social media platform.

'Not really,' I say. 'I'm at least a decade older and not nearly as petite and pretty.'

'Don't put yourself down.' Jazmin elbows me in the ribs.

'On X they're speculating whether Jackie fell victim to that serial rapist who's evaded the police in the south of England for the past year or so. God, this is horrible,' Sophie says, turning her phone off.

I shiver at the thought.

'How long has she been missing?' Jazmin asks.

'I don't know, but the police only turned up the day before yesterday.' I notice that Ruby is still staring at her phone.

'It says here that Jackie Walker has been missing for four days.'

'Four days?' I exclaim. I wonder why the police only arrived the night before last. That's really strange.

'Alright, enough of the speculation. We've got a book to discuss,' Sophie says, corralling us back into our chairs and producing the tome that we all have pretended to read.

The book chat doesn't last long. We're soon onto gossip, talking about mutual friends, errant husbands and school playground escapades – well, not me regarding the latter, at least.

'Oh, I saw Rosa this morning,' Ruby says. I freeze. Rosa used to be a friend, that is until she married Jacob last year. She seemed so sanctimonious, happily slipping into my previous role, moving from her smaller house into ours. The assistant I caught Jacob bonking didn't hang around for long, but he quickly moved on to other women. Perhaps I wouldn't have minded so much if he'd chosen someone I didn't know, but Rosa and I had been friends, neighbours, in fact. She swooped quickly, having discarded her own husband a couple of years earlier. I suppose she's everything I'm not, gentle, subservient, keen to be a homemaker. I expect Jacob treats her terribly.

'Rosa was in Peaches and Cream, that cute little baby shop that's just opened in Storrington. She's six months pregnant.'

I feel like I've been punched in the stomach. I must pale, because Jazmin looks at me with an expression of concern. That baby should be mine. For the first few years of our marriage, Jacob wasn't keen on children, and then by the time he conceded, our sex life had tapered off, and it never happened. Yet he's been with Rosa for no time at all, and she's already pregnant.

Ruby glances at me. 'Oh God, I assumed you knew,' she says, her hand over her mouth. 'I mean, you do still see Jacob from time to time because of Ludwig, don't you?'

'Yes, but he hasn't told me Rosa's expecting. Good for them,' I say, except my girlfriends know I don't mean it. I'm hurting. No, it's more than hurting, I feel winded, jealousy so profound I'm not sure whom I hate more, my ex-husband, his new wife or myself.

'I'm sorry, Laila. It must be very hard,' Sophie says. I don't want her sympathy.

'It's fine. I mean, I can always go it alone, can't I? Plenty of women get pregnant at forty and manage to bring up a child by themselves.'

'Or maybe you'll have a baby with that hunk from next door,' Jazmin adds with a smirk.

'It's not easy getting pregnant at our age,' Ruby says, bringing the conversation down again. 'Gus and I wanted a third, but it hasn't happened.'

I clench my fingers together, thinking that that's just greedy. All I want is one.

'You could always adopt or go for surrogacy,' Sophie says. 'Ben's best friend is adopted, and he's an adorable little boy.'

But I don't want to adopt. I don't want to use a surrogate or a sperm donor. I want my own baby, to fall pregnant, to carry a child to term, to go through the agony and joy of childbirth, to bring up my child in the confines of a loving relationship, just like I experienced in my idyllic childhood being cared for by my loving mum and dad.

CHAPTER SEVEN

I'm wading through paperwork in my little office at Cassel, Everett and Parker when the phone rings.

'Call from the local police station for you,' Debbie, the office secretary, says.

This isn't unusual although generally the requests only come through when I'm the on-call duty solicitor, and today isn't one of those days. Debbie pages the call through.

'Laila Bowden speaking.'

'DS Farthing here. I've got a client who wants you to represent them. Will you come in?'

Again, that's not usual except I'm not on my local patch in this town, and I don't know anyone, so that in itself is strange.

'Sure,' I say, glancing at my watch. It's all of a ten-minute walk to the police station, but I want to finish off the notes I'm making. 'I'll be with you as soon as I can.'

'Thanks, Ms Bowden.'

HALF AN HOUR LATER, I'm back in the quaint little police station, where I'm beginning to feel at home. I'm greeted warmly by the officer at the front desk. 'I'll take you through to the interview room,' he says.

'What's the name of the client?' I ask. It's unusual for me to have no information.

'A Mr Finn Walker.'

I stop still for a second. Finn, my new neighbour. Missing Jackie's husband. I remember what Ruby said, how it's always the husband, and I wonder if the police agree.

'Have you charged him?' I ask.

'Nah. Just brought him in for questioning, but he wanted legal representation, so we've taken a pause.' He opens the door. 'In here. Give us a call when you're done.'

'Thank you,' I say before walking into the small, now familiar room.

Alone in the room, Finn jumps up from his plastic chair. His face is stubbled, dark rings under his eyes and a cold sore on his upper lip. He looks exhausted.

'Have they offered you a drink?' I ask.

'Yes, but I don't want anything. I just want to go home and for them to do their bloody jobs and find Jackie.'

I sit down next to Finn and take out a notebook and pen.

'I'm surprised to be here,' I say.

'You're the only solicitor I know, and when they asked me if I wanted one, I said yes. Got them to call you. That's alright, isn't it?' He leans sideways towards me, as if he's worried he's offended me in some way.

'Of course. I'm a criminal lawyer, and I'll do whatever I can to best represent you. My understanding is that the police want to question you and nothing more, is that what you think?'

'Yes. I mean, they've got nothing to charge me with because I've done nothing wrong. But you hear of these horror stories where the cops pin charges on the husband or the boyfriend because they're the obvious culprit, and I'm not taking that risk.'

'Can you talk me through everything that has happened?' I ask gently.

Finn sniffs and swipes at his eyes. 'It's been the worst week of my life.'

I sit patiently. I'm used to listening and putting clients at ease, so I lean back in my chair, my body language open.

'Me and Jackie had an argument, and she stormed out of the house. I mean, usually she'd take Melanie, but this time she just went, saying she was going to stay with her mum, who lives in Crawley.' Finn bites his fingernails and doesn't meet my eyes.

'Do you argue a lot?'

He sighs. 'A bit. Particularly these last few months. It's hard with a baby in the house. We're both sleep deprived.'

I just nod because I wouldn't know.

'Anyway, she didn't call me, didn't come home, and I just assumed she was in Crawley. And then, when I called her mum, she said Jackie had never gone to her. She hadn't heard from her in days. Obviously I went into a complete panic and rang everyone we know, but no one has heard from her. It's so out of character. I know she was pissed with me, but she wouldn't just leave Melanie behind. I think something terrible has happened. What if that rapist has got to her?' Finn swallows hard, his voice quivering.

'How long has she been missing?' I ask.

'Five days.'

That surprises me. It seems a long time for a mother not to make contact with her husband and young child.

'Have you been able to check her phone or her bank account?'

He shakes his head.

'The police will want access to her phone and to check if she's been using her bank account.' I place my hands on the table and lean towards Finn. 'Is there anything at all that you want to tell me because it's much better that I know now and there aren't any nasty surprises.'

'No!' he exclaims, almost bursting upwards from his chair. 'I didn't do anything, and I certainly didn't hurt Jackie. I love her. She's my wife, the reason for my existence, and she's a brilliant mum to Mel. We argue, but all couples argue from time to time, don't they? I genuinely have no idea what's happened to her.'

'Alright,' I say, appraising Finn. I never deign to be able to judge if someone is telling the truth, but he is definitely upset, and if I had to place a bet, I'd say he's being truthful. 'Just answer all the questions honestly, and if I think the officers are putting words into your mouth, I'll direct you to say no comment.'

THE INTERVIEW GOES SMOOTHLY ENOUGH. The police are on a fishing trip, and clearly Finn is their number one suspect. It's not surprising, really, especially as the optics of not reporting Jackie missing for three days isn't good. They seem to be taking her disappearance very seriously, which is positive. They promise to investigate her phone records, her banking details, and there's talk of doing a national appeal. I'm surprised, because there's no evidence that Jackie has actually come to any harm, or perhaps the police are withholding information from us. And as far as I can tell, there's nothing concrete to pin on Finn.

I expect they'll want to search his property in due course, but for now, he's a free man. Except he's not. He seems really broken. When we're shown out of the police station, he bursts into tears, crouching down and gulping in air to try to compose himself.

'I'm sorry,' Finn hiccups. 'It just feels like my heart has been ripped apart. I don't think I can live without Jackie.'

'I'm really sorry you're having to go through this,' I say. 'But we need to hold on to hope that she's just gone to stay with a friend for a while.' The words sound trite as soon as I've said them, because unless Jackie has a friend Finn doesn't know about, that's looking increasingly unlikely.

Finn stands up and wipes his eyes with the sleeve of his jumper. 'Thank you, Laila,' he says, his voice hoarse. 'I'm really grateful for your help. Have you got time to go for a coffee? Perhaps you could come back to the house and meet my mum.'

'I think it's best that we don't socialise for now, Finn. I'm your legal counsel, and we need to maintain a professional relationship. Look, if anything changes or you want some advice, here's my number.' I hand him a business card. 'Stay strong,' I say before giving him an awkward wave and heading back to the office.

It's late afternoon when I get a call from Jacob. I have no desire to talk to my ex-husband, so I let his call go to voicemail, listening to it five minutes later.

'A bit last minute, but Rosa's mum is sick, and we need to go and visit her tonight. Any chance you could have Ludwig? Call me.'

No please, no thank you. Just call me. No courtesy of telling me that his new wife is pregnant. But because I'm overjoyed at unexpectedly having Ludwig to stay again, I do ring him.

'I'll drop him off at yours at 6.30 p.m.,' Jacob says, without asking if it's convenient. At least he's not expecting me to collect the dog from our old home. That I would refuse to do.

JACOB IS ALWAYS PUNCTUAL, and true to form, the doorbell rings on the dot of 6.30 p.m. It strikes me how very different he is to Max. Jacob isn't comfortable without an armour of tailoring, and even at the weekends, he wears starched shirts and corduroys with creases down the front. His hair is receding fast, more noticeably every time I see him, and that at least gives me some macabre satisfaction, as he's a vain man. When he's in London, he goes for a shave at a barber's shop and gets his nails buffed. Despite his personal trainer, he's developing a beer belly, and I wonder whether he'll have to exchange his Savile Row suits for a larger size. Max, although supremely confident in his own skin, doesn't seem to have the sartorial hang-ups of my ex, and I wonder if he even owns a suit.

After allowing me to give him a brief stroke on the head, Ludwig trots into the house, but Jacob hovers on the doorstep and obviously has something he wants to say to me.

I cross my arms and tilt my head. 'Yes.'

'I've heard that you're representing Finn Walker, the husband of the woman who's disappeared.'

I'm taken aback. That news has spread within a matter of hours. I glance out onto Violet Lane.

'You'd better come inside,' I say, standing backwards to let him walk into my hallway. I don't suggest we continue through the house, and I just lean against the closed front door, eyeing him with what I hope is a steely expression. 'Yes, and?'

'Are you sure you've got what it takes to represent someone in what might become a high-profile case? You haven't got a big firm behind you to keep you on track.'

'Excuse me!' I exclaim, throwing my arms up into the air. Why does Jacob always want to start an argument? 'What's it to do with you anyway?' I quip.

'I just wanted you to know that if you get out of your depth, you can pick up the phone to me. Can't see decrepit William Parker being much of a support.'

'Thank you, but I don't need you or your firm,' I spit tightly. 'I'd like you to leave now.' I tug the door handle and swing the door open.

'Keep your hair on, Laila.' Jacob gives his annoying fake little laugh. 'I'll collect Ludwig at 6 p.m. tomorrow.'

I slam the door so hard, the whole house trembles. I'm livid. Firstly, how on earth does he know that I'm representing Finn, and secondly, how dare he question my ability. I stomp to the kitchen and pour myself a large glass of wine, but after a couple of sips, I remind myself that Jacob knows exactly how to push my buttons, and he's doing this just to get a rise out of me. It also reminds me why it was so imperative I left May, Maclachlan and Thacker.

In the first few years of our marriage, Jacob and I were seen as the power couple. He was the second generation of Mays to become a partner, and it was generally considered that he was a better lawyer and more high-flying than his father, who had recently retired.

Except when our marriage broke down, it soon became apparent that any dreams I had of making partner would never come to fruition. My ex-husband would veto it, and before long it was obvious that he didn't want me in the firm at all. The cases assigned to me became easier and less high-profile, I was excluded from important meetings, and my name was removed from email lists. And most of the employees, solicitors and support staff alike, knew which side of their bread they needed to keep buttered. Jacob May was their senior partner, and I was a nobody.

As each day passed, I felt more ostracised, and my future in the firm was bleak. I considered suing for unfair dismissal, and I may well have had a case, but our divorce was acrimonious enough, and I didn't want to tarnish my professional reputation, especially as financially I knew I had to stand on my own two feet. No one likes to employ someone who was litigious towards their previous employers. So I took the only option available to me, and I left the firm with my head held high.

Ludwig nudges my leg, and I stroke his head.

'Okay, boy. Let's go for a walk.' He wags his tail and heads for the door. We have a decent walk across the playing fields and up onto the Downs, and afterwards my head feels clearer, and I've dismissed Jacob's irksome manner. I'm heading along Violet Lane when Phyllis appears, walking in the same direction, carrying a wicker basket filled with fresh fruit.

'Ah, Laila, it's good to see you,' she says enthusiastically. 'And who is this?' She bends down to stroke Ludwig's head.

'He's my dog, but I only have him part time. Unfortunately I have to share him with my ex-husband.'

'You're a very beautiful boy.' She strokes Ludwig's head.

When she straightens up, she says, 'How about a sherry for you and a bone for your dog? Have you got time for a quick one?'

I glance at my watch. I'm hungry and need to make myself some supper, and I'm rather hoping that Max might call me or, even better, stop by. I'm about to excuse myself when I see the expression on the older woman's face. She's clearly bursting to tell me something, but I wonder if she feels she can't standing out here on the street for all to hear.

'Just a very quick one, as I need to get home,' I say.

I follow her into her house, which is as immaculate as the first time I visited, but today she leads me into her kitchen. It's made out of pine and has seen better days, but again, it's spotless without a single appliance on the worktops. She strides to a pine dresser and removes two small cut glasses. Then she opens a cupboard and takes out a bottle of sherry. I'm not keen on the drink, but it seems I don't get a choice.

'A small one for me, please,' I say. Phyllis tips in much too much of the brown liquid.

'Have a seat.' She pulls out a chair for herself at the round pine table and takes a large swig of her drink. 'It's terrible what's been happening. Have you heard any more?'

I shake my head because there is no way I'm telling Phyllis that I'm Finn's solicitor.

'The thing is, those two were at each other's throats day and night. Slamming doors, shouting, you name it. I mean, I like Finn. He's always happy to help out, fixing things that are broken around my house, but it wouldn't surprise me one little bit if they had an argument and things got out of hand. You know what I'm saying?' She leans towards me, almost as if she's hoping that I'm going to confirm her suspicions.

'I know not all relationships are like mine and Roy's, but

there's been a number of occasions I've wondered if I should intervene. I just hope they find dear Jackie. Such a sweet girl.'

'What did you tell the police?' I ask.

'Only that the two of them argued a lot, because that's the truth.'

This conversation is making me feel increasingly uncomfortable, so I manage to steer it away to less controversial subjects, and after twenty minutes I make up an excuse and say that Ludwig needs feeding. But I leave Phyllis' house with a heavy heart, and now I'm questioning everything Finn told me. Was their relationship really on the rocks? Finn admitted that he and Jackie argued a lot, so is Phyllis right, and things got out of hand? Or is she just an interfering neighbour with nothing better to do than gossip?

BACK AT HOME, I've just finished eating an omelette and am wondering whether to watch something mindless on the television when my phone pings with a text message.

Are you home?

It's Max.

Yes.

I'm smiling now.

What are you wearing?

What do you want me to wear?

I press send before realising what I've just written. I've just sent my very first flirtatious text. I groan out loud, and Ludwig turns to stare at me.

> I want you so badly.

I feel heat between my legs, a throbbing just at the thought that Max wants me.

> Take off whatever tops you're wearing and play with your nipples.

Oh God. I can't believe we're sending these messages.

> You still there?' I'm so hard, I'm gonna have to sneak off to the bathroom.

Wow. I wonder if he's going to ask me to send nude selfies. I really don't want to do that. Not because I'm a prude but because of all the horror stories of compromising photos being bandied around. Okay, maybe I am a prude, but I'm not going to do it.

And then the phone rings, and I realise Max is calling me on a WhatsApp video call, and I'm sitting on my sofa, my breasts exposed, my nipples hard, my cheeks flaming bright red. I hold the phone up so he can only see my face.

'Where are you?' I ask. I can see white tiles behind him.

'In my mother's bathroom. Gross, I know, but I can't stop thinking about you. Can I see your breasts? Can you put the phone somewhere I can see you? You don't mind, do you?' he asks.

I kind of do, but I know that I'm just being prudish, that this sort of behaviour is normal today. What if I say no? Will Max think I don't like him? After a brief hesitation, I lean my phone up against a vase of flowers on the coffee table and turn the screen so it's facing me. I'm self-conscious and put an arm across my chest.

'You're so beautiful,' Max moans. 'Look how hard I am.' He lowers his phone so I can see his bulging boxer shorts.

I let out a groan.

'I want you so badly.' And then he pushes his boxer shorts down and releases himself. He's breathing hard now. 'Touch yourself, Laila,' he says. 'I want to see you. I want you to imagine that I'm inside you.'

I do what he says. And soon we're both writhing, eyes closed, just in the moment, roaring to simultaneous climaxes.

'You're completely beautiful,' he says as he wipes himself dry. 'Beautiful, beautiful Laila. I'm missing you so much.'

I'm not sure what to say. I've never done this before, and I feel dirty, ashamed. But on the other hand, it was exciting. Our little secret.

'You didn't record this?' I ask, pulling a blanket from the back of my sofa to cover myself. I suddenly feel panicked.

Max laughs. 'Of course I didn't. I wouldn't do that to you. I'm not some teenage kid, desperate for a fuck. Although I am desperate to be with you. I'm missing you, Laila, and want to feel your skin against mine. And doing this together is the next best thing.'

'When are you coming home?' I ask.

'Tomorrow or the next day. I've booked us into a lovely little hotel for the weekend. I can't wait to have you all to myself for two solid days.'

I smile because I feel the same way. It'll take my mind off being without Ludwig. I hear a woman's voice in the background. Is that his mother or someone else?

'I've got to go now, Laila. Sleep tight.'

I groan. What have I done? I barely know this man, yet I'm prostituting myself for him. Or am I? Isn't this just what people do today when they can't be together? I don't know, and I can't imagine asking any of my married friends. I put Ludwig to bed and take a long shower. Max makes me feel so good about myself, but I remind myself it is only sex. I cannot let myself fall for him.

CHAPTER EIGHT

I switch on the television whilst I'm making breakfast. Jackie's disappearance makes the headlines on the local news and is a small bulletin towards the end of the national news. On the one hand this is good, because the police are taking it seriously, but I'm worried for Finn on so many levels. He's clearly distraught that Jackie is missing, but we can't get away from the fact that he is the prime suspect. And the level of scrutiny that this case is going to receive means that my professional reputation is on the line. Nerves flutter in my stomach. I do agree with Jacob on one thing: I doubt William Parker is going to be much support.

When I open the front door and look to the right, I gasp. There's a police cordon a few metres down Violet Lane, and beyond that a small crowd of people have gathered. The media has arrived too, journalists with microphones and large cameras. I glance at Finn's house and see that the curtains have been pulled across all the windows facing the street. Deciding against leaving via my front door, I step back inside and send Finn a message.

Are you alright?

He doesn't answer. But a moment later my phone pings
with a message from Max.

Take your weekend stuff to work, and I'll
collect you from there at 5:30 p.m. Assume
that Violet Lane is a circus with all the
media. Probably best to avoid home for a
few days. Any probs let me know.

I'm immediately conflicted. I've just taken on an important case, my first high-profile case with Cassel, Everett and
Parker, plus I'm supporting my neighbour. What if Finn
needs me over the next couple of days? But then again, I am
entitled to a private life, and oh my goodness, I really, really
want to go away with Max. Finn has my telephone number,
and he can call me if there's any major development. It's not
like I'm going to Outer Mongolia. And so I decide to go. I
decide to take Ludwig with me to work and just hope that's
okay. I also send a message to Jacob, telling him to collect the
dog from my office at 5 p.m.

I chuck some clothes and my wash bag into a small suitcase and, with Ludwig attached to his lead, leave through the
back door, walking through my garden and out of the gate at
the rear of the property, onto a field at the back. Trying not to
muddy my shoes, we stride quickly back onto the narrow
road that runs behind the houses, in between the lock-up
garages, and then slip down an alleyway onto the high street,
relieved not to have been spotted.

MY COLLEAGUES ARE ENCHANTED by Ludwig, who laps up all the attention. I promise William that Ludwig's presence is a one-off, and he just smiles benevolently. I love having the dog at my feet, his presence so soothing.

At 5 p.m. on the dot, I glance out the window onto the street and see Jacob's Range Rover pull up next to the pavement. I hurry downstairs with Ludwig, opening the boot so that he can jump in. Jacob and I don't say a word to each other. I feel a pang of loss as I watch the black vehicle speed away, and traipse back upstairs with a heavy heart.

Exactly half an hour later, Max sends me a message.

> Waiting downstairs. In a black Lexus.

Well, that's a relief. I wasn't sure about going any distance on the back of Max's bike, and an adventure with Max will take my mind off Ludwig. I quickly tidy my desk, then hurry downstairs, excited and slightly nervous about seeing him again after a few days.

As I emerge onto the street, I see the black car partially mounted onto the pavement. Max hops out of the driver's seat and kisses me chastely on the cheek before taking my bag and popping it into the boot. He then opens the passenger door for me. Quite the gentleman.

'New car?' I ask as he pulls away from the pavement.

'No, a rental for the weekend. I thought you'd prefer it to the back of the bike.'

'Thank you,' I say, touched by his thoughtfulness. 'Where are we off to?'

'I've rented a gorgeous little cottage that backs onto the New Forest with views to Beaulieu River. Let's hope it matches the photos online and the excellent reviews.'

The journey takes a little over two hours, and we chat non-stop, initially about poor Jackie and then onto more cheery subjects. I don't mention that I'm Finn's solicitor.

The cottage is adorable and surprisingly remote. It has a big, thatched roof, but inside, the walls are wattle and daub, housing a kitchen with all the mod cons, a bedroom with a huge bed piled up with cushions and a living room with views across the river.

'It's gorgeous,' I say as we stand there admiring the view.

'Not as gorgeous as you.' Max wraps his arms around me from behind and kisses my neck. He barely needs to touch me before I go weak at the knees. What a cliché. After a quick kiss, he carries in the bags from the car. To my surprise, he's brought food and drinks with him and sets about making us supper. I offer to help, but he's insistent I lounge on the sofa with a large glass of red wine. I could get used to this.

'So you're a good cook as well as all your other talents,' I say forty minutes later, savouring the pasta bake that Max has produced.

'I love cooking but rarely have enough time to do it. Besides, it's not much fun cooking for one.'

After the meal, Max lights the open fire, and now that it's dark outside, he tugs me down onto the sofa, where he stretches me out and strokes my hair and then massages my feet whilst we chat. I feel completely relaxed and a million miles away from work and Violet Lane.

As our conversation fades, he starts making love to me, this time with a gentleness and patience that I haven't experienced before. His movements are slow and languid, and we kiss for what seems like hours before he starts exploring the rest of my body with both his lips and fingers. Afterwards, I feel like I'm a puddle of molten lava, and I literally can't move.

Max covers me with a blanket and snuggles in next to me.

'Do you want children?' he asks. The question takes me by surprise, and I find myself tensing slightly. Not only has it come out of nowhere, but it seems much too early in our relationship to be talking about such things.

'Um, yes. But it's probably too late for me.'

'Too late?' he scoffs. 'You've got the face and body of a much younger woman.' Max strokes my neck. 'Besides, plenty of women get pregnant at forty and older.'

'I always thought I'd have a family, but it just never happened, and now... Well, I don't have any expectations.' I pause. 'And you?'

'I think you'd make an amazing mother.'

That statement seems a bit incongruous because I'm not sure Max knows me well enough to pass such comments.

'Do you want children?' I ask.

'Of course. I want to give them the loving family life that my mum gave me.'

'Tell me about your childhood,' I say.

'I didn't know my dad, but honestly I never missed him. My mum was a mother, father and grandparents all rolled into one. She was amazing, juggling three jobs so I never wanted for anything. We were such a tight unit, but when I was thirteen, she met my stepdad, and things weren't the same after that. He was a mean bastard and decided to make my life hell. When Mum got sick, he buggered off. In many ways she's better without him.'

'That must have been so hard for you. And how is your mother now?'

He sighs deeply. 'She's in a care home. They look after her well, but it's horrible how her mind has faded while her body is still strong. I suppose as a medic, I know too much, and it's difficult to maintain hope.'

'Do you see her often?' I can't help but think about the white tiles behind Max when we had our embarrassing phone sex.

'I visit at least once a week and more if possible. Tell me about your family.'

And so I do, describing my lovely childhood and how my heart broke when Dad died too young, and how I love my stepdad, but that he'll never replace my real dad.

WE MAKE love again in bed and then languidly in the morning. During the day, we take a long walk with fabulous views of the estuary before meandering inland. We go out for supper to a stunning two-rosette restaurant, where Max insists on paying for everything, and then we make our way back to the cottage. It has truly been the perfect day.

I awake suddenly, my heart racing. It takes a moment to remember where I am, whom I'm with. Max's fingers are stroking my inner thighs, probing upwards. He is stiff against me, and for a moment I wonder if he's fully awake.

'Max?' I ask, feeling a little uncomfortable.

'Mmm,' he murmurs before kissing me hard on the lips, his tongue probing my mouth, the full length of his strong body pressed up against mine.

I give in to his urgency, and then he's on top of me, thrusting forcefully, over and over, deep inside me, and it's almost painful. I let out a moan, and he plunges in even harder, and then I feel pressure on my neck.

'Max?' I try to speak again, attempting to shift underneath him, but he's strong, and then his left hand is around my neck, pushing downwards, pressing on my windpipe. It hurts.

'Max!' It's hard for me to talk. Is he even fully awake, or is this a semi-sleeping Max? Perhaps he has that condition that I've read about but can't remember the name of, when a person has sex without being conscious.

'Darling, Laila,' he groans.

His thrusts are getting even stronger, faster and painfully deep. He's holding my hands up above my head, his right hand gripped tightly around my wrists so I can't release them. He's slamming into me, my head bashing against the wooden headboard. It's getting increasingly hard to breathe.

'Max.' I try to speak and then shake my head to the side, away from him, but it's as if he can't hear anything, almost as if he doesn't know what he's doing. My body and legs are completely pinned down, but weirdly the weight of him feels good, the way he's pulling out more gently now, rubbing my clit, sending waves of pleasure through me. But then he's slamming back down, the pressure on my throat increasing again. I try to gasp, to say something, but no sound comes out.

A terrible fear grips my heart. Is this some pseudo-erotic game, or is he actually trying to strangle me?

And then there's a huge groan, and Max releases me, rolling to one side of the bed. I gasp for air, letting out a little sob. *What the hell was that?* Yes, the sensations rolling through my body were exquisite. Except Max was rough. Really rough. Tears leak from my eyes as I try to comprehend the way that fear and pleasure were so tightly coiled together.

A light flicks on.

'Hey?' Max's face is above mine, a look of concern on his handsome features, his right hand stroking my hair with a gentleness that was completely missing a few moments ago.

'What was that?' I ask, sitting up in bed, shifting away from him, pulling the duvet so it covers my naked body, my fingers tentatively feeling my own neck.

'Darling, what do you mean?' He also sits up in bed, his torso glistening with a fine sweat.

'That was too much, Max! It felt like you were strangling me.'

'Hey,' he says, grabbing my hand, his fingers making circles on my palm. 'Of course I wasn't! I would never hurt you. Never.'

He glances down and away, and a strange expression flits over his face before he turns to me again and gently cups my face with both his hands, leaning his forehead against mine.

'God, Laila. I'm so sorry you thought that. I didn't mean to scare you. I just wanted you to experience the most intense orgasm of your life. I should have discussed it with you beforehand, told you what we were going to do. I never want to hurt you. That was my bad.'

'You frightened me,' I say.

'Oh my darling.' He pulls me towards him in an awkward hug, placing butterfly kisses on my face. 'I would never do anything to harm you. Firstly you're so beautiful and precious I couldn't bear the thought of hurting you, but also, I'm a paramedic. I know how the human body works, and I would never go too far. Never. Will you forgive me?'

I nod because I can't trust myself to speak. Was I overreacting? I think of Jacob and how boringly vanilla our love life was. A quick wham bam in the missionary position was all my ex wanted. Even in the early days we were never passionate, not like Max is. But then again, I never felt unsafe with Jacob, at least not in the bedroom. He rarely told me he loved me and certainly never told me that I was beautiful and precious. My head is a mush, and my body aches so much it's as if I've been in a car crash. I simply don't know what to think.

I slide out of bed, grab my nightdress, put it on and walk towards the en suite bathroom. Max moves as if he's going to follow me.

'Please just give me five minutes,' I say, holding up the palm of my hand. He looks hurt, but stays in bed.

I lock the bathroom door behind me and take a hot shower, trying to understand what just happened. How could I feel so turned on yet scared in the same moment? Was it because I've never experienced truly passionate sex, or is it because Max and I don't know each other well yet, and I'm not one hundred per cent trusting of this semi-stranger? I could see the hurt and concern on his face, the way he seemed genuinely shocked that I'd been scared. I can't work out if I'm overreacting.

After a few long minutes letting the hot water ease my soreness, there's a knock on the bathroom door. 'Are you alright?' Max asks.

I switch off the shower and quickly dry myself, opening the door a few moments later. He's standing there, wearing his boxer shorts, the look of concern still etched across his face.

'I'm so sorry if I scared you,' he says, taking my hand and tugging me back towards the bed. 'So deeply sorry. I'll never do that again.'

I'm quiet as I slip under the duvet next to him.

'Can I make it up to you?' he asks, looking at me with that crooked grin and sparkling eyes, which, despite everything, makes me feel aroused again.

'How?'

'Please let me.' His voice is a hoarse whisper, as if he's full of desire, and as I look down at him, I see that his boxer shorts are already tenting. And then he's slipping under the duvet, and before I can stop him, his head is between my legs, gently licking and teasing and probing until I'm bucking underneath him. He brings me to the most intense orgasm I've ever experienced, and I let out a scream before collapsing back onto the mattress. Slowly he emerges from the duvet, a grin on his face. He leans over to switch off the light.

'Sleep well, sleeping beauty,' he says before wrapping his arms around me and cradling me until I drift off.

CHAPTER NINE

There's an awkwardness between us the next day. Max is cooking me breakfast, a big fry-up, which makes my stomach grumble.

'I just want to apologise again,' he says, batting those long dark eyelashes. 'Believe me when I say I would never hurt you, Laila.'

I don't know how to reply, but something has shifted inside me. Yes, I still like Max. I enjoy his conversation, my body responds to his touch as if I'm the keyboard underneath his magical fingers, but now I'm not sure that I trust him. I promised myself that I wouldn't put myself in a position where I could be hurt. Of course, when I was imagining myself in a future relationship, I was more concerned about protecting my shattered heart. It never crossed my mind I might be physically hurt. And yes, I do believe Max when he says he wouldn't knowingly hurt me, but there's an uneasiness now.

As the day goes by, he must sense it too, because he suggests we return home straight after lunch, and I lie, saying that I have a mountain of work to catch up on before Monday.

Neither of us have much to say on the drive home, so Max switches on the radio, and when we arrive in South Gridgley, it's a relief. The press has gone from Violet Lane, or perhaps it's just because it's Sunday afternoon and they have better places to be, and there's no obvious police presence either. I haven't heard from Finn, and there's been nothing on the news to suggest that Jackie has been found, but I know how these things work. There's another bigger story or a more pressing police case, and the attention shifts.

'I had a glorious weekend,' Max says as he unloads my belongings from the rental car. 'Thank you. And again, I'm so sorry about last night. I hope you won't hold it against me.'

I smile uncomfortably and let him follow me into the house, where he dumps my case and gives me a brief kiss.

'I have to return the rental car, and I reckon we both need our sleep tonight. Can I see you tomorrow or Tuesday evening?'

'I've got a really hectic week, Max. Can we touch base Wednesday or Thursday?'

'You're not giving me the brush-off, are you?'

I smile awkwardly because in a way, I am. 'No. I'm genuinely stretched at work.'

'Alright, then.' He places a chaste kiss on my lips. 'I'm going to miss you,' he says.

AROUND 10 A.M. on Monday morning I get a call from Finn. The police have asked him to attend an official interview, and he wants me to join him. I drop everything and head for the station. We have a quick chat in the now familiar interview room. Finn is upset, pacing the tiny room, dark rings under his eyes and bitten fingernails.

'They want to search my car, take it in, look for evidence or something.'

'Is that a problem?' I ask.

'Well, no.' He wrings his hands. 'It's just so intrusive. They should be out there looking for proper suspects. Looking for Jackie.' He drops down onto the chair heavily. 'What should I do?'

'Unless you have something to hide, I strongly recommend that you agree to all police requests.'

'I don't have anything to hide.' His voice is indignant.

'In which case, it's good to cooperate with the police because then they can eliminate you as a suspect and concentrate their efforts more productively. That's the way you should look at it.'

Finn slumps. 'Alright. It's just they're looking in the wrong direction. They should be out there searching for Jackie. Using helicopters to scour fields and forests, divers to look in rivers. And what if she's been left for dead, or perhaps she's been kidnapped and is being held in someone's basement.'

'I'm sure they will be considering all angles, and that's something we can discuss with them.'

I'm almost relieved when there's a knock on the door and DC Vicky Mortimer and DS Stefan Kolinsky enter, sitting down on the chairs opposite us. DS Kolinsky explains that this is a voluntary interview, and Finn is free to leave should he so wish. The reality is, Finn isn't really free to leave. The interview is recorded and can be used in evidence in court, so it would be very bad optics indeed for Finn to walk out. After the formal preliminaries of explaining who we all are and that the interview will be recorded, DS Kolinsky starts with the questions.

'Can you tell us more about the state of your marriage?'

Finn glances at me, an expression of indignation on his face. I smile back at him and nod to indicate it's alright for him to answer.

He lets out a puff of air. 'We love each other; it's just we've been going through some tough times. Yes, we argued. We are both overtired from broken nights. Melanie isn't a great sleeper.'

'Is it right that your wife was having an affair?'

Finn stiffens. 'I wouldn't call it an affair.'

I also sit upright. He hasn't mentioned this to me.

'What would you call it, then?' DS Kolinsky asks.

'It was a fling. A mistake. We were trying to patch things up. Both of us want our marriage to work.'

'And who did your wife have this fling with?'

'Max. Maxwell Critchley who lives at number 32 Violet Lane. He's our neighbour.'

I freeze.

What the hell?

CHAPTER TEN

What the hell?

Jackie was having an affair with Max? My Max. I try to keep my face expressionless so as not to show how shocked I am. My heart thuds, and my hands start to shake. I sit on them and try to concentrate on what Finn is saying.

'And how long was this affair going on for, to the best of your knowledge?'

'I don't know.' His voice catches. 'Not long, I think.'

'Why didn't you tell us this before, Mr Walker?' DC Mortimer asks.

'Because the police always blame the husband, and I'm hoping that Jackie will still be found safe and well. If you knew she'd cheated on me, you'd think I harmed her, wouldn't you? Just like you're blaming me now.'

'Your wife has been missing for nearly two weeks now, Mr Walker, and we have no decent leads. I would have thought that this was a vital piece of information you would want us to know. Or have you kept this information from us because you were so angry your wife was cheating on you that you harmed her?'

Finn hangs his head. I'm finding it hard to concentrate, to formulate what, if anything, I should tell him to say.

And then Finn starts crying, his shoulders heaving, tears rolling down his unshaven face. 'I would never hurt Jackie. Never. And she would never leave us. She just wouldn't. She loves Melanie too much, and me.'

'Did you hurt Jackie because you found out about her affair?'

We all listen to Finn's sobs, and I wonder if he's about to confess.

'Now would be a good time for you to tell us everything, Finn,' DS Kolinsky says, leaning back in his chair.

'No, I would never hurt her.' Finn sniffs and looks at me. I give him a gentle nod. 'You've got to believe me. I don't know where she is, and I've got a really bad feeling. You shouldn't be interviewing me. I know who did it. I know who's hurt my Jackie. It's Max. Max Critchley.'

I'M NOT sure how I get through the police interview, and much of what is said after Finn makes his pronouncement is lost to me. Hopefully I'll get a transcript from the police. I try to be as professional as possible, but my mind is in turmoil. Is there any truth in what Finn is saying? Is he just a desperate and jealous man trying to deflect the blame? And did Max and Jackie really have an affair?

At lunchtime I have to get outside, to breathe in some fresh air and clear my head. I buy a sandwich from a local café and stride towards the playing fields behind the high street. I pass a woman sticking pictures of Jackie up on lampposts with the word *Missing* in bold letters. It gives me a terrible jolt, and I stop still and stare.

'Hello,' the young woman says, a quizzical look on her face. There's something familiar about her. And then I remember I saw her pushing little Melanie in her pram. 'Oh hello,' I say. 'I'm Laila, and I live at number 30 Violet Lane.'

'Ah, yes. You're Finn's solicitor.' She's not wearing sunglasses today, and she looks pale. She's holding a large stack of flyers and a roll of Sellotape.

'Are you a relative?' I ask.

She shakes her head. 'No, I'm Ellie. I'm Jackie's best friend. We've known each other since we were kids, and she's more of a sister to me than my own. I'm a registered childminder, so I'm helping Finn take care of Melanie, just until Jackie comes home.' Her eyes well up. 'I'm glad you're his solicitor. It's so unfair that the police are pointing their finger at him.'

'I'm so sorry about everything,' I say, trying to banish the memories of this morning's police interview. 'Can I do anything to help? Put up some flyers, perhaps?'

'I think I've got it in hand, but we're planning a vigil the day after tomorrow at the church, praying for Jackie's safe return. None of us are religious or anything, but we wanted to do something proactive. Perhaps you could spread the word? I mean, hopefully Jacks will be home by then so we can cancel it, but just in case.' Her voice tapers out.

'Of course I can help spread the word,' I promise. 'And don't hesitate to ask for help if I can do anything else.'

'Thanks. You're kind,' she says. 'At least Finn has lovely neighbours. It makes all the difference.'

I guess Finn hasn't shared his concerns about Max with

Ellie. We smile weakly at each other, and I walk away. On second thoughts, I don't think the fresh air and stunning views of the Downs are going to help my peace of mind, so instead I turn around and head back to the office. Better to lose myself in work.

I'M IN TURMOIL. Max hasn't said anything to me about having a fling with Jackie, but then again, would he really have told me? Perhaps he is embarrassed to have had a relationship with a married woman. And what are the implications? It's quite possible that Finn is just deflecting, and I'm sure if the police think there's a grain of truth in what Finn is saying, they'll interview Max.

I think back to Phyllis' barbecue. I remember Jackie appearing tense, but Max and Finn were happily manning the barbecue together. There didn't seem to be any friction there. Or did I miss the undercurrents? I recall Jackie's strained reaction to whatever it was Finn whispered in her ear. Did that have any significance?

I'M glad that I told Max I'm busy for the next few days except it doesn't stop him trying to get my attention. On Monday evening, I arrive home to find a huge bouquet of flowers on my doorstep with a note that thanks me for a 'glorious weekend'. On Tuesday, I find a tinfoil-covered dish, again deposited on my front doorstep with a little note from Max saying he's working late, but wanted me to have a scrumptious dinner, and hopes that his beef stew will hit the mark. On Wednesday morning, I get a WhatsApp from him with a MP3 attachment. It's a beautiful piano piece.

It's only when I reach the end that Max's voice floods my ears. 'Laila, this makes me think of you. I hope you enjoy it.'

All this attention does nothing to ease my mind, so I call Jazmin.

'How was the dirty weekend away?' she asks, an eagerness to her voice.

'It was good.'

But my friend picks up on the hesitation in my voice.

'What aren't you telling me?'

'Nothing.' I don't tell her about the forceful sex because I know what she'll say. Run. Run now. I don't tell her about Finn's revelation in the police interview because that would be breaking client confidentiality. 'He's just doing a bit of love bombing right now,' I add weakly.

'Has he told you he loves you?' she asks, surprise in her voice.

I think about it. Actually, he hasn't, but actions speak louder than words, don't they?

'A bit early for that,' I mutter. 'He's sent me flowers, last night he left home-cooked food on my doorstep, and he's recorded me a piano piece.'

'And what exactly are you complaining about?' She laughs. 'He really seems too good to be true.'

That statement hits me because on so many levels Jazmin is right. He's attentive, kind, loving, and talented, not to mention his ravishing good looks. But now there are two hiccups. The rough sex he was deeply apologetic about, and Finn's accusation. Is that something I can simply ignore? The trouble is, this man has got under my skin. I haven't been showered with this much attention, ever. I've never felt so good about my body, so very alive, loving sex. Max is like an addiction. I can't stop thinking about him, and I crave his touch. Is he really too good to be true?

BY THURSDAY, I know I'm going to have to make a decision. It's not like I can sneak out my back door and creep through the garden every time I leave the house, just to avoid Max. So when I receive a message from him, first thing in the morning, I open it with some trepidation.

> I'm meeting with some of my mates after work. Would you like to join us? I'd love you to meet them.

My initial reaction is no. Why would I want to do that? Except, what is the alternative? I could confront him directly with Finn's accusation, but then I'd be breaching client confidentiality and putting my career at risk, or I could try to find out more about him in a subtle manner. Alternatively, I could step away from the relationship completely. That would be the most sensible course of action, certainly what I should be doing. But in my heart it's not what I want. I've fallen for Max. I enjoy his company, and most of all he makes me feel amazing. I know I should recuse myself from Finn's case, except he hasn't been charged with anything, and is there really any reason for me to do that at this stage? Or I could just tell Max that our fledgling relationship is over, except that's not what I want either. Yes, I'm going around and around in circles.

Over a strong coffee and a couple of pieces of toast, I try to make up my mind. It's weird because I'm normally decisive, seeing life in black and white. But today, there are too many shades of grey. Maybe I *should* meet Max's friends. On the one hand, it means I don't have to be alone with him, and it will give me some breathing space. But perhaps even more importantly, it'll give me a better feel for him, seeing how he acts around them, what sort of people he chooses to surround himself with. And perhaps they will give me the reassurance I need that Max is a good person and that his behaviour in bed was just overenthusiastic sexual play and Finn's accusations are nothing but lies.

My phone pings again with another message from Max. It's a question mark emoji followed by a kiss emoji. He's obviously waiting for my answer. Before I can change my mind again, I write:

Sure. I'd love to meet your friends.

Fantastic!!! We're meeting at the Fox and Hounds pub at the far end of South Gridgley, 7 p.m. See you there!

THE REST of the day is difficult, and I find it hard to concentrate, so when, late in the afternoon, Max sends me a message, it's like a jolt.

Can't wait to show you off to my friends!!

I groan. I could still cancel, I suppose. But then I think about Jacob and his friends and how they should have been a warning to me, except I was young and naïve, and I thought I was in love. Now there are no excuses, and I know that Max's friendships will give me a good insight into him. I am a very different person more than a decade on.

Jacob and I met through work. It was a legal awards dinner to which I'd only been invited at the last minute because the partner I worked for was ill, and she requested I fill her shoes. I had nothing suitable to wear and ended up renting a fabulous dark red satin dress that clung to me in all the right places. The only other person I knew on the guest list was Jazmin, and during the initial drinks, we clung to each other like limpets. I could feel plenty of eyes on me, and I knew I looked good, not at all like many of the dowdy women in their long-sleeved velvet gowns.

At dinner, Jazmin and I were separated, and I was placed between a partner who must have been close to eighty and seemed to doze off, his chin sinking precariously low towards his soup, and Jacob. My soon-to-be husband was reasonably good looking – and he had a full head of hair back then – but most of all, he was uber confident. He had that air of superiority that comes with attending an expensive boarding school, followed by Oxford University. It helped that he'd recently been chosen as one of the thirty under-thirty rising-star lawyers.

For the whole of that meal, Jacob seemed transfixed by me. Perhaps it was because my upbringing was so different to his, or perhaps it was simply that he fancied me rotten. After the meal, he led me over to his friends. A bunch of braying solicitors who were indulging in the kind of drinking games that I thought we'd left behind at university. It should have been my first warning because I didn't warm to any of them.

Our relationship moved quickly. He encouraged me to apply for a job at Cassel, Everett and Parker, which I got. Six months later, we were engaged, and our wedding day was one week short of a year since we'd first met.

I can't deny that the warning signs were there. Every-thing had to be on Jacob's terms. He found my friends boring and banal, so I dropped most of them. It was only Jazmin who stuck by me, prepared to tolerate Jacob's derogatory remarks, able to retort with barbed comments even sharper than Jacob's. I think secretly he admired her, was even a little in awe of her brilliant mind, not that he ever articulated such a thought.

I was quite literally swept away by him. He promised me a world that I could barely imagine. Luxury holidays to far-flung places; a beautiful home in the country; the chance to discuss the law at home; sparkling children running around our garden. I really thought that I was going to experience a lifetime of mental stimulation, that I had found my equal. Unfortunately Jacob is a deep-rooted chauvinist, something it took me a while to realise.

I should have known the man I was marrying before our wedding because with hindsight the signs were all there. As his family had money and mine didn't, he announced that he would be paying for the wedding. All Mum and Dad (or me, as was in fact the case) had to do was pay for my dress. And as he, or more accurately, his mother, Bella, was in charge of organising everything, I felt like a spare part. We had a guest list of two hundred, except three-quarters of those were Jacob's family and friends, or friends of his parents who just had to be invited because they were invaluable business contacts.

I didn't warm to any of Jacob's close friends. Mostly, they came across as opinionated, entitled snobs who at best just about tolerated me, but mostly ignored me.

And so I have learned my lesson. Your partner's choice of friends matters. It's a reflection of them, and if I'd paid more attention to that a decade ago, my life might have turned out differently. That's why it's the right decision to meet Max's friends. It'll give me an insight into him.

Back at home, I throw on a sweater and jeans, eat a quick

sandwich and head for the pub. It's a quaint old-world type of establishment with dark beams and low ceilings and a rabbit warren of rooms. A photo of missing Jackie is pinned to the wall in the entrance lobby, and it's disconcerting, but I stride in quickly and stand on tiptoes, glancing around at all the clusters of jolly drinkers.

Max stands up and waves at me, and despite everything, my stomach flutters. He's wearing a tight white T-shirt and low-slung jeans that make him look younger than usual. I weave between the tables, and as I get close, he steps forwards, placing his hands on my shoulders and bending down to give me a kiss on the lips. He then turns me around and, holding me close, says, 'So, everyone, this is Laila, the woman I can't stop talking about.'

I smile awkwardly. There are ten people seated around two circular tables pushed together. Eight men, and two women, with a couple of the men still wearing their green paramedic's uniform. Max introduces me to everyone although most of their names escape me almost immediately. He then pulls out a chair for me and hurries to the bar to get me a glass of white wine.

A petite woman called Saffron, with short bright blue hair, leans towards me. 'We're so happy to meet you, Laila. Max has been insufferable the past fortnight. It's been Laila this and Laila that.'

'Oh really!' I laugh awkwardly. In many ways I'm flattered that Max must have been thinking about me as much as I've been thinking about him, except then I remember Jackie. Perhaps he was obsessed with her, but because she was married, he couldn't share his feelings. Or was Finn lying? I go over and over the same narrative. How do I even know Finn was telling the truth? Perhaps he's just looking for somewhere to place the blame. My confused thoughts are interrupted by Saffron, and I focus my attention on her.

'We've never met any of his girlfriends before.'

'Are you also a paramedic?' I ask her.

'Yes. Most of us are. It's a stressful job, so we tend to hang around together. You develop a wry kind of humour in our line of work, which some people don't get.'

'I guess you have to to survive.'

'Yes. It's a kind of armour that really can't be taught. Some people survive working in high-stress situations, and others don't. Anyway, Max said you're a solicitor?'

'Not as exciting as being a paramedic,' I say.

'It's only exciting when we manage to save people.' She looks rather wistful, and I try not to think of the terrible things she has experienced. 'Max is really good at his job. Super calm under pressure.'

He reappears with my drink and drags a stool to perch next to me. Despite everything, it's a relaxed and fun evening, and his friends and colleagues are generous in involving me in their banter. They're a very different crew to Jacob's friends, teasing each other, laughing with abandon, happy to talk about both their pasts and their futures.

'Did you all train together?' I ask Saffron.

'Some of us did. I don't know where Max trained. He's only been part of our gang for about eighteen months. But honestly, it's like he's been here forever.'

'Oh,' I say, surprised. 'He didn't mention he was new to paramedics.'

'Sounds like you've been spending too much time in bed and not enough time talking,' a tall man sitting opposite me interjects, with a wink and a grin. 'But Max is an old hand paramedic, aren't you, mate?'

'What's that?' Max asks, turning away from a conversation with the man to his right.

'Just saying you're new to us, but you're not new to the job. How long have you been a paramedic?'

'Goodness, coming up for a decade now. I'm definitely one of the old-timers.'

'Guess it was a bit different in the big city to here in the countryside.'

'A lot less knife crime here,' Max says.

'I didn't realise you were new to Sussex,' I add, wondering why Max has never mentioned that.

'I'm a convert to small-town life.' He laughs, as if this omission is completely normal. 'Saffron's right. I've been here for eighteen months and loving every minute of it. I wouldn't return to the big smoke if you paid me.'

The conversation ebbs and flows. From time to time, thoughts of Max and Jackie and Finn permeate my thoughts, but generally I feel surprisingly relaxed, laughing with these people as if I've known them a lifetime. It's only when I glance at my watch and realise it's gone 10 p.m. that I say it's time for me to leave.

'Well, you're not going home alone,' Max adds, placing a kiss on my cheek. He holds my hand and helps me to my feet.

I say my goodbyes, promising to see them all again, and we walk out of the pub. I hope that I will see Max's friends again, but if my relationship with Max doesn't last, then I suppose it's unlikely.

'They liked you,' Max says, putting his arm around my shoulders and pulling me in tightly.

'How do you know?'

'I can tell. We're all pretty close. It's the nature of the job.'

'You didn't tell me you've only moved to Sussex recently.'

'I think we've had more important things to talk about and do, haven't we?' He nibbles at my ear, and I gently push him away. It does bother me that I know so little about Max, especially in light of Finn's accusations, but at least I'm reassured that his work colleagues like him.

As we approach Violet Lane, I disentangle myself from Max because I can't afford to be seen with his arm around me. I pretend to be fumbling in my handbag for my keys, and I don't think he twigs that I've consciously moved away from him. Fortunately, once again we see no one on Violet Lane. There are lights on in all the houses, but it's so quiet. We're in front of my house when Max asks, 'Can I come in? It's been a complete nightmare not being able to touch you this evening.'

I laugh. 'You sound like a teenage boy.'

'I feel like one. You're my addiction, Laila.'

I hesitate. Every cell of my body is screaming out for Max's touch, except my rational, lawyer's brain is trying to pour cold water on my desires. If Max was having an affair with Jackie, then he's been lying to me. And if what Finn said was true, then should I be scared of this man? I think about his hand on my throat, but then the gentleness of his touch afterwards, his caressing words, the way he made my body burn with desire, his genuine kindness. That visceral need to be touched, to be loved, to actually feel good about myself banishes the negative thoughts. But has Max been lying to me?

My key is in the lock, and I can sense Max so close to me,

it's making every nerve ending in my body burn. The scent of his aftershave melts my insides, and then I feel a gentle touch in the centre of my back.

'Come on in, then,' I murmur quickly before my rational brain takes over again. I unlock my door and step inside, hopeful that no one has seen us. Max kicks the door closed and is kissing me before I've even had a chance to switch the hall lights on.

He pushes me back against the wall, his body pressing hard into mine, and once again, there's that sense of urgency. His hands are everywhere, exploring and probing, tugging off my clothes.

When I'm just in my underwear, he steps back, and I see his eyes glisten in the dark light. 'God, you're beautiful,' he murmurs. And then he scoops me up into his arms and carries me up the stairs, all the while I'm protesting, chuckling, asking him to put me down, but he's too strong, and somehow he manages to place distracting little kisses up my neck as he walks.

'You're going to drop me.' I laugh.

'Never. We're surgically attached to each other. You're the yin to my yang, or whatever the saying is. I want to take care of you and make love to you for ever and ever.'

And then, before I can really register that his words are just too much, he's gently laying me down on my bed. In seconds, he's ripped his own clothes off and is lowering himself down on top of me. Once again, our lovemaking is urgent and passionate, and I get completely lost in the scent of him and the exquisite sensations that surge through me over and over until we're both screaming out loud and collapsing in a breathless, giggling heap.

As I lie there, exhausted, unable to move, waves of happiness pouring through me, Finn's revelations come back to mind, and I know that somehow I'm going to have to talk to Max and put my mind at rest. Except how can I without betraying my client, without breaking the code of ethics that has been so deeply ingrained into me?

'Shit.' Max sits up on the bed suddenly, shuffling upwards.

'What is it?' I ask, turning to switch the bedside light on. He's looking down at himself, his beautiful naked body.

'The condom broke.'

I sit up too, any embarrassment about being completely naked vanishing. 'Are you sure?'

'Um, yes. I'm so sorry, Laila. This hasn't happened in years.'

'I'll take the morning-after pill,' I say, although at my age and stage I doubt I even need to do that. The chances of me getting pregnant are close to zero.

'So sorry, sweetheart. But rest assured I don't have any nasty diseases. I'm careful about sex and get myself checked every so often.'

That never crossed my mind. But I suppose if you're sexually active and single, that would be the sensible thing to do. It's just I haven't been in this position in over a decade. And then, despite me trying not to, I think of Jackie, and Max's accusations. Did my lover sleep with her? And if so, did they use protection?

'Hey, you're tense.' Max is stroking my back. Except I'm not tense for the reason he thinks. 'I'm really sorry about this. I hope you're not too worried or annoyed. Let's have a hot shower and head back to bed,' he says, gently taking my hand and leading me to my en suite bathroom.

By the time we're back under the duvet, having made

love again in the shower, I'm completely exhausted and almost immediately fall into a dreamless sleep in Max's arms.

I awake with a start, sitting bolt upright in bed. Max is still asleep next to me, snoring gently. The doorbell is ringing repeatedly, as if someone is pushing their finger on it, briefly releasing and then pushing again. What the hell?

I jump up and pull on my dressing gown.

'What is it?' Max asks sleepily.

'There's someone at the door,' I reply. 'I'm going to look out the window of the spare room.'

I hurry across the hallway and walk into the spare room that has windows looking out onto Violet Lane. I leave the lights off so that I can see. A uniformed police officer is standing on my doorstep. My heart sinks. What on earth is he doing here in the middle of the night? I hurry back to my bedroom.

'Stay in my bed and close the door, please,' I instruct Max. The last thing I need is for the police to realise Max is here.

'Why?' he asks, his brow furrowed.

'It's a client. These things happen, I'm afraid.' Not true. We lawyers go out of our way to protect our personal information from clients, and I've never had a client either know my home address or visit me at home. I remove my dressing gown, pull on a jumper and jeans, rush down the stairs, lift up the chain and unlock the door.

'I'm sorry to disturb you, ma'am,' the officer says.

'What's happened?' I glance up Violet Lane towards Finn's house and see that all the lights are on in the windows, two police cars parked outside. I look at my smartwatch. It's 2 a.m., so why all the activity in the middle of the night?

'Your client Finn Walker requires your presence.'

'Why?'

'I'm sorry to tell you that the body of Jackie Walker has been found.'

'Oh no,' I say, leaning against the doorframe for support. 'I'm so sorry.' I grab my keys from the bowl in the hallway and follow the officer across the road. Finn's front door opens, and he's there, crouching down onto his knees. He buries his face in his hands. His hair is messy, and he's wearing a T-shirt and jogging bottoms, as if, like me, he's just got out of bed. Another police officer is standing behind him in the hallway.

Finn can barely get his words out, he's sobbing so hard. 'They've found Jackie's body.'

'I know. I'm so terribly sorry,' I say.

Finn gets up now and swipes the back of his hand across his nose. His voice is juddering. 'They found her caught up in a reed bed in the River Arun. My poor baby.' He sobs again. 'And now these guys' – he throws his hand towards the police officer standing behind him – 'are pointing their fingers at me. They're saying I must have done it. They've got a warrant to search my house, and they're ripping the place apart.'

CHAPTER ELEVEN

It's a horrible night. I stay with Finn for a while, but there's nothing much I can do to support him. The police have a warrant, and they're entitled to search his house, yet they still don't charge him. I assume they're on a fishing trip and awaiting results of the post-mortem. About 3 a.m., I return home and gently awaken Max. The time has come to tell him that I'm Finn's solicitor.

His reaction surprises me. 'I'm so proud of you,' he says, hugging me tightly.

'The thing is, with everything going on in Violet Lane, I don't think we should be seen together. It could be a bit awkward, with me being Finn's lawyer. And the police are likely to want to interview all the neighbours again. They've found Jackie's body.'

Max tenses. I watch him carefully, looking for any hints that Finn might be correct, that Max had feelings for Jackie, that he might have something to do with her disappearance and death.

'Oh, that's terrible,' he mutters. 'What a tragedy.' He lets out a puff of air and relaxes back onto the mattress, his eyes fluttering closed. Is this the reaction of a guilty man or the reaction of someone who had feelings for the deceased? I'm not sure. Or is Max pretending to fall back to sleep because that's the best way to conceal his true thoughts?

'So are you okay if, publicly, we keep our distance?'

His eyes flicker open. 'If that's what you need for your job, but not for too long, please. I want us to be official, Laila,' he says. 'But right now, I'm really, really tired. Can we sleep?'

Max seems to drift easily back to sleep. I don't. I toss and turn all night long, my imagination getting the better of me, images of Jackie's battered and bloated body filling my head. In the morning, I'm bleary eyed, and my bones ache. Max brings me coffee in bed.

'It's on the news,' he says. He's got the local radio playing on his phone, and unsurprisingly, the press have got their teeth into the story. As I look at the news on my phone, all the headlines say something similar: 'Young mum found butchered in river'. Apparently Jackie was found with stab wounds, murdered. A police spokesman promises that 'no stone will be left unturned in the hunt for Jackie's killer, and he or she will be promptly brought to justice'. I hope the spokesperson is correct.

'There's the vigil for her this afternoon,' I murmur.

'I'll be there,' Max says as he dresses in yesterday's clothes.

'Me too. But we'll need to keep our distance.'

Max doesn't reply, seemingly lost in thought. I wish I knew what he was thinking, whether he knows things he's not telling me.

WHAT WAS MEANT to have been a vigil for Jackie has now taken a sombre tone and morphed into a memorial for a much-loved young woman. The service takes place at 6 p.m. in the evening. I reckon the whole town must be in attendance, not surprising I suppose, since apparently there hasn't been a tragic, high-profile death in South Gridgley for several decades. The church is small, and any expectation of holding it inside is quickly banished. There are hundreds of people milling around the graveyard, most of them carrying flowers or a candle or even a teddy bear, which I find a little bizarre. Soon there is a huge semicircle of lit candles flickering in the fading light. I attend with my work colleagues, and like most other businesses in the town, we finish work early to show our respects. A large photo of Jackie has been pinned to an ancient cedar tree, and Finn, Ellie, plus a handful of other people, who I assume must be Jackie's relatives and closest friends, huddle together next to the vicar.

There is such sorrow in the air, yet there's also tension. Lots of poorly concealed whispers about Finn, pointing fingers at him, barely concealed suggestions that he murdered his wife.

Despite the hordes of people, I can sense Max. He's standing off to my left, talking to a couple of people I don't recognise. I catch his eye and nod at him, then turn away, conscious of his eyes on my back throughout.

'Laila,' an unfamiliar voice says. It's Jamie, my neighbour. I've only seen Jamie and Rico once or twice since our initial introduction at Phyllis'.

'Good to see you, but not under these circumstances.'

'I know. It's terrible. I came down from London to pay my respects. I've been crazy busy with work, so I haven't spent much time in South Gridgley.'

'How are you and Rico?' I ask, because I can't think of anything else to say.

'Rico has been travelling a lot. He was sorry he couldn't be here today.' From Jamie's expression and the way he's talking, I sense that there's more to Rico's absence.

Just after 6 p.m., the vicar coughs into a microphone and starts talking.

'We are gathered here today under the very worst of circumstances,' he says. 'To remember the life of Jackie Walker, a beloved wife, mother, sister, daughter and friend, taken from us much too early. The news of Jackie's death has shaken this community to its very core. Such a terrible event has never happened in South Gridgley, certainly not within our living memory. We say our prayers for Jackie and that she may rest in peace, and our thoughts and prayers are with her beloved family and friends, who are suffering such a grievous loss. As many of you will know, this is a police investigation, and Detective Sergeant Stefan Kolinsky would like to say a few words. Afterwards, we will hear from Ellie, Jackie's best friend, and then we will join together in prayer.'

The vicar steps to one side, and it's only then that I notice DS Kolinsky. Unlike the previous times I've met him, he is wearing a jacket and tie and looks particularly sombre. He leans into the microphone.

'Thank you, Vicar. The tragic death of Jackie Walker is now a murder investigation. Whilst I would like to reassure the community and further afield that there is no suggestion that there is further risk to members of the public, we have no suspects at this moment in time.'

There's a rustling amongst the crowd, with all eyes turning towards Finn, accompanied by low, murmuring voices. Finn's gaze is firmly to the ground.

'As such, there will be a heightened police presence and visibility in the coming days in the area as enquiries are ongoing and we gather evidence to bring an offender to justice for Jackie's family. Should you have any information that you feel might be of relevance to this investigation, I urge you to contact me or my colleagues. Thank you.'

Kolinsky shuffles to one side, and then Ellie stands in front of the microphone. She's smartly dressed in a long black coat and boots, her face pale but made up. She looks older than the woman I met the other day.

'Jackie is my best friend,' she says before her voice cracks. She sniffs. 'Jackie was my best friend. I miss her so much, and I will miss her for the rest of my life, as will Finn and their beautiful daughter, Melanie. Finn wanted to talk today, but it's just too much for him.' She glances over at Finn, who nods at her, and she throws him a weak smile. 'Finn is a good man. Do not listen to the unfounded rumours. He was a loving husband to Jackie, a wonderful father to Melanie, and a friend to me and many others.'

I notice that DS Kolinksy is frowning. I wonder if Ellie is going off script.

'Please help the police bring the murderer to justice. There have been rumours about Jackie becoming the victim of a serial rapist, of her taking her own life and all sorts of other horrible things on social media. But the chances are that someone here knows something. Please help us by contacting the police, even if you think it's the tiniest thing that might be irrelevant. It could be the key that helps bring the evil murderer to justice.' She pauses then, and the evening is so quiet, you could hear a leaf drop from a tree. Then she turns and walks towards Finn, slipping her arm into his.

The vicar takes over for the next ten minutes, leading everyone in a couple of prayers before explaining that there will be an official funeral for Jackie when the police have concluded their investigations. I overhear a woman's whisper behind me.

'Finn was always leery. He lost his virginity at twelve. Can you imagine that?'

'What are you saying?' another woman asks.

They move away, and I don't hear the answer.

Jamie throws me a knowing look, as if this isn't news to him. He opens his mouth as if he's going to say something, but Phyllis appears and drags Jamie away. The crowd dissipates quickly, many of the candles blowing out fast, as a wind has picked up. I glance around to look for Max and to my dismay see Finn making a beeline for him. I weave through the groups of remaining people just as Finn appears in front of Max, who is deep in conversation with the same couple he was talking to earlier. Everything about Finn is tense. His fingers are clenched into fists at his sides, tendons protrude on the side of his neck, and his jaw is set forwards, his bloodshot eyes fixed on Max.

Max glances up. 'I'm so sorry, mate,' he says. 'This is the most terrible, terrible news.'

I reach Finn just as he's lifting up his fist, clearly about to punch Max in the face. Somehow, I manage to grab Finn's upper arm and tug it downwards, throwing myself off balance.

'Finn,' I say, holding his arm tightly and using his strength to right myself. I ignore Max, who throws me a confused glance. 'Finn.' I speak loudly and firmly. 'I need to have a word with you, urgently.'

The tension releases from his body as quickly as if I'd pricked a balloon. He sighs as he turns towards me.

'Come on,' I say, my hand still resting on his upper arm, guiding him back towards the church.

'What was that bastard doing, turning up here? He shouldn't be here. The police should have him locked up in a cell.'

Finn's words sicken me.

'Anyway, what do you want?' he asks. 'I wish you hadn't bloody well stopped me.'

'I had to defuse the situation and make sure that you don't get into further trouble. How would it look to the police if you got done for grievous bodily harm, beating up Max?'

Finn grunts. Then Ellie appears and slips her arm into Finn's. 'Shall we get you home?' she asks. 'Melanie will be wondering where you are.'

THE NEXT MORNING, I get another call from the police and a further request to go to the police station. Finn has been arrested. It doesn't surprise me. It's obvious that the police have been homing in on him from day one, yet I wonder if they're right. Sure, Finn could be an excellent actor, but my gut feeling is that he's innocent. But if he's innocent, does that make Max guilty? When I arrive back in the familiar small room, Finn looks utterly broken. His stubble is now a ragged beard, his eyes are red with heavy grey rings underneath them. He's wearing a long-sleeved T-shirt that looks like it hasn't been washed in weeks. His right knee is jumping up and down, and he's sitting on his hands.

I have seconds with him before Kolinsky and Mortimer

enter the room, just enough time to tell him that he should respond by saying no comment to their questions. After the formalities of taking our names and explaining that this interview will be recorded, they waste no time.

'Finn Walker,' DS Kolinksy says, 'we are arresting you on suspicion of the murder of your wife, Jackie Walker. You do not have to say anything. But it may harm your defence if you do not mention when questioned something which you later rely on in court. Anything you do say may be given in evidence.'

Kolinsky shuffles some papers on the table.

'Can you explain the traces of Jackie's blood that we found in the kitchen of the home you shared with Jackie?'

This is news to me. Finn pales, glances at me, and I nod.

'No comment.'

'Can you explain why you took three days to report your wife missing?'

'I've already told you–'

I place a hand on Finn's forearm.

'No comment.'

The questioning continues in a similar vein, going over many of the issues that the police covered in previous interviews. Finn follows my instructions of saying no comment, but I can tell he's getting more and more agitated.

'I need to say something,' he says eventually, obtusely ignoring me and staring straight at the detectives. 'I've been framed. I didn't do it, but I know who did. And he's framed me.'

'Who do you think murdered your wife, Finn?' DS Kolinsky's voice is laden with sarcasm.

'Max Critchley. I've already told you that. Have you interviewed him yet? Because you're wasting your time focusing on me. I didn't do it; he did!' Finn is leaning right across the table now, half out of his chair, his face, which was pale, is now puce. 'He's a creep.'

'Sit down, Mr Walker,' DS Kolinsky instructs him. Finn sinks back onto the plastic chair, which creaks under his weight.

'Why won't you listen to me?' he asks, more to himself I think than as a question for the police. Meanwhile I'm feeling increasingly uncomfortable.

'Ms Bowden?' DS Kolinsky says.

I've completely missed his last few sentences. 'Sorry,' I mutter. 'I think I've got a migraine coming on.'

'In which case it's just as well we're finished here,' he says, his lips pressed into a straight line. 'We are formally charging Mr Walker, and he will be held in police custody pending the bail hearing.'

'No!' Finn says, jumping up from his chair. 'They can't arrest me. I haven't done anything wrong.'

Except the police clearly think he has, and they claim to have found evidence of Jackie's blood in their kitchen. Right now, there's nothing I can do for Finn. He's led away in handcuffs while I promise to do everything I can to get him off the charges, knowing that my words are meaningless.

I wander back to the office dejectedly. Everything is a mess. What would Finn think if he knew that Max and I were an item? I can't begin to imagine his rage, and frankly, he'd be entitled to be furious. I feel like I've been backed into a corner, and I don't know how to get out of it. I could resign the case, stating a conflict of interest, but I should have recused myself sooner, straight after the first time Finn accused Max. Yet I didn't. And now it's too late. My reputation is at stake – no, worse than that, my whole career. I could be reported to the ethics committee of the Law Society. And what of Finn's accusation?

I try to imagine Max hurting Jackie, and I can't. Except my mind harks back to when he put pressure on my neck, how he explained that he knows the human body. If anyone would know how to kill someone, it would be Max. Except the police said that Jackie was killed with stab wounds. That doesn't seem like the modus operandi of a medical professional or a professional killer, but more like a frenzied crime of passion. But could Max have lost control?

My head is a jumble of conflicting thoughts. I want to stay on this case, to concentrate on supporting Finn, because at least it'll mean that I'm privy to any information that might affect Max. I'll then be in a position of power, able to make sensible, informed decisions. And if the evidence really does point towards Max, then I will extricate myself from the relationship and report him straight to the police. Surely that's the best result for everyone involved?

THAT EVENING, Max turns up at my doorstep with a Chinese takeaway and a bottle of wine. For a moment I wonder if I should come up with some excuse, except I'm so weary, I'm not quick enough. In fact, it's more than that; despite everything, I actually want to be in Max's company.

'I thought you might need cheering up,' he says before spooning the food onto plates that he's removed from my cupboard. Max is increasingly at home at my place. 'I gather Finn has been formally charged.'

'Yes,' I confirm.

'What evidence have they got against Finn? Must be pretty major to arrest him.'

'I'm afraid I can't disclose anything.'

Max grabs my hand and brings it up to his lips. 'It'll be all over the media soon enough,' he says. He may be right, but it still doesn't mean I can share details of the case, especially considering Finn's accusations.

I'm quiet as we eat.

'Do the police know what Finn's motive was? Was it a crime of passion?' Max asks.

'Hey, don't push me,' I say. 'I really can't disclose anything.'

'Fair enough. Sorry if I'm making you uncomfortable. It's just quite something to be the neighbour of a man accused of killing his wife.'

'How well did you know Finn and Jackie?' I ask, trying to keep my face impassive.

Max hesitates. He's about to take a sip of his wine but places the glass back down on the table. 'Hardly at all. Obviously we met at neighbourhood social events, and I waved at them when we passed in the street. But that's it. Besides, I haven't been living here long, less than eighteen months.' He takes that sip of wine. 'But thank goodness I did move to Violet Lane; otherwise we may never have met. I'd love to do another weekend away. Have you got any thoughts as to where we could go next?'

I notice how adeptly Max has changed the subject. Was that done on purpose because he didn't want to baldly lie to my face, or was that a natural segueing of the conversation? An unease creeps down my spine. As much as I like Max, and I really do, there's a niggle that maybe Finn is telling the truth and maybe Max is deflecting. Could I have got my boyfriend that wrong? Because although we haven't articulated it, we are definitely in a relationship. I've met his friends, we've been away together, we're spending several nights of the week in each other's arms. We're making plans for the future. I look at this beautiful man and how he's gazing at me, and I know that however painful it might be, I need to take a step back.

After our takeaway, during which Max does most of the talking, I start clearing the dishes away.

'Is everything alright, sweetheart?' he asks, getting up and placing a hand on the small of my back.

'I'm sorry. I'm just tired and wonder if I'm coming down with something. Think we need to take a rain check on tonight.'

He hesitates for a moment as if he can tell that I'm giving him the cold shoulder. 'Can I get you anything? Paracetamol, Lemsip?'

'It's kind of you. I think I just need an early night. I barely slept last night.'

'Let me check if you've got a fever.' He places the back of his hand against my forehead. 'Feels normal. Shall I check your blood pressure?'

'No, really. I'm just exhausted. It's kind of you.'

'You want me to leave?' He scrunches up his face with disappointment.

'Of course I don't,' I lie. 'But it might be for the best tonight so I can catch up on sleep and halt it if I'm going down with something.'

'Alright. But don't hesitate to call me if you feel worse.'

Later, as I'm lying in bed, trying to make sense of everything, I'm jolted with a sudden thought. I completely forgot to get a morning-after pill. With Finn's arrival, the finding of Jackie's body, and Finn's arrest, it slipped my mind. Is it too late? I do a quick search online and discover it can be taken up to seventy-two hours post sex. I'm fast running out of time, but I'm not going out now in search of a pharmacy that might be open twenty-four hours. It'll have to wait. At my age, I don't suppose the risk is very great anyway, and frankly, it's the least of my worries.

CHAPTER TWELVE

I toss and turn most of the night, thinking about Max, wondering if anything that Finn has said might be true. Did Max have an affair with Jackie? And was Max pumping me for information about the case last night because he has something to hide? I could ask him directly, but I really don't want to. Undoubtedly he'd be dismayed if I start accusing him of having an affair and potentially being a suspect in Jackie's murder. That would be the death knell for our fledgling relationship. And of course, I would also be committing a massive breach of legal ethics.

About 4 a.m. I decide that my best bet is to talk to some of the other neighbours. I think of Jamie and wish I'd had the chance to question him more. This is a close-knit community, and someone surely will have seen what was going on. He may not have been here much the last couple of weeks, but he's known this community a lot longer than me. Perhaps if he's still here and hasn't hopped back to London, I'll invite him over for coffee. With that decision made, I slip into an uneasy sleep.

If I was lying about feeling ill last night, this morning I really do feel dreadful. Frankly I'd like to skive off work for the day, but as I'm so new in the job, I simply can't. With heavy limbs and a throbbing head, I'm locking my front door when I see Ellie tugging a pram out of Finn's house.

'Laila!' she shouts across the street when she notices me, waving frantically with one arm. 'Can I have a word?'

She seems to be struggling with the pram, which looks like a complicated modern contraption with levers and over-sized wheels. I cross the road towards her.

'I'm so glad I saw you,' she says a little breathlessly.

'How are you doing?' I ask, because frankly she looks as exhausted as I feel.

'Honestly, none of us are coping well. Jackie's mum was meant to be looking after Melanie, but she's too distraught. She can't bring herself to be in their house with Jackie gone.' Her voice cracks, and she swipes her eyes with the back of a hand. 'And with Finn in custody, it's a complete nightmare. He was falling apart before he was falsely arrested, so I hate to think what state he's in now. He asked me to move in for a few days so I can look after Melanie. It's the least I can do.' She smiles weakly at Melanie, who is gurgling and happily playing with a plush toy cat.

'You've got to get Finn off. I've known him for years, and he hasn't got it in him to hurt Jackie. Sure, they had their problems, but Finn's not a violent man. I mean, a few nights ago there was a spider in the bath, and I hate spiders. You should have seen how carefully he picked it up and popped it outside. Most men would have killed the thing, wouldn't they?'

I'm not sure that saving a spider would be a mitigating

factor for murder, but I smile gently at Ellie. It's obvious she's being sincere.

'I'll do everything I can, Ellie. But ultimately it's up to the police.' I glance at my watch. 'I'm sorry, but I've got to get to work.'

'You're going down the high street, aren't you?' she asks. Clearly everyone knows where I work.

I nod.

'I'll walk with you.'

She manages to straighten up the pram, and she pushes it in front of us as we walk side by side along the pavement. I wonder if this would be a good opportunity for me to find out more about Max.

'I heard on the grapevine that Jackie was having an affair. Is that true?'

Ellie glances at me with a surprised look on her face. 'Did Finn tell you?'

I have to be careful what I say. 'He mentioned something.'

Ellie lets out a puff of air. 'They were having problems, Finn and Jacks. But they were working through things. Jacks had even booked in for some marriage guidance counselling. She knew that I'd have her back come what may. Being a childminder, I see lots of new mums, and that first year in a kid's life is hard, you know.'

No, I don't, but I keep quiet.

'But Jackie loved Melanie and Finn, and the two of them were determined to make their family work.' She stops the pram for a moment and removes a paper handkerchief from her sleeve, blowing her nose. 'God, I miss her. She was one of life's truly good people. I could call her day or night and she'd be there for me. And Jackie was so funny. She'd have us all in stitches over the littlest of things.'

At the end of the high street, she says, 'I'm going this way. But please, Laila, do everything you can for Finn and for our little Melanie. She's my godchild, aren't you, cutie?' She ruffles Melanie's downy hair. 'They don't deserve this.'

We say our goodbyes, and I hurry towards the office. It isn't until I'm sitting at my desk, the only noise coming from the hum of my computer, that I realise Ellie never actually answered my question. I'm still none the wiser as to whether Jackie really was having an affair and, if so, whether it was with Max.

I HAVE a busy day in the office, including preparing a bail application for Finn, which is likely to be rejected. The CPS very rarely allow people charged with murder out on bail. I'm just packing up the papers on my desk when Max calls me.

'I've got something for you. But you need to come over to my house. Are you free?'

'I'm still at work, but I can pop over in about an hour.' I'm worried about Ellie seeing me enter Max's house. 'I'll come in via the back gate.'

I imagine that Max is rolling his eyes, or perhaps I'm being unduly concerned. 'I'll leave it unlocked.'

An hour later, I'm at Max's open patio door.

He gives me a kiss and then says, 'Sit down,' gesturing to his sofa. He hands me a glass of wine, but I notice he isn't drinking.

'What's going on?' I ask, a flutter of nerves in my stomach.

He ignores the question, and still smiling widely, he sits down at his baby grand piano. He takes a moment, closing his eyes before positioning his hands over the keyboard. And then he starts playing, his body moving in time with the music. It's a beautiful, melodic tune that starts off quietly before building to a huge crescendo and then quietening again with a simple, haunting melody. When he's finished playing, he slowly opens his eyes and grins at me.

'Well?' he asks.

'It was beautiful. Really beautiful.'

'Just like you. I wrote it for you.'

'You what? I didn't know you composed music too!'

'From time to time when the inspiration hits. And you're my inspiration.'

I'm dumbstruck. No one has ever written me a song or a poem, and I'm not even sure I've had much more than a post-card with any sentiment of love on it. I realise that Max is staring at me, waiting for a further reaction, and I'm completely thrown. This man is just too good to be true. Then I remember what Dad used to say: if something seems too good to be true, it generally is. But at the same time, my heart feels full, and it's hard not to smile.

'Let's eat, and if you're lucky, I might play it for you again, and you can record it on your phone.'

'Thank you,' I say. I'm now sitting on his knee, and we kiss, a deep, romantic kiss, and when we eventually come up for air, I think to myself, oh dear God, have I really fallen in love with Max? I know I'm playing with fire, but I can't switch off my feelings.

'Will you stay the night with me, here?' he asks.

I hesitate, but he's not giving me the chance to say no. He's got hold of my hand and is leading me upstairs.

'I delivered a baby this afternoon,' he mutters.

'Oh.'

'It was one of the most beautiful experiences of my life. I hope you can experience that one day, Laila.'

'What, being a midwife or having a baby of my own?'

'Having a baby of your own, of course, sweetheart,' he says as we reach the top of the stairs. He cups my jaw with his hand and kisses me, deep and lovingly. Then he tugs me into the bedroom, and we stand there in front of the window, our bodies pressed tightly together, his hands holding my head, and I lose myself in him once again. It isn't until we pull away that I glance out the window. Unlike in my house, Max's bedroom is on the street side, and his window looks straight out across Violet Lane to Phyllis' house. And Phyllis is standing framed in one of her upstairs windows, her eyes directly on mine. Without a doubt, she has just witnessed Max and me in a passionate embrace.

CHAPTER THIRTEEN

'Laila, can I have a word?' William Parker has popped his head around the door to my office. For a horrible moment, I wonder if he's discovered my conflict of interest.

'Of course,' I say, pushing some papers to the side of the desk.

He steps inside. 'I think I've mentioned it before, but Cassel, Everett and Parker are long-standing sponsors of the South Gridgley fete.'

I feel my shoulders relax.

'We check all the sponsorship agreements, manage the committee meetings and generally help in any way we can. In return, our company logo is on all the official documents and posters advertising the event. As you're new here, I thought it would be a good idea for you to represent us this year. It'll give you the chance to meet the local dignitaries and to do your bit for the community. What do you say?'

I would like to say absolutely not, I can't think of anything I'd less like to do, except I don't. 'Of course, I'd be happy to help.' I force my lips into a smile.

'Jolly good,' William Parker says, clapping his hands. 'I'll let the powers that be know you're taking over. It's not too onerous, but you will have to attend the committee meetings, and they do go on for a bit. But I'm sure with your tact, you'll be able to keep them all on track. Right-eo, better get on, then.'

I suppose it's not the end of the world getting involved with a community exercise, especially as I intend to stay living here for the next few years. But generally, I avoid committees at all cost.

I'M tired when I get home, and I'm missing Ludwig horribly. There's an envelope lying on my doormat with my name typed on the front, but no address. I open it up, remove a folded piece of A4 paper and promptly drop it. The words are typed in capitals and say:

I KNOW WHAT'S GOING ON. YOU'RE AN EVIL WOMAN. GET OUT OF THE TOWN.

What the hell!

I study the piece of paper, holding it gingerly between my finger and thumb, as if it's going to combust. I read it again. My first thought is perhaps it's not meant for me. Except I think it probably is. But I'm not an evil woman, am I? And then I remember Phyllis. She saw Max and me embracing last night. Has she written this? Except she seems such an innocuous person and has been so friendly. I'm not sure what to do and resort to messaging Max, telling him I received a poison pen letter. He promises to come over as soon as he's back from work.

A couple of hours later, Max is sitting at my kitchen table. Despite everything, the bulk of him makes me feel secure. I show him the letter.

'I suppose I should take it to the police,' I say. Although I doubt they'll do much.

'I expect it's some delusional loony with too much time on their hands,' he says, carefully folding the page back up and placing it on the table.

'Do you think it could be Phyllis?' I ask. I don't mention how she saw us yesterday evening.

'No.' He shakes his head emphatically. 'She's only ever been nice to me. Having said that, when I first moved into Violet Lane, people viewed me with suspicion too. South Gridgley is a small place, and there are folk who have lived here for generations. Maybe the person wanted to buy this house, but you outbid them.' He shrugs his shoulders. 'It could be anyone, but I suspect it's nothing.'

I appreciate Max's reassurance, but I'm not so sure. I don't think I've ruffled any feathers in the short time I've lived here, but perhaps inadvertently, I have.

'Maybe it's to do with the case,' Max says. 'Perhaps someone is angry towards you for representing Finn.'

I nod, but that doesn't really fit with the note, *I know what's going on*. It seems more likely that it's directed towards me because I'm in a relationship with Max. I think of the gossip I overheard at Jackie's service and shudder.

WHEN I'M at the police station, I show one of the constables a copy of the letter sent to me, and after establishing that I've received no other threats, he confirms Max's thoughts. It's probably nothing. He logs it, and I'm allocated a crime number, nevertheless. I need to forget about it.

It's Saturday night, and Max has invited me out for supper at a new restaurant in a hotel set at the foot of the Downs, a remote location with beautiful views across rolling hills. Thoughtful as ever, he has ordered a taxi so neither of us has to worry about driving.

'I love the countryside here,' Max says as we drink gin cocktails in an airy lounge with wide windows that look onto a mature, colourful garden. 'I always dreamed of living somewhere like this, having a big garden, maybe a pony or two and kids running around, climbing apple trees, making dams in streams and me growing vegetables.'

'Really?' I laugh. 'I'd imagined you as more the city type.'

'I used to be, but now I want something different. A family.'

I don't say anything because that's what I want too. But this conversation is premature.

'You want children, don't you?' he asks. He knows I do.

I nod. 'If I can, but as I said before, it might be too late for me.'

'Is it too soon to say that I'd like children with you?' Max's face flushes slightly. I try not to let my jaw drop open because I'm horribly conflicted. Yes, it's way too soon to be having this conversation, but on the other hand, I'm desperate for a family. He must notice my reticence because he picks up the menus and hands me one. 'Let's discuss it later. We'd better order some food.'

Max seems a little distracted during the meal. Normally he's so attentive, his eyes never straying from my face, making it seem as if I'm the only person in the world for him. But this evening, it's as if his concentration is elsewhere.

'Are you alright?' I ask as he pats down his jacket pocket for the tenth time.

'Yes,' he says. 'Just a challenging day at work.'

'Oh no,' I add. 'Did you lose someone?'

'No, nothing like that.' He takes a large swig of wine and then thumps the glass on the table. A couple sitting next to us glance over and stare. I've never seen Max uptight like this, and I wonder whether it's because I didn't engage in the conversation about wanting children. Perhaps I need to bring the topic up again and tell him how I really feel, except I'm not sure how I feel.

And then Max pushes his chair back a bit, and for one horrible moment, I think he's going to get up and leave. But no, he's walked to my side of the table and is standing next to my chair.

'I was going to do this later, over dessert and champagne, but I can't wait,' he says. He fumbles in his jacket pocket and produces a very small navy-blue box. To my utter bemusement, he gets down onto one knee, opens the box and holds it out in front of him, looking at me with a soft gaze.

'Laila, I know we haven't been together long, but when you know, you know. I've fallen head over heels in love with you, and I want to spend every moment of every day with you. Will you be my wife?'

I clasp my hand in front of my mouth as he opens the box. Inside is a sparkling emerald-cut diamond ring. It's beautiful in its simplicity and much more stylish than the ostentatious sapphire that Jacob gave me. I realise that it's not only Max who is staring at me, but most of the people in this dining room. The gentle hum of voices has silenced, and it's as if everyone is taking a collective inhale of breath. My cheeks feel as if they're burning, because this is so incredibly awkward. Max and I haven't even said we love each other, and an engagement, well, it seems crazily premature, really rather inappropriate. Yet there's yearning and passion in Max's eyes, and I know that if I say no, this will be the end of our relationship for ever.

'Come here,' I say in a whisper.

He shuffles closer to me.

I speak as quietly as I can. 'Ask me again in a few months.'

Max leaps up into the air, and before I know what's happened, he's scooped me up in his arms, and he's kissing me, and the restaurant is filled with rapturous applause. I didn't actually say yes, but it's as if I did. This is mightily awkward.

'Put me down!' I say, embarrassment scorching my face. He does, and I scurry back to my chair.

A woman at the next-door table leans over. 'Congratulations, dear. You've got quite the catch there.'

Is that how people will see us? Max being the catch? I feel a little affronted, but then a waiter appears with a bottle of champagne and fills both our glasses to the rim. Max moves back to his chair, but I'm conscious of all eyes on me.

'Can I put the ring on you?' he asks as he leans forwards across the table.

'Keep it,' I say. 'It's stunning, and I'd be very happy if you proposed again with this ring in a few months' time.'

Very briefly, Max scowls, but then it's as if I imagined it, because his face settles into one of adoration, big soft eyes, upturned lips.

He reaches for my hand. 'So it's a deferred yes?'

I laugh. 'Yes, a deferred yes.'

'You've made me the happiest man in the world, Laila.'

AFTER OUR MEAL, I expect Max to want to come back to mine, to seal his proposal and my delayed acceptance with one of his marathon lovemaking sessions. Slightly tipsy, it's certainly what I want. To make love, to spend the night in his arms, to feel secure and loved, and to forget everything – particularly Finn and the horror of Jackie's murder. Except he seems distracted, uptight even. The hand-holding in the cab home seems perfunctory, and he gazes out the window during the whole journey, and when we reach Violet Lane, he doesn't follow me up the steps to my house.

'Are you not coming in?' I ask, surprised, and in that moment forgetting that I don't want us to be seen together.

'I've got to work,' he says, unable to meet my gaze. I'm surprised because it's unlike Max to drink and then go on shift. And I'm not aware that he's received an emergency call-out.

'Alright,' I say. I wonder if I've offended him by not accepting his proposal outright. 'Thanks for supper and for popping the question,' I say.

He nods at me. 'I'll call you later,' he says, and before I can ask what he means, he's disappeared into his house.

I'm confused. Max has been acting really weird this evening. I thought his initial nervousness was because he was plucking up the courage to ask me to marry him, but his reaction afterwards was equally strange. It makes me uneasy, and I struggle to sleep, thinking about him and Finn and the threatening letter.

It feels like I've barely been asleep when my mobile rings. It's Max.

'I'm outside your patio door. Can I come in?'

I hesitate. This really is a booty call.

His voice sounds husky. 'I need you, Laila. It's been a tough night. Please.'

I get out of bed, pad to the window and open it. Max is standing in my garden, wearing his green paramedic's uniform. I throw the key down to him so he can let himself in. Then I snuggle back underneath the duvet, listening to his footsteps as he comes up the stairs.

'You don't mind, do you?' he asks as he sheds his clothes. 'Can I take a quick shower?'

'Of course you can,' I say. The patter of water is reassuring. A couple of minutes later, Max wriggles under the duvet. Despite the shower, his limbs feel cold as he wraps himself around me. 'It was a horrible night.'

'Do you want to talk about it?' I ask.

'No,' he says before pulling me into a deep kiss. 'I just want to lose myself in you, my future wife.'

His lovemaking is urgent, and I tell him to slow down.

'I can't,' he murmurs. 'I love you too much.'

And then, when he comes with violent shudders and a groan that could awake the whole street, he falls off me, lying on his back. Normally he's eager to make sure that I'm satisfied too, but tonight he just seems exhausted. I open my eyes and can see his face in the low moonlight streaming in from where I've forgotten to close the curtains. His eyes are glistening, and I think I see a tear slip down his cheek.

'Hey, what is it?' I ask, wiping his cheek dry.

'I love you too much,' he murmurs. 'Just too much. I would never hurt you, you do know that, don't you?'

I squeeze his hand because it seems like a strange thing to say, but then we're both exhausted.

'I'll protect you from whoever sent that letter.'

I'd forgotten all about it, but now it preys on my mind again. I move as if to ask him what he means, but Max is already fast asleep.

CHAPTER FOURTEEN

The unpleasant, anonymous letter preys on my mind all Sunday. I know it's a risk that comes with my job, but I've never experienced any threats from disgruntled clients before, and I'm struggling to believe it was left by any of my neighbours. I'm just hoping it was a one-off and perhaps put through my letter box erroneously. I'm also feeling a little concerned because by Monday mid-morning, I still haven't heard anything from Finn or the police, which is unusual for this stage of a case. I call DS Kolinsky.

'Just wanting an update on Finn Walker,' I say.

There's a long silence. 'Hello?' I ask, wondering if the line has been cut.

'Ah, Ms Bowden. I thought you knew.'

'Knew what?' I hope I haven't messed up in some way.

'You're no longer Mr Walker's legal representative.'

'Excuse me?'

'I'm surprised no one told you. He's now being repre-sented by May, Maclachlan and Thacker.'

I lean back in my chair and close my eyes. Jacob's firm

has taken over. I should have seen this coming, except I didn't.

'Any reason?' I ask.

DS Kolinsky snorts. 'I'd be the last to know, but I expect he wants a big, fancy firm to represent him. He's going to need all the help he can get.'

'Let me guess. Jacob May has taken on the case.' My words drip with sarcasm.

'Yes. Mr May is now Mr Finn's solicitor.'

We say our goodbyes, but I feel a sickening gnaw in my stomach. This is bad. Really bad for me and really bad for Cassel, Everett and Parker. William Parker is going to be devastated. But most of all, I'm furious. I jump up from my desk and pace the small office. Jacob has been trying to undermine me ever since our marriage unravelled. How naive I am to think that I could escape his reaches by moving to another firm. It's so damned unfair, especially since he gets the pick of the very juiciest cases. Couldn't he have let me have this one? It's not like it's going to be a big money earner for his firm. The chances are it'll be legal aid and financially not worth their while, so he's only swiped in to make me look bad. If I could scream out loud, I would.

Instead, I pick up the phone and call him. His mobile rings once and then goes to voicemail. I'm not going to let him get away with ignoring me that easily. I call Annie, his secretary, and put on a saccharine voice because I'm sure Jacob has told her all sorts of lies about me.

'Annie, how are you? It's Laila Bowden here. Formerly Laila May.'

'Ah yes. Hello.'

'I need to speak to Jacob. It's urgent.'

'I'm sorry, but Mr May is in a meeting. Can I take a message?'

I grit my teeth. 'How long do you think he'll be in the meeting for?'

She pauses for a moment before saying, 'If you wouldn't mind holding on, I'll check for you.' That is code for *Jacob isn't really in a meeting, but I'll have a word with him and see if he's willing to take your call.* A couple of moments later, she's back on the line. 'I'm sorry, but Mr May is in back-to-back meetings all day. I can pass him a message if you like.'

I don't like. 'It's fine,' I say through gritted teeth, because it really isn't. 'I'll catch him tonight.'

JUST BEFORE LUNCHTIME, I tell the team that I'm going out for a meeting and will be gone for a couple of hours. I don't say a word about the firing, so I assume they'll think I'm doing something regarding Finn's case. I hurry back home, collect my car and drive to May, Maclachlan and Thacker's offices. It's been a while since I've been here, and it feels strange to return to a place that is so familiar but no longer home.

I know my ex-husband, and I know his routine. Unless he's in court, every single day he leaves the office at 1 p.m. on the dot, power marches down the road to a very expensive sandwich shop called Penny's Pretzels (goodness knows why, as they don't even sell pretzels, and I'm not even sure that it's owned by someone called Penny). He orders a chicken mayonnaise sandwich with extra avocado and marches back to the office, where he eats said sandwich at his desk. He is a creature of habit. Of course, today he might be in court, but I'm pretty sure that Annie would have simply said Mr May is in court, rather than telling me he's in meetings. Or he might genuinely be in meetings and have sent Annie to collect the sandwiches, but I'm prepared to take the risk.

I park on the street rather than in the firm's car park and make my way to Penny's Pretzels, loitering outside the shop as a queue begins to form for lunch orders. I recognise a few solicitors I used to work with, but keep in the shadow of a doorway, pretending to be on my phone to avoid catching anyone's eye. And then at two minutes after one, I see him. He's wearing a pin-striped suit, a canary yellow tie, and his shiny black leather brogues clip-clop on the pavement. I intercept him just as he's about to join the queue.

'We need to talk,' I say.

'Well, hello to you.' Jacob seems amused to see me rather than annoyed. That's even more frustrating. He skirts around me as if to go into the shop.

'I want to talk to you now and not in the presence of other people,' I say, crossing my arms in front of my chest.

He rolls his eyes at me. 'What is so very important that we have to talk now, Laila?'

'Finn Walker,' I hiss at him.

'Ah. Got a spot of jealousy, have we?'

I glower at him and pace a few steps along the pavement. Jacob follows me. When we're away from anyone who might be listening in to our conversation, I turn to him. 'Why do you always try to ruin everything for me?' I know I sound petulant, but Jacob brings out the worst in me.

'You can't blame me for your own misfortunes,' he says.

'What do you mean?'

'That you're more than capable of ruining everything for yourself.'

'Finn Walker was an important client for me, especially

as I'm trying to establish myself at a new firm. He's nothing to you.'

Jacob stops walking and swivels towards me, jabbing a finger in my direction. 'It's you who has screwed up, and congratulations, you've achieved that all by yourself.'

'What do you mean?' For a horrible moment I wonder if I've missed a vital point of law or unintentionally been negligent.

Jacob grins at me in that pompous, all-knowing manner that grates on my nerves. 'When you fuck the person your client thinks is actually guilty, your client is unlikely to trust you any longer and consequently will seek new counsel.'

My jaw drops open, and I stare at Jacob, horror flooding through me. *How did Finn find out?* I stay silent.

'Ah, so you're not even denying it.' He rubs his hands together, and it infuriates me that he's backed me into a corner. Yet again. 'You should choose your lovers a bit more carefully, Laila. Not shack up with the first man who shows any interest in you.'

'You don't know anything,' I spit.

'And that's where you're wrong. I reckon I know everything. Frankly, Laila, you're lucky that we're not reporting you to the ethics committee at the Law Society.'

I stare at him, speechless. This is utterly humiliating.

'I trust this conversation is over now. I'm hungry and need to get a move on. See you when I drop off Ludwig.' He turns on his heel and strides back towards the sandwich shop, leaving me feeling like a complete idiot.

Shame and fury course through me in equal measures. I hate that I've given Jacob a reason to be pompous, to get one over on me, and I loathe the fact that he knows about my personal life and how I've let it impact on my professional life. How I wish I hadn't confronted him. I should have just accepted Finn's decision and moved on, except now I've made everything ten times worse.

I shuffle dejectedly back towards my car, wondering how Finn found out about Max and me. I wonder if it was Phyllis. Of course, someone else might have seen us together, but Phyllis seems the most obvious culprit, as she definitely saw our embrace. But as much as I would like to blame this situation on Phyllis or on Jacob or even Finn, I have to accept that this situation is all of my own making. I should have resigned the case as soon as Finn mentioned Max's name.

I drive slowly back to South Gridgley, dreading having to tell William Parker that I've lost Finn as a client. I wonder if he'll fire me; after all, I'm still in my probation period. And then what? If I lose my job, how will I pay the mortgage on the house? I check myself and tell myself that I mustn't catastrophise. One step at a time.

As luck would have it, I run straight into William Parker when I get back to the office.

'Can I have a word?' I ask.

'Of course, Laila,' he replies cheerily. 'My door is open to you at any time.'

I follow him into his bookcase-lined office with its wide oak desk inset with leather. He sits down and gestures for me to take a seat opposite him. I don't sit.

'I'm afraid I've got bad news. I've lost Finn Walker as a client. He's moved to May, Maclachlan and Thacker.'

There's a beat of silence before he says, 'Oh. Well, that's a shame.'

Understatement of the year. I expect him to grill me, to request that I explain exactly what happened, to analyse the precise steps I took or failed to take to nurture the client, as would have been the case when I was at May, Maclachlan and Thacker. Except he doesn't. He steeples his hands together and sighs. 'Well, I suppose it was inevitable. This is a high-profile case, which will be even higher profile if Walker pleads not guilty and goes to trial. We're not a big enough firm for such a case. The bigger firms are like sharks; they were bound to circle and pounce.'

His face sags with disappointment, yet it's his kind words that make me feel truly terrible. I hesitate for a moment, wondering if I should admit that it actually is my fault, that I dropped the proverbial ball. Surely it's better to come clean? I'm about to speak when he stands up and marches around his desk, placing a hand on my shoulder.

'These things happen, Laila. Worry not. We win some, and we lose some. I've been in this game long enough to accept the odd disappointment. We're dealing with people in this business, and people are fickle.'

I throw him a weak smile. William Parker is a good man, and I wonder how such a sanguine, mild-mannered individual has lasted so long in the cut-throat legal world. I leave his office feeling even more terrible than I did when I went in.

CHAPTER FIFTEEN

'Aunty Laila!' Zara careens into me as I walk into Jazmin's house laden down with gifts for my goddaughter. Zara bounces up and down in front of me, excitement making her jiggle like a marionette. 'Are they for me?' She points at the gifts that I've wrapped up in pink, glittery paper. They match her sparkly pink fairy dress.

'No,' I say, keeping my face straight. 'They're for your mum. It's her birthday today, isn't it?'

'It's not!' Zara squeals. 'It's my birthday. I'm seven.'

'Oh, silly me!' I exclaim. 'I completely forgot.'

'No, you didn't,' she says. She's dancing around me, her excitement contagious.

'You're right. I didn't forget. And yes, these are for you.' I place the gifts on the kitchen table.

She squeals. 'Can I open them?'

'Shall we ask your mum?'

'Ask me what?' Jazmin walks into the room carrying a platter of sandwiches. She looks mildly harassed, which isn't surprising since she's about to welcome twenty-five six- and seven-year-olds into her house.

As much as I love Jazmin and her family, this isn't really how I want to be spending my Saturday afternoon. However, as Zara's godmother and Jazmin's best friend, I couldn't say no when she asked me to help. Besides, this has been my role for each of Zara's birthdays. It's just it really drives it home that I'm the singleton without children. Which reminds me, I never got around to taking the morning-after pill. I'm not too worried though; besides, getting pregnant would be a dream come true.

Before I can ponder it anymore, the guests start arriving. Overexcited children with weary-looking parents, who grab a glass of wine the second it's offered to them. Having lived with Jazmin and Yves, I know quite a few people here, including the women from my book club.

'Laila,' Sophie says, releasing her hyperactive son to race into the garden, 'how are you?' We do the obligatory air kisses, and she grabs a glass of white wine.

The afternoon is frenetic, filled with screeching children, loud music and weary, moaning parents.

After the party I have a little moment when I feel relief that I don't have children. This afternoon has been exhausting, and it's not like I've had to be responsible for anyone in particular. But then I quickly change my mind. I'm sure it's fundamentally different looking after your own children as opposed to other people's.

'Drink?' Jazmin asks, collapsing onto the sofa at the far end of their kitchen.

'I'll make myself a cup of tea,' I say, realising that I've been serving everyone else this afternoon and not drunk much myself. 'Do you want one?'

'No. I need a triple gin and tonic.' She laughs and pats the sofa next to her. 'Come and sit down and tell me the latest.'

I sigh. I've already told Jazmin that I was fired from Finn's case and how Jacob had gloated, throwing my relationship with Max in my face. She was sympathetic.

'What's the latest with Max? Have you asked him about his affair with Jackie?'

I squirm.

'Oh, Laila! Really?'

'I haven't said anything yet. I don't want to mention anything or throw around false accusations.'

'If Finn told the police about the affair, then he must be pretty sure it was going on,' Jazmin says.

'And the police wouldn't have arrested Finn if they didn't have strong evidence against him,' I add. 'So how can I believe a word that Finn says? He's likely just making up stories to deflect from his own guilt.'

'Look, you know Max best, but it's my job as your bestie to make sure you don't get hurt. What do you really know about the man? Yes, you've met his colleagues in Sussex, but what about his old friends or his family? You need to be sure that this man is who he says he is.'

'But why would he be hiding anything?' For a moment I'm taken aback. I know Jazmin has only met Max briefly, but I thought she liked him.

'Let's try to find him on social media,' she says, stretching her legs out on the sofa so her shins are crossing my knees. She produces her phone, and her fingers whizz across it. 'Has he got a Facebook profile?'

'I don't know,' I admit. I recall trying to find him on

social media previously to no avail, but it's not like I looked very hard.

'Well, I can't find him. Haven't you googled him, Laila?'

'Of course I have.' I think of that *London Standard* newspaper article of him giving evidence at the inquest for the horrible accident.

'Well?' Jazmin peers at me.

'I haven't found much.'

'Because there isn't much,' Jazmin mutters. 'He's a ghost online. Don't you think that's weird in today's day and age? Everyone has a digital footprint unless they've worked very hard to hide it.'

'What are you suggesting?' I'm getting a bit annoyed with my friend now.

'That he warrants further background checks. Talk to his family and his old friends. Track down his colleagues and his ex-girlfriends.'

'But why?' I shift away from Jazmin.

She grabs my hand. 'Because you're serious about this man, aren't you? And I don't want you getting hurt.'

I think of how I was going to tell Jazmin that Max asked me to marry him, but now I'm glad I haven't mentioned anything. 'I don't want to sneak around behind his back.'

'Then ask him outright. Say that you've heard a rumour he had a relationship with Jackie, that you're not judging or anything, but is it true? There could be many reasons why he doesn't want you to know, not least because he was having a fling with a married woman who has now been murdered. Even though Finn has been charged, it's still mighty suspicious.'

I clench my jaw. I don't like what Jazmin is saying, but it's the truth.

'Alright,' I say reluctantly. 'I'll ask him tonight.'

'And try to find some of his old friends or colleagues. And old girlfriends.'

AS I DRIVE HOME, I know Jazmin is right. Max and I are having this crazily intense affair, and if I do marry him, I need to know more about the man. The Finn and Jackie situation is awkward in the extreme, but I can't have secrets with my future spouse. And for that matter, do I even want to get married again? My marriage to Jacob was a disaster. I certainly can't afford a repeat. I wonder if Max and I would be better off living together, being a couple without formalising it.

A warm shiver goes through me as I try to imagine our life together. Perhaps we'd be allowed to knock through our houses and create one big one, but probably not. The houses are listed, and it's doubtful any major structural changes will be permitted.

What if I really could get pregnant, or perhaps I am already? Max seems as keen as me to start a family, so that's another reason to progress with our relationship quickly. Except I'm not going to commit myself to someone having only known them a few weeks. That's ridiculous.

As I'm musing this over, I turn the car into Violet Lane and sense straight away that something is different. Music is blaring out from someone's house. Initially I think it's coming from Jamie and Rico's house, except their cars aren't parked on the lane, and the shutters are closed, as they always are when the men aren't there – which is most of the time. As I park the car, Phyllis comes out her front door, and I see she's talking to Ellie. There are a couple of other people milling around who look suspiciously like journalists. Max's bike is in front of his house, so he's also at home.

I climb out of my Mini, and Ellie shouts, 'Laila! Over here.' There's a levity to her voice, and from the other side of the road, it looks like her cheeks are flushed, and she's beaming. What has happened?

I hurry towards her.

'Fantastic news!' she exclaims. 'Finn is back home. He's been released, and he's no longer a person of interest to the police.'

'Oh,' I say, completely startled. How on earth has this come about? Has Jacob performed some miracle, or have the police obtained new evidence?

'Aren't you happy for us?' Ellie's brows knot together.

'Of course I am. I'm sorry, I've had a really full-on day, and I'm not completely with it.'

Phyllis throws me a strange look.

'So what changed?' I ask.

'Incontro – whatever the word is.'

Phyllis laughs. 'Incontrovertible evidence,' Phyllis adds. Yet when she shifts her gaze from Ellie to me, I note that she's no longer smiling.

'Yeah. Evidence has come to light that Finn wasn't anywhere near Sussex at the time of Jackie's death. It's what he's been saying all along.'

'Fantastic news, isn't it?' Phyllis says. Except there's a strange expression on her face as if she's judging me somehow. As if she knows that I might not think this is such great news because if Finn had nothing to do with Jackie's murder, does that swing the spotlight back onto Max? Or am I reading something into this that isn't there?

CHAPTER SIXTEEN

I spend the rest of the weekend restless and unsettled. Max hasn't returned home. He sent me a message on Saturday night to say that he's on a late shift and will be spending Sunday with his mother. The conversations I need to have with Max can't take place on the phone. I need to look him in the eyes, judge his reactions and tread very lightly.

And then there's Finn. Because I no longer represent him, I'm not privy to the evidence. I wish I could know why the police have let him go, and what exactly has come to light. I go for a long walk on the South Downs and miss Ludwig horribly. It seems almost wrong to be walking without him. When I get home, there's an envelope lying on my doorstep.

A prickle of unease flutters down my spine as I pick it up and note my typed name with no address, just like the last letter. Picking it up, I walk to the kitchen, open the envelope carefully and extract a typed sheet of paper. There is no doubt that this has been sent by the same person as before.

Be careful who you're sleeping with. You might be next...

Phyllis. It must be Phyllis. She saw me with Max. She was a bit off with me yesterday, almost as if she was judging me. But why is she doing this? And what if I confront her and it wasn't sent by her? Then I will have destroyed any remnants of goodwill with my neighbours. Besides, Phyllis is a gossip, and anything I tell her will be the talk of South Gridgley in no time.

After debating it for a few minutes, I decide to take this latest letter to the police. As I already have a crime number, there's no reason not to reach out for help. I want to feel safe in my new home and be welcomed into the South Gridgley community. Carefully placing the letter into a see-through plastic bag as if it's some vital evidence, I place it in my handbag and march along the streets to the police station. But it's Sunday, and the police station is closed. Of course they're closed at the weekend. I groan as I run my fingers through my hair. I should know better.

I debate taking both letters to the main police station in Brighton, but reckon they have more important matters to deal with. Besides, I know a few of the officers in the South Gridgley police station, and what with Jackie's murder, I reckon they're more likely to help me. It will have to wait until tomorrow.

I'm meandering back home, lost in my own head, when I come face to face with Finn.

This is awkward. I haven't prepared myself as to how I'm going to react to him; whether he'll say something to me about my relationship with Max, be angry that I might not have acted in his best interest.

'Hello,' I say but it comes out a bit like a squeak.

'I'm glad to run into you,' Finn replies. I brace myself for the likely admonishment. 'I hope there aren't any bad feelings.'

'Bad feelings?' I repeat, surprised.

'I dumped you for a bigger firm without any explanation. But at the end of the day, I got the outcome I needed. Hope you didn't mind too much.'

I bite my lip as I realise that perhaps he doesn't know about my relationship with Max. Surely he wouldn't be talking to me so warmly if he knew the truth?

'Are you heading home?' he asks.

I nod.

'I was just out for a breath of fresh air, so I'll head back too, then. Perhaps we can walk together?' He's looking much better than the last time I saw him. Finn's face is clean-shaven, and although he still looks wan, his eyes are no longer bloodshot, and he's dressed in clean jeans and a neat cotton jacket.

'I'm glad you got off,' I say awkwardly, because the truth is rather more nuanced than that. Yes, I'm pleased for Finn but terrified it throws Max back into the picture.

'Thank God,' he mutters. 'I mean, I knew the evidence would prove that I didn't do it, but it took its time. I wouldn't wish what I went through on my worst enemy. Being held in the cells was hell.'

'So what evidence did come to light?' I ask.

'Do you want to have a coffee?' He nods his head towards a little cafe that I pass every day but haven't yet been inside.

'Sure,' I reply, remembering how Finn wanted us to have a coffee that first day after I was appointed his solicitor.

He opens the door for me, and I step inside. I'm hit by the delicious scent of roasted coffee.

'What would you like?' he asks.

'Just a cappuccino,' I say.

'There's a little courtyard garden out the back. Go grab us a table there.'

I walk through the small, beamed coffee shop and out through an open door. There are six tables in the little courtyard, four of which are occupied. I sit down at a small table, my back to the wall, which is bedecked with hanging baskets and a profusion of geraniums.

Finn appears quickly, carrying two cups of coffee. I notice that a couple of women to my left stop talking and stare at Finn. I suppose he'll be notorious for a long while in this close-knit community.

'Thank you,' I say, taking my cup from him. He sits down and then leans forwards and talks in a conspiratorial whisper.

'It's going to take some time for the locals to trust me. Reckon they still think I'm guilty despite being cleared by the police. I guess they think I shouldn't be carrying on living my life after such a tragedy. But what am I meant to do? Sit at home day and night, wallowing in my grief?'

'I don't think anyone can judge how someone else should react,' I say. 'No one can possibly imagine what you're going through.'

A sadness settles on his face. 'That's true. My heart will be broken for the rest of my life, but I've got to carry on for Melanie's sake.'

'Where is she?' I ask.

'With Ellie. Thank God for our Ellie.'

'The important thing is that you're home now and able to

look after your little girl. What evidence did the police find to exonerate you?'

He takes a sip of his coffee, and I notice that his hand is shaking. 'Well, after they found Jackie, they did a post-mortem.' He swallows so hard I can hear it, and then grimaces before continuing.

'After that, they got an exact time of death, and I was able to prove that I was building a garden room for a client in North Wales at the time of Jackie's murder. I mean, I told the police that, but they didn't believe me. It was like all the events conspired against me. My client, Dave, is abroad, and the police couldn't track him down. What are the chances of someone being untraceable in today's day and age? But Dave was on a bloody riding holiday in Outer Mongolia or some-where in the middle of the wilderness without any telephone reception or internet. So the police thought I was lying.

'Anyway, Jacob May hired a private detective, who traced the travel agent, got in touch with some rep on the ground and eventually got a signed affidavit from Dave that I was on his site in Wales for the three days when it happened. I was staying with Dave in his house when I wasn't working on his garden room, so I couldn't have had anything to do with Jackie's murder. It was as solid an alibi as it could be, but just a bugger that my client had taken himself off on that fancy holiday.'

'Didn't the police have other evidence too? A trace of blood in your kitchen, was it?' I know full well that that was the case.

'Yeah, but just a trace. It probably happened when Jackie cut her finger on a knife in the kitchen. The autopsy confirmed she had a cut on her index finger and residue of adhesive from the plaster. The plaster itself must have come off in the water.' He lets out a little sob and stuffs his knuckle in his mouth. 'Sorry,' he mutters.

'Please don't apologise,' I add. We're both silent for a few moments as we sip our coffees.

'Look, Laila, I know this isn't any of my business, but I've heard you're seeing Max.'

I swallow. So here it is.

'The thing is, I don't want two murders on Violet Lane.'

My jaw drops open. That's a very overly dramatic statement.

'He's not a good guy, is Max. He comes across as the modern-day hero, all chiselled looks and ready to help everyone, except I don't trust him one inch.'

I sigh. 'I know you don't, Finn. But what evidence do you have against him?'

He throws his hands up in the air. 'That's the problem. I don't have any concrete proof. He's clever and has tied things up well, but I know he did it, and I don't want you to get hurt too. I couldn't live with myself without warning you.'

Finn does not sound rational, and of course, that's perfectly understandable. His wife has been murdered, and he is visibly grieving. But to throw around unfounded statements like that? It's like he's deflecting onto the only other person who could possibly be a suspect. Frankly, it makes him sound a bit deluded.

'Have you sent me any letters, Finn?' It suddenly hits me that perhaps Finn has been trying to warn me off Max.

'Letters?' He scrunches his face up. 'No. What sort of letters?'

I keep my gaze on him, but Finn doesn't flinch. 'It doesn't matter,' I say. 'I've received some strange, unpleasant letters, hand-delivered. I'm sure it's nothing.'

Finn keeps his eyes on mine, and I'm fairly confident that he's telling the truth. He doesn't touch his nose or ears, he doesn't twitch in his seat, and his pupils don't change size.

'Has Max told you that he was sleeping with my Jackie?'

I shake my head.

'I knew about it.' He sighs and briefly close his eyes. 'Jacks wasn't good at lying, but then when she got pregnant–'

'What?' I interrupt. 'She was pregnant?'

'Yes.' His voice cracks. 'We didn't only lose Jackie, we lost our second child too.'

'Oh no. I'm so sorry, Finn.' This is quite the shock.

'She told Max that she was pregnant. The bastard knew. Anyway, she offered to get a paternity test done when the baby was born, but I said no. I love Jackie, and I'd love the wee babe whether it was mine or not. We were going to see a counsellor, get our marriage back on track for the sake of our babies.'

I feel sick. If what Finn is saying is true, Max could have been the father of Jackie's unborn child. Does that change things? Yes, of course it does.

'Have you told the police all of this?' I ask. My voice sounds unnaturally high-pitched.

'Of course. It all came out in the interviews.'

That makes me feel even worse. Not only is Max implicated, but Jacob knows all the tawdry details. I bet he's loving it.

'I'm confident that the police will be questioning Max again, and that's why I think you should get out of the relationship as soon as you can. You seem like a good person, Laila, and you need to look after yourself.'

There's a long awkward pause, and I just want to get out of here. I shift my chair backwards.

'Thank you so much for the coffee, but I really need to get back home. I've left washing in the machine, and it'll probably shrink if I leave it there too long.' That's complete nonsense, of course. I just feel as if the courtyard walls are closing in on me, and the fresh afternoon air is becoming increasingly stifling. I've got to get away from Finn.

He throws me a look of pity. 'Sure, no problem. I'll see you around.'

I almost trip as I hurry out of the coffee shop, weaving between Sunday strollers and hurrying back to Violet Lane. I tug open my door, and as soon as I'm inside and alone, I sink to the ground, Finn's warnings about Max swirling around in my head like toxic smoke. It feels like I've been punched in the stomach. Finn is accusing the man I thought I might marry of murdering his wife. And although he doesn't have any evidence, he's planted such horrible doubts in my head. Is this just a jealous man lashing out, or is there any truth in his words? I need to talk to Max. Soon.

CHAPTER SEVENTEEN

Except Max doesn't come home, and as Monday drifts into Tuesday and I don't hear from him, my resolve to confront him fades. Jazmin mentions that it's their wedding anniversary, but they're not going to celebrate it because they can't find a babysitter. That's my excuse for getting away from Violet Lane. I offer to move into their house for two nights so they can go away, and my lovely friend jumps at the opportunity.

I'm busy at work and am inundated with paperwork, having to check all the sponsorship agreements and contracts for the upcoming village fete. I'm also not feeling great. At first I wonder if I'm going down with a bug; the nauseousness and weariness never seems to go away. But as the days go past, and I don't feel any better, I assume the cause is being overtired and worried.

During my lunch hour on Monday, I went to the South Gridgley police station and showed them the second letter. I didn't get much response, just a further logging of the case and instructions to remain vigilant. I guess everything fades into insignificance when there's a murder investigation underway.

Max contacts me late on Tuesday, sending me a long message apologising for not calling. Apparently he's been on difficult shifts, and his mother took a turn for the worse. He says he'll be home on Wednesday evening and asks if we can meet up. I tell him no. I'll be at Jazmin's. And actually it's quite a relief not to have to face him.

Living back at Jazmin's gives me a distance, and I decide to follow her advice and do some proper probing into Max's past. From the newspaper article, I know he was a paramedic in West London but nothing else. The next morning, when I should be working, I start my investigations. It takes me the best part of an hour making numerous phone calls until eventually I find the department where Max used to work. Using LinkedIn and sheer doggedness, I discover that his boss was a man called Thomas Estrader. And eventually, I reach him by phone.

'Good morning. My name is Lillian Smith.' It's the first name that pops into my head, and I haven't got a clue where it's come from. 'I understand that Max Critchley used to work for you.'

'Yes,' he says hesitantly.

'I was wondering if you'd be willing to give me a reference?'

'Is he moving into the private sector?' Thomas Estrader asks.

'Yes,' I say, wondering whether references for the NHS work differently. 'How was he as a paramedic?'

There's a beat of hesitation. 'He had excellent practical skills, calm in an emergency. An excellent nurse.'

'That's good to hear. And his personality?'

'Yeah, well. As I said, he was a good paramedic.'

'Was he trustworthy?' My heart is thumping in my ears.

'I'm not keen on giving references, you know. Max was a good enough bloke. If that's all, I've got a meeting to get to.' He hangs up on me.

I sit back in my chair and frown. That was a strange conversation, almost suspicious. Thomas Estrader seemed happy to praise Max's technical skills, but he was evasive in the extreme about his personality and trustworthiness. That is not good and does nothing to ease my worries. How can I find out more?

I have an old colleague who works on the legal side of the health sector, negotiating with trade unions, supporting staff in employment tribunals. I wonder if she could help me. We haven't spoken in a couple of years, but I call her anyway, and she promises to see if she can uncover any information on Max Critchley. Now all I can do is wait.

That evening, after reading the girls a bedtime story and waiting until they drift off to sleep, I decide to do some more digging on social media. Now that I know where Max used to work, I hope I can find out the names of his colleagues. I start on LinkedIn, searching for paramedics at Max's old NHS Trust. A few names pop up, so I check out the time-lines of when they worked there and then hop over to Face-book and Instagram, searching their names on both social media platforms. After that, I check out the names of their followers, and before long I've found two paramedics who look like they're a similar age to Max.

I'm scrolling through the Instagram profile of a man called Jason Leigh, carefully scouring the faces of his friends, flicking through scores of photographs. And then bingo. I see Max. He's standing with five other people, Christmas decorations hanging from the ceiling of a bar, all of them with beers in hand. My heart almost stops. He has his arm around a woman. A woman with dark hair and blue eyes. A woman who looks a bit like me. And a bit like Jackie Walker. She is staring up at him with an expression of adoration. It makes me queasy to think that Max has such an obvious type.

Fortunately, Jason Leigh has tagged my lookalike, as he's tagged all the people in the picture. Firstly, I click on the tag attached to Max's name, but it goes nowhere, confirming what I already know, that Max isn't on social media. As he was tagged, I assume he used to be on Instagram, so I wonder why he's deleted his account.

And then I click on the face of Tara Monteith. Tara is all over social media, posting frequently. Pouting in bathroom mirrors, out on the town with her friends and occasionally taking photos at work, a hospital where she's dressed in a nurse's uniform. I'm sure that taking selfies at work must be contrary to protocol.

I go back through her Instagram, further and further, and it takes long minutes of scrolling to flick through thousands of photos. And then I stop. There's a photograph of her and Max, their arms around each other, her looking up at him with a trout pout and adoring Bambi eyes. She's captioned it 'My luv'. I scroll backwards and find plenty more of her and Max. They were clearly in a relationship. I do the maths from the dates where he features, and I reckon they were seeing each other for approximately five months.

There was a period of maybe a fortnight about eighteen months ago when Tara didn't post at all, which was extremely unusual for her. And then there's a photograph of her, all dolled up with enough foundation to paint a house, and a caption that says, '*Picking myself up on a night out with my gals*'.

I've got two options. To ask Max outright about his ex Tara Monteith, or to try to talk to her directly. The latter seems a much more attractive solution right now, although I need to tread carefully, as I don't want her reaching out to Max to tell him that I've been poking around in his past. I dismiss contacting her on social media, which would certainly be the easiest option, and try to find her telephone number. Except I can't. She's listed on the electoral roll as living at an address in Clapham, London. Of course there's no knowing if she's still there, but I wonder whether it's worthy of a trip up to London to scope her out. But then I discover that she's working at Chelsea and Westminster Hospital.

I call the hospital in the morning and ask to speak to Tara. It takes a while to track her down, but eventually I'm directed to the correct ward. And I get lucky. The phone is answered on the fourth ring.

'Ward E, Tara speaking. How can I help you?' Her voice is saccharine.

'Good morning, Tara. My name is Laila Bowden, and I'm in a relationship with Max Critchley. I realise I shouldn't be calling you at work, but would it be possible to have a quick chat about him?'

There's a click and then silence.

'Hello?' I ask, but quickly realise that Tara has hung up on me. Is that because I rang her at work or because I wanted to talk about Max?

CHAPTER EIGHTEEN

I'm back home now, and I slept badly. I've woken up feeling nauseous and barely make it to the toilet before violently throwing up. As I splash water over my face, I realise I've been feeling sick, particularly in the mornings, for a good week now. And then it hits me. Am I pregnant?

With everything that was going on, I never got around to taking the morning-after pill, so it's possible, although not likely. A flutter of excitement grows as I consider the possibility. I know I shouldn't get my hopes up, but it would be a dream come true. Except then I think of Max. He has made it perfectly clear he wants children with me, but there are too many doubts in my mind about him. Not least that Finn suggested Max might have got Jackie pregnant. And although I really like Max, do I love him? If I could strip away all the doubts, I think the answer would be yes. But we're far away from that. Besides, I'm jumping to conclusions. I'll pick up a pregnancy test on my way home from work.

FRUSTRATINGLY MY AFTERNOON MEETING OVERRUNS, and I need to hurry to get to the fete committee meeting. The meeting for the South Gridgley fete is held in a conference room at the Partridge Arms, the local hotel. It's the first time I've attended in person, and it's not something I'm looking forward to.

I arrive five minutes early, and the chairperson, Florence Green, welcomes me warmly, thanking me for my time and expertise. She talks me through the agenda and shares information on the other committee members. I'm surprised when she mentions Max. He's in charge of health and safety, apparently. It's the first time I'll have seen him in several days and I feel an uncomfortable flutter of nerves in my stomach.

As other people start arriving, we're handed cups of coffee by a server, and we all mill into the large conference room, taking seats around a large oval table. Max hasn't arrived yet, and I'm relieved when strangers sit either side of me. I'm talking to an accountant on my left when Max strides into the room. I try not to catch his eye, yet every nerve ending seems alight to his presence. To my dismay, he sits down directly opposite me. How on earth am I going to concentrate?

The agenda is ridiculously long, and added to that, we have to approve the minutes of the previous meeting. Every time I glance up, Max seems to be looking at me, that frustratingly attractive grin on his face, as if he can read exactly what I'm thinking. I wish he'd stop making eyes at me.

Florence starts by introducing me to the other committee members.

'So before we start, Laila, do you have any questions?'

'Actually, I do,' I say. 'Should the fete even be going

ahead this year, considering the tragic murder of Jackie Walker?'

There's an audible intake of breath.

'Laila makes a good point,' Max adds.

'I've preempted this,' Florence explains. 'I've spoken to Finn Walker, and he has confirmed the family wants the fete to go ahead. Jackie used to love it. For the past couple of years she was responsible for running the face-painting stand. She was very good at it.' There's a long pause while we all think about Jackie.

The accountant sitting next to me says, 'This town will never be the same again, but we need to carry on and not live in fear. That is the best way we can respect Jackie's memory.'

A couple of people say, 'Hear, hear.'

I glance up at Max, but his eyes are lowered, and his face is expressionless. As William Parker warned me, the meeting goes on for nearly two hours. It's tedious, and many of the other committee members argue between themselves over the most ridiculous items. From time to time I glance up and catch Max's eye. He winks at me.

WHEN IT'S time to leave, I say my goodbyes and hurry out of the hotel, avoiding Max, who thankfully is in conversation with Florence. As I emerge out onto the street, grateful to be breathing in some fresh air, a hand grabs my upper arm.

'Laila,' Max says, 'aren't you going to wait for me?'

'Sorry, I just–' I let the words peter out. I can hardly tell him that I want to nip to the chemist before it closes to pick up a pregnancy test.

'I've missed you,' he says, and stares at me expectantly. Except I'm not sure how to respond. Yes, in many ways I've missed him too. Just breathing in his scent makes my body crave his, but now I have concerns, worries that I can't voice to him. Although perhaps now is exactly the right time to ask the questions. 'Are you heading home?' Max asks.

I nod.

'Can I come with you?'

'Of course.'

'I sense things aren't quite right,' Max says.

'There's a lot going on. Let's talk when we're back home,' I say.

We walk in silence along the high street and turn together into Violet Lane. My heart sinks as I see Finn approaching us. Finn's eyes narrow, and he clenches his fists, striding towards us, his jaw jutting forwards. I pray he doesn't start a fight.

'You need to stay away from him, Laila,' Finn says when we're just a couple of metres apart. 'I've warned you.'

Max takes a step closer to Finn, invading his personal space, their noses just inches apart. 'What did you say?' Max's voice is low and tight.

'I told your girlfriend that she needs to get away from you. I know what you're really like, Max Critchley. You bastard.'

'What the?' Max says. And then, before I can intervene, Finn pulls his arm back and throws a punch, catching Max on his nose. Max staggers backwards before quickly gaining his balance, and he rushes towards Finn. I think he's going to knock out the smaller man, except a female voice yells, 'Stop! I'm calling the police!'

Phyllis has emerged from her front door, her phone in her hand. Max halts suddenly. There's blood pouring from his nose.

'Piss off, you interfering old woman!' Finn jabs his finger at Phyllis, who pales, and for a moment I wonder if she's going to faint. We all watch as Finn marches towards his front door, tugs it open and slams it shut with such force, the vibrations can be felt on the street.

'I told you I don't trust that man,' Phyllis mutters. 'Did he do that to you, dear?' She peers at Max. 'Should I call the police?'

Max has removed a handkerchief from his pocket and is holding it up against his nose to stem some of the bleeding. 'Please don't, Phyllis,' he says. 'No point in causing any more upset. Besides, Finn isn't acting rationally. He's grieving, and we need to give him some leeway.'

'But punching you like that? It's not acceptable.' She stands with her hands on her hips.

'I know. And I'm sure I'll get an apology when he's calmed down. Anyway, I need to staunch this nose bleed, so if you'll excuse us.' Max turns, and I follow, raising a hand at Phyllis, who narrows her eyes at me.

'Will you come and help me?' Max asks, and I see some rare vulnerability in him.

'Of course,' I say.

I follow him into his house and glance back at the other houses, but both Phyllis and Finn are safely inside their own homes.

We walk into Max's kitchen. 'I'm sorry if Finn has been giving you grief,' he says, pulling out a first aid kit from a kitchen drawer with his left hand. 'Could you get some ice out of the freezer for me?'

He directs me how to help him, and soon enough the bleeding stops, although I expect he'll end up with a black eye. 'Is there anything else I can do?' I ask.

'Come here,' he says, beckoning me over to him. He then pulls me down onto his legs, so I'm sitting on his knees, facing him. 'God, I've missed you.' Max clasps his hands behind my head and draws my face down to his. A second later he's kissing me, gently at first and then more insistently. He shifts underneath me, and I can feel his hardness growing as his hands push my jumper up, and he runs his fingers gently over my bare skin. 'I want you so badly.' Max is breathing heavily now. I climb off him.

'Upstairs?' he asks as he levers himself up from the chair. He takes my hand.

'I'm not sure,' I mutter, except there's something so delicious about this man, and even though my head is saying hold fire, my body is craving more.

'Please, my darling,' Max says, tugging me towards the stairs. And I let him lead me up the crooked staircase and into his bedroom, where the bed is neatly made up.

'Take your clothes off,' he says. I don't move.

He smiles that crooked grin, his eyes glistening, his teeth so very white, the beginnings of a bruise marking his left under eye. 'Alright, I'll do it for you.' Slowly he unbuttons my blouse, his eyes on mine as his fingers work their way down my front. Then he's on his knees, unbuttoning my skirt, tugging it downwards, working his fingers into my lacy knickers. A shiver followed by heat runs through my core.

'You want me, don't you?' he says, feeling my wetness. My body is betraying me. I expect Max to tug me towards the bed, except he doesn't. He bends downwards onto his knees and reaches under his bed, pulling out a box from beneath the mattress. 'Shall we have some fun?' he asks, grinning at me. 'Come and choose.'

I kneel down next to him, my bare legs on the soft carpet.

Max takes the lid off the box, and for a moment I don't fully appreciate what I'm seeing.

'Oh,' I say as I realise with some dismay that this is a box full of sex toys.

He removes a pair of handcuffs and a weird-looking contraption that I assume is some sort of vibrator, but not before I catch a glimpse of leather, silk fabrics and metal chains. I know Jacob and I were very boring and vanilla, but is this normal? I haven't got a clue.

'Are you up for this?' he asks, his face expectant.

'I'm not sure.'

'We won't do anything that makes you feel unsafe,' he says, and immediately that makes me feel nervous. The relaxed eagerness I felt just moments ago has morphed into a disquiet as I remember his hand on my neck.

'I'm not into this kind of thing, Max,' I say, unable to take my gaze off the handcuffs that are hanging from his fingers. He stares at me, as if he's weighing up whether or not to try to convince me otherwise, and then for a horrible moment, I wonder if he's going to force me. Grab my wrists, lock them to his bed and force me to do all sorts of things I'm uncomfortable with. Or worse.

'Don't look so worried,' he says, lifting my chin up so that my eyes meet his. He brings his lips down on mine, and his kiss is so gentle.

I can't do this. Any desire I had has vanished, and it's not because of the sex toys, it's all the turmoil that's going around in my head.

'I sprang this on you,' he says as he stands up, holding out his hand for mine. 'The toys can come out another day when you're more comfortable.'

'I'm sorry,' I say, 'but I'm really tired.' I let my words hang.

'Don't be sorry. I love you how you are, and you set my body on fire. I don't need any of that stuff. Feel how hard I am.' He guides my hand downwards, but for the first time, I don't want to make love with Max. There are too many questions buzzing around my head, and that's killing any desire.

I pull my hand away. 'Can we do this another time, Max? There's so much going on, and I'm completely exhausted.'

The disappointment is written all over his face as I step away from him.

'I'm sorry,' I repeat.

He turns away from me and pulls on a jumper. 'It's fine. We all have off days. I'm tired too.'

I would like to ask Max so many things, except now isn't the right moment. Hurriedly, I get dressed. He accompanies me downstairs, and at the door, he places a gentle kiss on my lips and murmurs, 'Sleep tight, gorgeous.'

CHAPTER NINETEEN

The next morning, feeling sick once again, and with my period increasingly late, I stop off at the pharmacy on my way to work and surreptitiously purchase a pregnancy kit. It's like a hand grenade in my bag. I have back-to-back meetings during the morning, but just before lunch I take my handbag with me to the ladies' toilets. With trembling hands, I remove the stick, read the simple instructions and pee. The next three minutes are some of the longest in my life, not only hoping that one of the other women from the office don't come in to ask if I'm alright, but waiting to see if my dreams might be coming true.

And they are.

I'm pregnant.

I don't know whether to laugh or cry. This is exactly what I wanted, except is it? I have so many doubts about Max. Could we be a family? Yes, if I knew I could trust him. And then I wonder about bringing up this child alone. I could do that. I'm strong, independent, and although I'm not as financially secure as I'd like to be, there are many, many single mothers in a much more precarious position than me. Whatever happens, I'm having this child.

I walk back to my office wanting to skip with joy. Except I know that I can't tell a soul about this. I'm not going to share the news with Max until I'm sure about our relationship, and I'm not naive. It's extremely early days, and the chance of a miscarriage at my age is high. No. This is going to have to be my secret for a few weeks, at least.

But what it does do is focus my mind. I've been putting off confronting Max for days now. Tonight I am going to ask him outright about Jackie and his previous relationships. I'm going to ask why there's such animosity between him and Finn, and get to the bottom of why Finn is making such accusations. I'm also going to demand to meet Max's family and friends from before he moved to Sussex. I send him a message, asking if he's free to come to mine for supper this evening.

WE'RE EATING a simple chicken and potato dish, Max is drinking wine, and I'm on water. I told him that I've decided not to drink mid-week. He looked at me askance but seemed to accept it. I take a deep breath and blurt out the question that has been weighing so heavily on me.

'Did you have a relationship with Jackie Walker?'

Max's fork hovers in mid-air. He opens and closes his mouth before neatly placing his cutlery back down on the centre of his plate. Leaning his elbows on the table, he sighs and looks at me.

'Yes, I did. Although it wasn't a relationship. It was a one-night stand that we both bitterly regretted. How did you find out? Phyllis or Finn?' he asks.

'Phyllis?' I frown.

He harrumphs and takes a sip of wine. 'It seems that Phyllis saw us together and told Finn. As you've discovered yourself, she's Violet Lane's gossipmonger. Finn and I had a massive bust-up but agreed to let it go for the harmony of Violet Lane.'

'When did this happen?' I ask, recalling the afternoon of Phyllis' barbecue and how the two men seemed quite harmonious back then.

'A few days before Jackie disappeared. I can't remember which day.' His eyes shift to his plate, and I'm not sure that I believe him. 'Why are you asking?'

'Why am I asking?' I exclaim. 'Because you and I are in a relationship, and I want to know more about you.'

'I don't make a habit of sleeping with married women,' he says curtly. 'As I already said, it was a huge mistake. We had both drunk too much and were feeling vulnerable. It happened before I met you.'

'Did you know that she was pregnant?'

'What?' Max pales.

'Jackie was pregnant when she died. Was that your baby or Finn's?'

Max is very still. 'I have no idea. She didn't tell me she was pregnant.' His face turns from pallid to puce, and I'm pretty confident that this news has come as a shock to him. 'Maybe she was already pregnant when she slept with me.'

Of course, I don't know how many weeks pregnant Jackie was. I can't stop myself from rubbing a hand protectively over my own stomach. How many weeks pregnant am I? It can't be more than five or six weeks. How long ago was it that the condom broke?

Max's phone pings with an incoming message. It's lying

face down on the table. Normally he picks it up straight away, except now he ignores it.

'Do the police know that you had a relationship with Jackie?' I ask.

The sinews in Max's neck go taut, and his phone pings again. 'Why are you asking that?'

Nerves flutter in my stomach, and for an instant I wonder if I've pushed him too far. Max is so on edge, shifting uneasily in his chair; I've never seen him like this.

'I just assumed. Never mind.' His phone pings for the third time. 'Are you going to answer that?'

He grabs the phone, looks at it, and I think I see further anger flash across his face. 'It's my mother.'

'Is everything alright?'

He angles the phone so I can't see it, and reads through a message, then slams it onto the table, once again face down. 'I'm going to have to go.'

'Oh no. Is she okay?'

'Nothing major, but the folk at the care home have asked if I can pop over.'

'Where is the care home?'

'In Haywards Heath.' He stands up, grabs his plate, which still has food on it, and walks to the kitchen cabinets. Pulling open the bin, he shovels the remaining food into it and then dumps his plate in the sink.

'Maybe I could come with you? I could drive so you don't need to take your bike.'

'It's fine. I can get there faster on the bike.'

'I'd love to meet your mum.'

He shakes his head. 'Another time, maybe.'

'Are you sure you're alright, Max?'

Tension oozes from his every sinew, and it doesn't take a

detective to realise he's not telling me the truth. Either my questions about Jackie have completely rattled him, or there's something going on with the messages he just received on his phone.

I stand up too and carry my plate to the dishwasher. I open it and stack both Max's and mine inside. Max hovers awkwardly.

'Sorry, but I've got to dash. I'll catch you tomorrow or the next day. Okay?' As if he's just remembered his manners, he strides towards me, places a chaste kiss on my lips and squeezes my upper arm. 'Ignore Finn, please. He's a trouble stirrer, and Jackie was really unhappy with him.'

I nod and stand still for a moment. It hits me that when I first asked how well he knew the Walkers, Max said not very. That was clearly a lie.

I listen as Max walks to my front door, and it closes behind him. I wonder. Is he really dashing off to see his mother? What if I follow Max? What if I see where his mother is staying and go and talk to her about her son? Is that even ethical? Without much thought, I'm grabbing my bag and coat and hurrying towards my car. I fling myself onto the driver's seat just as Max emerges from his house, and slip down as low as I can, praying he doesn't spot me. Glancing up, I see him pulling on his bike's helmet and swinging his legs over the seat. Max roars past me without a sidewards glance.

I start up my car's engine and quickly edge out of the parking space, keeping my distance as I drive behind him down Violet Lane. I expect him to glance in his mirror, to see me and stop. Except he doesn't. He rides out of South Gridgley, strictly keeping to the speed limits, and I stay far enough behind him so that hopefully he won't notice me. At the main road, he indicates right, which is strange because the way to Haywards Heath is to the left, but perhaps he knows some shortcuts that I'm not aware of. I follow, keeping another car between us.

It's hard to keep track of him up ahead because he's nimble and overtakes a slow-driving car. But then I see him at the roundabout that leads onto the A27, and now I'm convinced he's not going to Haywards Heath. Max is heading south whereas Haywards Heath is north. Why did he lie to me?

Within moments, I've lost him. He roars up onto the dual carriageway and disappears into the distance. And I check myself. What the hell am I doing following my boyfriend? How would he react if he knew?

I've followed him on a whim because I think he was lying to me when those text messages came through. Perhaps his mother has been taken to the hospital in Brighton, and that's why he's not going to Haywards Heath. Or perhaps he's been called into work. But if so, why not tell me the truth? It's as if those phone messages completely threw him, and he made up the first excuse that came into his head.

I take the next turning off the dual carriageway and head back home. I'm sure Max lied to me tonight, and it gets me thinking. What else has he lied about?

THE NEXT MORNING, I send him a message.

> How is your mum?

He replies almost immediately.

> A fuss about nothing, as is often the case.
> Sorry about that. X

He's put a kiss after his message for the first time.

> You free later?

> Doing some gardening this afternoon and
> then going over to mum's for my regular
> Tuesday 5pm supper. Sorry. Tomorrow
> evening?

He's being very forthcoming as to his plans, much more so than usual, and it sparks another idea. What if I try to follow him again? Surely this time he really will be going to Haywards Heath?

I leave work early and park my car at the far end of Violet Lane, once again slipping down low in the driver's seat. I'm wearing a baseball cap and have tucked my hair up under it. The largest, oversized pair of sunglasses that I own are on my face. Max passes me on his bike just after 4:30 p.m., and this time I'm ready. I'm determined not to lose him even if it means getting a speeding ticket. I just hope that he doesn't look in his mirror and recognise my blue Mini.

Once again, he heads south, and once again he rides up onto the A27, except today it's rush hour, and the traffic is heavy. I wonder if Max will weave in and out of the cars, but he doesn't. He waits in turn with all the other vehicles. And then he's turning off the A27 and heading towards Hove. Definitely nowhere near Haywards Heath.

My heart thuds as I stay as close to him as I can, forever hopeful that he doesn't glance in his mirror and spot me. He rides his bike respecting all the speed limits and indicating well in advance. We dip down the hill into residential streets, turning left and right so that I've no idea where exactly we are. And then he's indicating to the side of the road. I carry on past him at a crawl, stopping just a few cars down, maintaining a good view of him in my rear mirror.

He parks the bike, climbs off it and pulls off his helmet, tucking it under his arm. Then he's striding along the street, and for one horrible moment, I think he's going to walk straight past my car. Except he doesn't. He crosses the road directly opposite my Mini, stops, climbs up three steps and rings the doorbell of a house. I have a perfect view, except I've slid down the seat and just pray that my face isn't visible through the window.

It's a stucco-fronted building that has seen better days, white paint flaking off the walls, and a navy-blue door with two storeys above. There are net curtains across the downstairs windows. He waits, and then the door swings open. A woman stands there, probably in her mid-thirties. She's wearing smart jeans and a white cotton sweater, but it's her facial features that make me gasp. She has black hair and startling blue eyes, with a warm and pretty smile that lights up her face. This woman bears a shocking resemblance to Jackie, to Tara, Max's ex-girlfriend, and to me. Is my boyfriend having a relationship with this woman too?

Before I can blink, they're inside, and the door is closed. My heart is thumping because this doesn't seem right. There is no way that this residential house is a care home. Or is it? Did I misunderstand Max when he said his mother was in Haywards Heath?

I wait about ten minutes and then slide out of my car. With my heart in my mouth, I run across the road and glance up at the house. There is nothing on the door to suggest it's a commercial property, and there's just one doorbell, so it's not even broken up into separate apartments. But then I get nervous. It's dangerous for me to be loitering on the pavement. What if Max comes out and sees me? How could I explain myself? I hurry back to my car and slither down into the seat once again.

I wait. The minutes slip by, and I make little promises to myself. If Max hasn't reappeared after thirty minutes, I'll leave. But thirty minutes comes and goes. I adjust again. If he hasn't appeared after an hour, then I really will go home. Except I don't have to wait that long. The door swings open about fifty minutes after he went in, and there he is again, although I don't get a glimpse of the woman this time. He walks jauntily towards his bike, climbs on it and roars away.

I stay put, debating what I should do. I could speak to this woman directly except that would be extremely creepy, and the chances of it getting back to Max are high. As I'm deciding what to do, the door opens again, and the dark-haired woman steps out. She's wearing a thin jacket now with a leather crossbody bag flapping at her side. She walks briskly, and before I give it any further thought, I'm out of the car and following her.

The woman is talking as she walks, and I realise she's got ear pods on. At least that's likely to stop her from realising I'm walking behind her. Every so often she glances at her wrist, and considering how quickly she's striding, I assume she's late.

Perhaps three minutes later, she's ringing the bell on a gate to a children's nursery called Tippety Toes. I cross the road and hover behind a tree, hoping that I don't look too conspicuous. I take out my phone and pretend to be busy texting, but all the while, I'm glancing up. The woman disappears inside, but a mere two minutes later, she's back again, clutching the hand of a little boy. He can't be more than two or three years old, and he's bouncing up and down, grinning as he talks to his mother. But there's something about his features that catches my breath. Is it his dark eyes or the mop of dark hair, or perhaps the shape of his little mouth in his miniature jaw? I feel sick as realisation dawns. I'm looking at a mini-Max.

A sharp cramp spears my stomach, as if my own embryo is reminding me that I'm also carrying a mini-Max. I lean against the tree to support myself as I watch the mother and child disappear around the corner, walking back the way I've just come. Is Max a serial cheater? Am I just one of many dark-haired, blue-eyed women he's courting, and does he have a team of little children scattered all over England?

CHAPTER TWENTY

I'm not sure how I get home, but when I do, I feel totally broken. Max has spun me a web of lies. He's probably got a different woman in every town. And then, to compound my fears, I get a call from my old colleague, the one I asked to investigate Max.

After some frustrating chitchat, she gets to the point. 'So I found Max Critchley's trade union rep. There was some investigation into Max just under two years ago, but there is nothing on record to say what it was or why he was being investigated.'

'What does that mean?' I ask.

'Either the investigation was dropped, or he left his job.'

'That ties in with him leaving London and taking a para-medic position in Sussex. But if he was under investigation, would he have been able to get another job in the same field?'

'He clearly wasn't fired for gross misconduct or anything like that, so perhaps some quiet agreement was reached. I'm afraid there's nothing on file, or nothing that his union rep is prepared to disclose. Sorry I can't be of any further help. We must meet up for a drink sometime.'

We finish the call, but it leaves me feeling even more frustrated than before. Something happened, and it meant that Max either had to leave his job, or he chose to leave. Probably the latter; otherwise his previous boss wouldn't have given him a decent reference. I wonder if it has something to do with the ending of his relationship with Tara. I groan with frustration.

As the hours pass, I sink into a smog of self-pity. Jazmin's warnings about Max have turned out to be true. He clearly can't be trusted. He has a murky past, which I can't uncover, and worst of all is his relationship with Jackie. A woman who has been brutally murdered. I'm going to have to end this. Here I am, pregnant with a baby I so desperately want, yet its father is of very dubious character.

Over the next couple of days I descend into a fog of depression. I call in sick, something I never do. I lie in bed, watching mind-numbing daytime television on my iPad, getting up just to make myself the occasional piece of toast and a cup of tea. I switch off my phone. I pine for Ludwig. And I don't go to book club. Occasionally I switch my phone back on and find messages from Max and worried call me backs from Jazmin. I send her a text saying I'm not well and will be in touch in a few days.

On the third evening, I hear little stones being thrown up against my window, and I know that it's Max, trying to catch my attention. The doorbell rings a couple of times, but I ignore everything and everyone. I wallow in my misery, worrying how I'll cope when the baby is born, worrying how I'll cope if I have a miscarriage, worrying about how I can break up with Max when he's living right next door.

Wondering if I'll make a huge loss if I sell this house and relocate up to the midlands to be closer to Mum.

On the fourth day, I force myself to ring the surgery, and I make an appointment to see a doctor. I may not want to look after myself, but I am desperate to keep this baby, and I owe it to him or her to take care. My appointment is at midday, and I'm relieved that Violet Lane is its normal tranquil place with no one I know wandering the streets.

The medical centre is a ten-minute walk away, and it does me good to breathe in the fresh air and feel the gentle warmth of the sun on my cheeks. It's the first time I've attended this medical practice. The waiting room is generous in size with tall windows and an airy feel. When my name is called, I pad down the corridor to room 6.

'Come in,' the female doctor welcomes me warmly. 'How can I help you today?'

'I think I'm pregnant,' I say, sitting down heavily in the chair. 'In fact, I know I'm pregnant.'

'Congratulations,' she replies, throwing me a broad smile. 'Let's do a quick examination, then.'

After taking my blood pressure and my medical history, I complete another urine test, and as I anticipated, the doctor confirms that I am indeed pregnant.

'Please don't take this the wrong way,' she says. 'However, yours is a geriatric pregnancy, so you need to take extra care. That means that you're in a high-risk bracket due to your age, and you will need to keep stress to the minimum. Do you have any particular concerns?'

I want to scream yes. I have a million concerns. I don't trust my baby's father, I am all alone in the world, and my child may have numerous half brothers and sisters. Except I don't say any of that. I smile and thank her, and she tells me I need to book in for an ultrasound and regular check-ups with the nurse. And then I leave.

This should be such a happy moment. I should be planning how to break the wonderful news to Max. I should be telephoning Jazmin and telling her that my dream has, at long last, come true. I should be ringing Mum to tell her she's going to become a grandmother. Except I can't do any of those things. Instead, I feel completely alone, almost as ostracised from the world as I did during the dying-ember days of my marriage. I walk dejectedly, wondering what the hell I should do now.

Back at home I send William Parker a message to say I'll be in work tomorrow, but a heavy wave of apathy has settled on me, and I don't feel like doing anything. I haven't cleaned the house in days and have a mountain of washing and ironing, the fridge is almost empty, and despite the sunny weather outside, I just sink onto my sofa in the living room and sit there for hours.

Max telephones me, but I ignore the call. I can hear him playing the piano next door, and whilst before I loved the sound, today it grates on my nerves. I close the windows. He rings me again. I send the call to voicemail. Then he sends me a text message to say he's coming over. That's the last thing I want. Avoidance tactics aren't going to work, so I pick up the phone. I've no idea what I'm actually going to say to him, but I know this relationship needs to end.

'At last!' he says, answering on the first ring. 'I was worried something might have happened to you. Are you alright?'

'Yes, fine, thank you,' I say curtly.

'Can I see you?'

'No. I'm sorry, Max, but I need a break from this relationship. There's too much going on in my life at the moment, and I can't cope.'

'Oh, sweetheart. I thought you seemed a bit overburdened, what with your new job and the fete committee and caring for Jazmin's kids. Of course you're in overwhelm. I get that. But I'm here to support you. I realise I haven't been around much the last couple of weeks, but I can take fewer shifts, and I can help you cook and just be there for you.'

I dig my fingernails into the palms of my hands. This isn't the reaction I want.

'It's kind of you, but I don't want to be in a relationship.'

'I get it, Laila. It's all too much, too soon.' Except he doesn't get it. I want out.

Static fills the silence before he starts talking again. 'Perhaps we should just see each other at the weekends. Distance makes the heart grow fonder and all of that. A temporary stepping back. What do you say?'

I would like to groan out loud, but I can't. This isn't what I mean at all. I curse myself for having this conversation on the phone; it would be so much better if we were face to face, except I don't want to see Max right now.

'I love you so much, Laila. You know that I want to marry you, spend the rest of our lives together. And we're going to have such beautiful babies.'

I freeze. Does he know I'm pregnant? Surely he can't know? This must just be Max talking out loud.

'Look, Max, I'm feeling really under the weather and am going to bed now. Please just leave me alone for a bit. I need to step away.'

There's a very long silence, and I wonder if Max is still there. I think I hear a thump in the distance, but then he's back on the line. 'We need to talk, darling,' he says. And then he hangs up.

What the hell?

I wonder if he's going to call me back, except he doesn't. Five minutes later, the doorbell rings. I tiptoe to the upstairs bedroom, the only place I can see who is at the front door. Unsurprisingly it's Max. He's hopping from one foot to another, trying to peer into the living room, and then pressing the buzzer again. He lifts up the letter box and shouts inside, 'Please open up, Laila. I'm worried about you.'

I stand completely still; the only vibrations are my rapidly thumping heart. As I'm watching him, as discreetly as I can, standing just out of view and peeking around the side, I see Phyllis at her window. She's staring straight ahead, watching Max on my doorstep, and then she glances up and sees me at my window. Her face is expressionless, but she nods at me before disappearing out of view.

Max leaves eventually, but to my dismay he appears in my garden, no doubt having hopped over the hedge. He's knocking on my patio door now, peering inside. This is completely unacceptable behaviour. I stride to my bedroom window and open it, leaning out.

'Max, please get out of my garden. I need you to leave me alone.'

He stares up at me, eyes wide, his jaw slack. He looks genuinely shocked. And then redness seeps into his face, and I see a flash of anger. 'I'm only trying to help,' he says through gritted teeth. 'But if you want to be like that, then...' He turns his back on me and marches to the hedge, dragging one of my chairs to stand on. A second later he's disappeared.

I CAN'T SLEEP. I toss and turn, either too hot or too cold, my brain racing with thoughts and worries. Shortly after 1 a.m. I go downstairs and make myself a camomile tea. It does nothing to ease me into sleep. Maybe an hour or two later, just as I think I might be drifting off, something wakes me. I sit bolt upright in bed. What was that sound? A noise, like the slamming of metal, or was it something shattering? My heart is thudding.

I grab my phone and switch on the torch function. There's silence now except for the creaking of the floor-boards as I tiptoe across my bedroom. I stand stock-still in front of my closed bedroom door. What if there's someone there? I have nothing with which to protect myself. Is it Max? Has he broken in? Unsure what to do, I carefully open the door and creep onto the upstairs landing. The house is shrouded in darkness.

'Who's there?' I shout. 'The police are on their way.'

Should I call them even though I'm not sure anyone has broken into the house? As I hesitate, my nose twitches. I'm smelling something acrid, something burning. What the hell? I switch on the light above the stairs, and that's when I see it. Glowing orange, lying on the stone floor in the hall-way, is a burning fire lighter. The pungent smell is increas-ing, smoke rising from the red-hot brick, and I realise with absolute terror that I need to put this out immediately to stop my beautiful, old house from going up in flames, taking me with it.

I run down the stairs, skirt the smouldering brick and race into the kitchen, grabbing the kettle, which thankfully is full of water. Back in the hallway, I pour the water over the smouldering fire lighter. It doesn't completely extinguish it, so I run back and fill the kettle up again, hold a wet tea towel under the running tap and pelt back into the hallway. It fizzles and spits, but soon, other than the stench of burning, the danger has gone.

I let out a sob. If I hadn't been awake, if I'd slept through that sound, I might have died tonight. And this was no accident. Someone purposefully shoved a burning fire lighter through my letter box. They wanted to cause damage, or worse. Set my house on fire, perhaps hoping to murder me in the process.

I think of those two anonymous letters. Who would do this? Who wants to cause me harm? Max. Sure, he was angry with me yesterday evening, but would he really do anything as horrific as this? He's a paramedic. His job is to make people better, not kill them. He told me that he loves me. And am I safe right now? My head is spinning as I pick up my phone from where I dropped it on the staircase. I dial 999.

'What's your emergency? Police, ambulance or fire?'

'Police. Someone tried to set my house on fire.'

'Police and fire brigade, then. What's your address?'

'Number 30, Violet Lane, South Gridgley.'

'Are you or anyone in your household in imminent danger?'

'No, I put out a burning fire lighter. But someone tried to harm me tonight.'

'Okay. I will dispatch police and a fire engine.'

'I don't need the fire engine,' I say. 'I've put out the fire.'

'They'll still need to check your premises, and if it's suspected arson, then they will be investigating. Are you safe right now?'

'Yes,' I reply. But am I?

CHAPTER TWENTY-ONE

It takes ten slow minutes before I hear the wailing sirens. I'm sitting on the bottom step of my staircase, shivering despite having pulled on a thick jumper and jeans. I can't think straight; my head is buzzing with all the what-ifs, my eyes transfixed on the semi-burned fire lighter. A moment later, blue flashing lights illuminate Violet Lane, and I hurry to open the door, carefully stepping over the fire lighter. Two uniformed police officers bound out of their car, their walkie-talkies echoing in the quiet night.

'Laila Bowden?' the man asks. I wish it were one of the local officers whom I know, but it's not.

'Yes. Please come in.' I want to get them off the street to prevent them from waking up all the neighbours. And Max in particular.

A moment later, a fire engine arrives, and a fireman jumps down from the truck, pacing towards us. 'Is anything on fire?'

'No. I told the operator that I put it out, but someone

shoved a fire lighter through my letter box, and they clearly wanted to set my house on fire.'

'Right, let's have a check.'

The police officer and the fireman bend down to examine the charred remains on my hallway floor.

I'm standing there trembling, my arms wrapped around my torso, when suddenly Max appears in my open doorway, his hair up on end, wearing a thin T-shirt and jeans.

'Laila!' he exclaims. 'My God. What's happened? Are you alright?'

The second police officer puts his arm across the open doorway. 'Excuse me, sir. You can't enter.'

'But I'm Laila's boyfriend, fiancé.'

I wince at the description.

'I live next door, and I'm a paramedic.'

'That might be the case, but Ms Bowden doesn't require any medical assistance, do you, ma'am?'

'No, I'm fine,' I say in a shaky whisper.

'In which case, sir, you're going to have to leave.'

'If you need anything, anything at all, just shout, Laila. You can stay at mine.' And then, to my relief, he's ushered away.

Two firemen walk around my house and take detailed photographs of the embers, and fifteen minutes later, they leave. The two police officers lead me into my kitchen, where on automatic, I make a pot of tea. I try to drink from my mug, but every time I attempt to bring it to my lips, my hand shakes too much, and I spill it. I talk the officers through exactly what happened tonight and show them photographs of the two threatening letters.

'Is there anyone who might hold a grudge against you?' the taller police officer asks.

'No, I don't think so. I had an acrimonious divorce, but my ex is a solicitor, and this isn't his style. And of course, there's the horrible murder of Jackie Walker, my neighbour who lives just across the road. Perhaps this is something to do with that? I was Finn Walker's solicitor for a short while. Or perhaps it's all a mistake,' I add, although I don't really think that. 'I'm new to the area, so maybe someone is after the people who lived here before me.'

'That's certainly a line we can investigate. But you mentioned you're also a solicitor. What about disgruntled clients?'

I can think of a few, particularly a couple of cases that ended badly between me and my clients when I failed to get them off criminal charges, but that's all a while ago. Why would anyone want to threaten me now? But above all, how would they have found my new home address? I take great care to make sure my address is never in the public domain.

'There's a group of local youths who have been causing problems in South Gridgley, shoplifting, breaking into cars and the like. Maybe they targeted you because you represent the law.'

I suppose it's a possibility, but this doesn't seem like the actions of some impetuous youths. Somehow this seems more personal. Again, my mind drifts back to Max. Could he have posted the fire lighter because he was angry that I want to step back from our relationship? Surely not. He's a good person, isn't he? And just now he seemed completely panicked that I might have been hurt.

'Right, Ms Bowden. I'm going to have to talk to the officers assigned to the Jackie Walker case and the officers investigating your poison pen letters to see if there's any connection. In the meantime, your house is a crime scene, so you won't be able to stay here tonight. Could you go next door and stay with your boyfriend?'

So Max has got his way after all. I glance at the clock on the kitchen wall. It's nearly four in the morning, so I can't contact Jazmin. It seems that I have no choice. I collect my toiletries, some spare clothes and my bag, and the shorter police officer escorts me out of my house and up Max's steps. The lights are on in his bedroom upstairs, and when I ring the doorbell, he's there, opening up almost instantly.

'Oh, Laila,' he says, throwing his arms around me. And although I tense initially, soon I relax into his warm, comforting embrace, just relieved to feel safe and wanted.

'We'll be in touch in the morning and ask that you don't re-enter your house until you've heard from us.'

I thank the officer, and Max closes the door.

'What happened, sweetheart?' he asks, concern etched over his face, his arm around my shoulders.

'Someone threw a lit fire lighter through my letter box. I don't feel safe.'

Max hugs me so tightly, I can barely breathe. 'I will never let anyone hurt you,' he murmurs into my ear, holding me with one arm and stroking my hair with his free hand. 'Come on, let's get a drink and then go to bed.'

I let Max lead me to his kitchen, where he pours me a small brandy. I drink it, and only when the glass is empty do I remember that I'm pregnant and shouldn't be drinking alcohol. Does that make me a bad mother already? And what of the stress? I place a protective hand over my stomach and will my embryo to be strong.

'You're freezing,' Max says. 'Let's go to bed, and I can warm you up.'

'I don't feel like...' I wave my hands around.

'I have no intention of coming onto you, Laila. I simply want to hold you and make sure you're toasty and safe. Come on.' He holds his hand out, and because I'm so utterly exhausted, I take it and allow Max to lead me upstairs.

When we're in bed, he spoons up against me and cradles me in his arms. I have to admit that it does feel good to be held, and the shivers soon stop.

'What's really going on, Laila? Why are you pushing me away?'

I don't want to be having this conversation now, but if I don't, when will the time ever be right? I pull away from him and lie on my back. 'I need to know more about you,' I say, staring into the darkness of the room. 'Your past, your previous girlfriends. It's like there's this big blank in your life before you arrived in Sussex. What really happened? Why the big move?'

He sighs, and his breath is warm on the side of my neck. 'I was dating a woman called Tara. She was a paramedic, but she's a nurse now. It was pretty intense.'

'What does she look like? You don't even have any photographs in your house. Not even of your mother.'

Max pulls away from me, and I hear him shuffle in the dark; then his phone is illuminated. He swipes through it and brings up a photograph of Tara Monteith, the photograph of him with his arm around her that I found on Facebook.

'Dark hair, blue eyes,' I murmur. 'You have a type.'

Max laughs uneasily. 'I suppose I do. Although I have dated blonde women and redheads.'

'So what happened?'

'We were working together and going out together, and it got too intense. It wasn't an appropriate relationship, and then it ended really badly. I felt I had no choice but to leave my job in London because of it. I shouldn't have mixed work and play, not in that way, at least.'

'So you argued?' I ask, probing for more information.

'We really weren't compatible. Not like me and you. Tara is horribly needy and possessive, and it became too much. I tried to end things, and she went ballistic, accusing me of all sorts of stuff. It was dreadful, and I needed to get away.'

I feel some of the tension ease from my body. This explains why Max's ex-boss gave him a not-so-great reference. He can't have been impressed that two of his team were dating, and that must have impacted upon their work. Yes, it explains so much. Have I been worrying about nothing? After all, we both have pasts, it's just we haven't talked about them.

'Who did you date before Tara?' I ask.

Max laughs. 'Do you really want to know all the details of my checkered dating history? I'm thirty-nine years old, Laila, and I haven't been a monk.'

'No, okay. Fair enough.' I think about the dark-haired woman in Hove and her little boy, the miniature version of Max. Yet I can't mention her because then Max will know that I followed him.

'So are there any little Max offspring in the world?' I try to say it casually, but I'm not sure my tone of voice is right.

He snorts. 'Not that I'm aware of. No, seriously, of course not. I want children, you know I do. And I want them with you, Laila.' He puts his arms around me again and draws me to him, kissing the back of my neck. I tense. I just want to be held tonight, although it's barely night any longer.

The pale grey light of dawn is starting to seep in behind the curtains.

'Living on Violet Lane and all the Jackie stuff has got to me. And then with me being a target too, and the things Finn has been saying about you.'

He holds me tighter. 'I get it. I really do. But I promise you I had nothing to do with Jackie's death. And if the police are sure Finn didn't either, then we have to accept it. Let's face it, if she was prepared to have a one-night stand with me, perhaps she did the same with other men too. She was quite the flirt. Hear me out on this one. Let's say she had been playing away, but she was good at hiding it. Unfortunately Finn found out about her and me, and that's why he's been pointing his finger in my direction. But what if Jackie was sleeping with someone else none of us know about? He could be the murderer.'

I consider what Max is saying, and it makes sense.

'Have you mentioned this to the police?'

'No, but I might. I really think that Jackie's death has nothing to do with what's happened to you. Maybe the letters and fire lighter were meant for the people who lived in your house before you?'

'I thought of that,' I said. 'Who were they?'

'An elderly couple, nice enough. I don't want you to worry,' Max says. 'I love you so much, and I will keep you safe. All I want to do is marry you, Laila.'

I don't say anything.

'Tomorrow, I'm going to install some cameras in your house. I'll put some hidden cameras above both your front and back doors. Perhaps you should get an alarm installed too. I can do some research for you.'

'Thank you,' I murmur. 'I'm going to try to sleep now,' I

say, although I seriously doubt I'll be able to. Max, on the other hand, is breathing deeply within five minutes. As I lie there, I can't stop thinking about the letters and about that horrific fire lighter. The what-ifs go around and around my head, and I begin to wonder whether moving to Violet Lane was a terrible mistake.

CHAPTER TWENTY-TWO

My phone rings at 7.30 a.m., and I've barely slept. Max's side of the bed is empty, and I fumble to answer.

'Good morning, Ms Bowden. This is DS Stefan Kolinsky. I've been passed the details of the incident at your house last night, and I will be the investigating officer. We are taking this very seriously and will be sending forensics around this morning. After that, you should be allowed home.'

'I'm going to have to go to work today,' I explain. I don't tell him that I've skived off the past few days to wallow in a misery of my own making. 'But you can drop off my keys with my next-door neighbour, Max Critchley.'

Max appears in the doorway, bare-chested, holding a steaming cup of coffee. 'Thought you might like this,' he says, placing it on the bedside table next to me.

'Thank you.' I explain that I have to go to work, but DS Kolinsky will give my keys back to Max or shove them through his letter box if he's not at home. Max, meanwhile, promises to nip down to Brighton to buy some cameras and to install them for me before I'm back from work.

I HAVE SO MUCH CATCHING up to do in the office, and it's difficult to concentrate considering I'm bone-weary exhausted. At least I don't have to pretend that I'm unwell – I look a fright, with pale skin and grey bags under my eyes. Even William asks whether I'm well enough to be back at work.

At 5.30 p.m., I switch off my computer and leave the office. I have two missed text messages. One from DS Kolinsky telling me he'd like to talk to me, the other from Max saying he has my keys and, if he's out, he'll leave them under the flowerpot next to his front door.

I pick up some food in the Co-op and shuffle towards Violet Lane, but as I turn into the cul-de-sac, I let out an audible gasp. Once again there are blue flashing lights at the far end. I break into a run. Is my house properly on fire now? What has happened? Except there is no fire engine. Instead there are three marked police cars and an ambulance blocking the far end of the street. And they're not outside my house or Max's or Finn's. There are two uniformed officers standing either side of Phyllis' front door. I rush forwards just in time to see a man standing in the doorway. There is crimson blood stained all across the front of his shirt, and his hands are clasped together behind his back, secured with handcuffs.

Max.

I let out a gasp, but no one is interested in me.

A uniformed officer is reading Max his rights. Those

words that are so familiar to me, yet seem totally out of context here. My hand rushes to cover my mouth, and a dizziness makes my head swim and my knees buckle slightly. Max is standing in Phyllis' doorway, covered in blood, in handcuffs, and I listen as he is charged with murder. An officer pushes Max forwards towards the nearest police car while another officer opens the rear door. Max is shoved inside the vehicle. I will him to look up at me, to give me some sign that he's seen me here and that this is all some terrible mistake. Except Max doesn't look up. His head is bowed, and inside the closed police car, I can't see his expression.

I raise my eyes to look back at Phyllis' house. The police are crowded around the cars, so I edge forwards. The front door is open, and I can see a body on the ground, stretched out in the hallway, a glistening pool of blood underneath her grey locks, eyes staring upwards, sightless. My stomach clenches, and I think I'm going to vomit. I swallow bile repeatedly. There is absolutely no doubt that Phyllis is dead.

'Excuse me, miss, but you can't be here.'

'Wait!' I exclaim. 'What are you doing with Max Critchley?'

'You need to leave, miss.'

'But I'm Max Critchley's solicitor. I have a right to accompany him.'

'Okay,' he says slowly. He evidently doesn't believe me. I rush towards the police car and knock on the window, but the engine has started, and I just watch hopelessly as Max is driven away.

'I need to speak to whoever is in charge,' I say to a young officer. He eyes me warily, as if he thinks I'm some meddling neighbour with delusions of grandeur.

'Wait here, please.'

I do as I'm told, and a few moments later, DS Kolinsky emerges from Phyllis' house. 'This is a crime scene, Ms Bowden.'

'I know. I'm the solicitor representing Max Critchley, who I understand you have just arrested.'

He raises an eyebrow. 'Indeed we have arrested Mr Critchley. And we need to discuss the alleged arson attack on your house last night. Everything is certainly happening in Violet Lane, isn't it? If you make your way to the police station, you can join your client, and I'll be along shortly.'

'What's happened here?' I ask.

He purses his lips as if deciding whether or not to tell me anything. 'Mr Critchley was caught red-handed over Phyllis Hallett's dead body. I suspect all the goings-on in Violet Lane are somehow connected, and it appears that Max Critchley is our missing link. I look forward to discussing more down at the station.'

I can't believe it. Why would Max kill Phyllis? Yes, she's a nosey woman, but it doesn't make any sense. And that look in Max's eyes as he was arrested. Was that the look of a guilty or a desperate man? I turn around and jog back to the high street and literally run towards the police station. By the time I've arrived, I'm panting and dishevelled, but I don't care.

'I'm here to represent Max Critchley.' I scoot up to the front desk and speak breathlessly. 'I want to see him now.'

I recognise the police officer manning the desk, and he clearly recognises me, because I'm ushered through to the interview room in record time. Max is seated there, his hands still in chains, his head bowed.

'Max,' I say, reaching to touch his arm.

'What are you doing here?' His eyes are red, and his shirt is still covered in blood.

'I've told them I'm your legal representative. Is that alright?'

'I didn't do it, Laila. You've got to believe me! I'm innocent.'

'Alright.' I pace the little room, and only then do I think through the repercussions of what I've just done. I'm in – or at least was up until last night – a relationship with Max, he took care of me last night, and I accepted it. No, I was grateful for it. Officially, I might not be Max's girlfriend, but I am personally involved. I made this mistake representing Finn, so should I be Max's solicitor? I can easily get out of this situation, tell them that it's too personal, find a replacement counsel. But if I do that, I won't know what's going on. I'll be ostracised as I was before. If I remain Max's solicitor, then I can find out what's happened and then pass the case to a colleague. Besides, I've just told everyone that I'm representing Max. I'll look a complete fool if I change my mind. Exhaustion, shock and confusion are clouding my judgement, and for the first time, I simply don't know what to do.

Except then the matter is taken out of my hands as DS Kolinksy and DC Vicky Mortimer enter the room.

I sit down in the chair next to Max while they set up the recording equipment and read through the formal notices prior to the interview.

'I didn't do it,' Max repeats. 'I've been set up.'

'Alright,' I say. 'Let's listen to what DS Kolinsky has to say,' I suggest.

'So, Mr Critchley, you say that you are innocent. In your own words, talk us through what happened this afternoon.'

'I was at home, and I got a phone call from a withheld

number. I thought it might be someone connected with work, so I answered it. It was a voice I didn't recognise. A weird voice telling me that Phyllis Hallett was having a stroke and could I come over immediately. I raced out of the house straight to Phyllis', and the door was open. She was lying there on the floor, bleeding out. I tried to save her, but it was too late.'

'You are aware that we can check all of this. We'll be able to see on your phone if you received a call from a strange number.'

'I'm telling you the truth,' Max says. There's exasperation in his voice.

'You can say no comment,' I add.

'But I want to tell them what happened!'

'Can you explain why we found your front door closed?'

Max frowns. 'I thought I left it open, but perhaps I slammed it shut. It all happened so quickly.'

'It sounds like you were in a panic,' Kolinksy suggests.

'No, just in a hurry.'

'Which is strange because as a trained paramedic, you must know how to stay calm in these situations.'

'I do, but this was on my home turf, and Phyllis. She was stabbed, wasn't she?'

'You tell us, Mr Critchley. Surely as a trained paramedic, you would know not to touch any evidence, except you were found with a bloodied knife in your hand. Can you explain that?'

Max shakes his head and says nothing.

'For the purposes of the recording, Mr Critchley is shaking his head.'

'Who called the police, anyway?' Max asks. 'It wasn't me. I didn't have time.'

'We received an anonymous tip-off that there was suspicious activity at number 41 Violet Lane, the property of Mrs Phyllis Hallett.'

Max interrupts. 'I was set up! Can't you see that? I got that strange phone call, which lured me over to Phyllis' house, and then you got a tip-off. I didn't do anything wrong. All I tried to do was save Phyllis.'

'Except you didn't, did you?'

Max's shoulders sink. 'I was too late. She'd been stabbed repeatedly, and because the knife was lying on her stomach and she had a wound there, I had to move it. Of course you'll find my fingerprints on the weapon.'

'Is there anything else you'd like to tell us, Mr Critchley?' DS Kolinsky asks.

Max stares at me, his eyes beseeching, except what can I tell him? I shake my head.

He turns to face the two officers. 'No comment.'

CHAPTER TWENTY-THREE

I'm a mess. The father of my child and possible future husband is in a police cell, charged with murder. Someone is threatening me in my own home. And my career is in danger of going down the pan. On top of that, I'm pregnant, feeling permanently exhausted and nauseous. I'm lying in bed, unable to sleep, when the first cramp sears through my stomach. When it comes a second time, panic washes over me. Am I losing the baby? Feeling completely lost and alone, I telephone Jazmin.

'Bright and early,' she says. I can hear the background noise of clattering plates and cutlery and her kids chattering.

'I'm not feeling good,' I say.

'Hey, what's up?' I hear the clip-clop of her heels as she walks into another room.

'There's something I didn't tell you. I'm pregnant.'

There's a pause before Jazmin exclaims, 'That's amazing news!'

'Except I think I might be losing the baby. I've got terrible cramps, and I'm nowhere near twelve weeks yet.'

'Oh, darling,' Jazmin says. 'Do you want me to come over?'

'If it's not too much of an inconvenience, yes, please. I think I need to go to the hospital.'

'And lover boy Max isn't at home?'

'I'll tell you everything when I see you.'

'Alright. Let me sort the girls out, and I'll be with you in about forty-five minutes. If the cramps get worse or you pass blood, call 999.'

'Thanks, Jaz,' I say.

In the car to the hospital, I tell Jazmin everything. About how Max asked me to marry him, how he was overvigorous in bed (although I did play that one down) and how he's been arrested on suspicion of murdering Phyllis. Nothing much riles Jazmin, but even she appears shocked. 'The most important thing is your and your baby's well-being,' she says. 'The rest we'll deal with another time.'

The cramps have settled down a lot, and as we enter the hospital, I dare to feel hopeful. Perhaps I'm not losing this baby after all. I feel bad that Jazmin is having to miss work to accompany me, but she reassures me that she'll catch up on paperwork tonight, and instead we talk about her kids during the long wait for me to be seen.

Eventually I'm assessed by a midwife and sent for an ultrasound.

'Both you and baby are doing absolutely fine,' the midwife reassures me afterwards. 'But you need to rest. This is your body's way of telling you to slow down and take care. Have you been under a lot of stress?'

Jazmin answers for me. 'Yes, she has.'

'Well, I need you to take more care. Pregnancy is hard on your body, and the little one growing inside you needs you to be stress-free and rested. Please make an appointment to see your GP in a week's time.'

I surprise myself with the intense relief I feel. Despite everything, I want this baby. With or without Max.

I GET through the days on automaton. I organise for an alarm system to be installed, and it makes me feel safer, able to sleep at night. Ludwig comes to stay for a few days, and he is the best tonic of all. Otherwise, I'm focusing on work, taking on more and more cases so I can block out the Max situation.

He has been charged, not just with Phyllis' murder but also with Jackie's murder. I genuinely believe the police's evidence for the latter is circumstantial and won't hold up to scrutiny in court, but they do have evidence. They have matched Max's DNA and sperm to a handkerchief found in Jackie's pocket. It seems that her body had not been submerged in water as I had previously thought, but was decomposing caught up in reeds at the side of the river. Max is vigorously denying any involvement, explaining that yes, he and Jackie did have sex together, so that was the reason his DNA was found.

I try to do the maths, to work out when Max might have last slept with Jackie. Was he already courting me? Except nothing seems sure.

Max is in prison; unsurprising for someone charged with two murders. And just when I think things can't get any worse, I'm notified that the director of Public Prosecutions has requested a DNA analysis of Jackie's foetus. The several-day wait for the results to come through is interminable, and I spend all of my time working, trying to block out my emotions. Then the results arrive. Max Critchley was indeed the father of Jackie's unborn child. And I'm devastated.

It feels like I can't trust a word that Max told me. I'm doubting everything, feeling like I've been played for a fool. How could I have let Max into my life, my heart and my head? I'm a complete idiot, and now I'm the one carrying his baby. Everything he told me must have been a lie. Except there's one thing I can't make sense of. He had a reason for killing Jackie: rage that she decided to return to Finn, to make her marriage work; rage that he wouldn't be part of his child's life, when it's clear that he is desperate to be a dad. But why did he kill Phyllis? That's the thing I can't reconcile. What was his motive?

I go to see William Parker. 'I'm sorry,' I say, sitting heavily in the chair opposite him. 'But I'm going to have to hand over Max Critchley's case to someone else.' I feel such shame as I speak. 'I have a personal relationship with him, and there's a conflict of interest. I'm sorry to be letting you down.'

He sighs. 'You're not letting me down, Laila. You're doing what's in the best interest of your client. Of course, it grieves me to have to give up the business. I can't take the case on at my age or stage, and there's no one else in our team who is qualified to handle it. I suppose we'll have to hand it over to another firm. Who are you thinking of, Jacob May?'

'Absolutely not,' I say. I mention the name of a female colleague in a Brighton-based firm, someone I have great confidence in.

'You have my blessing,' he says, and smiles at me gently. I sense his deep disappointment, but at the same time, William Parker is gracious.

AND THEN THERE'S my own confusion. Do I want to keep this baby, knowing that Max might be a killer? Some days the answer is no, but mostly it's yes. I'm desperate for a child. Besides, nurture is far more important than nature, and I can give this baby a great life. And then I remind myself that Max hasn't been proven guilty. At least not yet.

CHAPTER TWENTY-FOUR

I remember the first time I visited a client in prison. I was in my mid-twenties, and it was absolutely terrifying. All of the security checks and the clanging of metal doors and the constant locking and unlocking. But worse was the noise. I felt like pressing the palms of my hands over my ears to block out the cacophony of shouting, wolf whistles, stomping of feet and hard laughter. And then I was all alone with my client, a suspected murderer, in a small room with just a prison guard waiting on the other side of the door.

I suppose I have become a little immune to prison visits over the years, but this one is different. My client is my lover, the father of my unborn child, the person I thought I might spend the rest of my life with. The pressure is immense. On the one hand, I need to know if he's innocent; on the other, it shouldn't matter. I have come to see Max to tell him that I'm passing his case to a colleague, and I've no idea how he's going to take the news.

He's already in the small room. It stinks in here of stale

sweat and disinfectant, the fluorescent lights too bright. But the shock is Max. He looks unkempt and exhausted. He has a livid purple bruise on his right cheekbone, and his pale grey sweatshirt and joggers look tattered and dirty.

'Oh, Laila,' he murmurs as I sit down opposite him. 'I'm so happy to see you.' A tear drips down his cheek, and it shocks me. 'I didn't do it. I didn't kill anyone, I promise you. It's all a terrible mistake, and you have to get me off.'

I take a deep breath, knowing that I have to go for the jugular and tell him immediately. 'Max, I can't be your solicitor anymore. I'm too close to the case, too involved. I've assigned your case to a colleague of mine. She's really, really good, and she'll do everything in her power to help you.'

'You can't walk away!' Max's eyes plead with me, his voice edged with desperation. He shifts towards me, lifting his cuffed hands onto the table, and for a brief second, a bolt of fear runs through me. I have to remind myself that this is Max. He is – was – my lover, and I really don't think he's going to hurt me.

'I need to do what's best for you and also what's best for me,' I say. Now I'm sitting here, looking into this man's eyes, the man I thought I loved or at least might love, the doubts seem to fade. Yet the police have charged him, and they don't do that unless they are very confident of their evidence. Could I be wrong? Could Max be a wicked person? I know for sure that he's lied to me, but lies don't mean that he's a murdering psychopath.

Max sighs. 'I also want what's best for you, Laila. I've had a lot of time to think in here, and I'm worried you're not safe in your home. Those letters and the fire...' His voice fades. 'What if the person comes back?'

'They haven't come back, and I've installed an alarm,' I say. There's a pause before I add, 'So it wasn't you?' My voice sounds snide.

'Of course it wasn't me! I love you, Laila.' He leans forwards, and once again, I instinctively lean back. 'I want to protect you, and I can't when I'm stuck in here. I'm convinced Finn has something to do with all of this – Jackie's death, the threats to you. Maybe you should go and stay with Jazmin.'

I don't answer. There haven't been any more threats, and although that fire lighter was extremely scary, I'm not willing to give in to an invisible threat that may or may not happen. Besides, the police have cleared Finn. And why would he come after me? He's a free man now.

Max interrupts my thoughts. 'Oh, I didn't get around to telling you. I connected the cameras in your house. There are two on the exterior of your house – one above the front door and the other above your patio door.'

'I didn't see them,' I say, having forgotten all about them now that I have the safety of an alarm system.

'They're concealed cameras. You wouldn't know they're there if you weren't looking for them. You'll need to download an app called WatchZnZ. The footage is backed up to the cloud and deleted after thirty days. The password is MaxnLaila3032.' He looks a little bashful. 'Our names and house numbers.'

'Yes, I get that.' Max is making me feel unnerved.

There's an uncomfortable pause. 'I didn't kill Jackie, and I didn't kill Phyllis,' he reiterates.

'Except you are a liar, aren't you?' I can't stop the words from tumbling from my mouth.

VIOLETS ARE BLUE   213

His jaw drops open, and his eyes narrow. 'What do you mean?'

'I know you weren't visiting your mother on Tuesday nights. In fact, do you even have a mother?'

He opens his mouth, but I put my hand up to stop him.

'I know you left your previous job under a cloud, and your ex-girlfriend Tara refuses to talk about you. Is that because she's scared? Did you do something bad to her? Strangle her perhaps during sex? You tell me that I should trust you, that you're a good person, but actions speak louder than words. And the thing is, Max, I don't know what to believe.' Tears prick my eyes, and I know that all the confusion and the disappointments have come to the surface, and if I don't get out of here now, I'm going to break down and tell Max about the baby. I can't let that happen.

I stand up suddenly, pushing the chair back so that the legs scrape against the vinyl floor.

'Don't go, Laila. Please!'

I shake my head and turn away from him, knocking on the door. The prison guard opens it immediately.

'You can't go! We haven't finished talking!' Max shouts.

'All okay in here?' the guard asks.

'Fine,' I say, bunching my fingers into fists and biting my lip so hard I draw blood. 'I'd like to leave now.'

'Laila!' Max exclaims, but the door swings shut, and his voice is obliterated.

I'D LIKE to go straight home, to shower away the imaginary stench left on my body from my visit to the prison, but I have a midwife's appointment. I'm at the doctor's surgery, in the waiting room, along with another ten or so patients. My midwife is running late, and I'm passing the time by playing a word puzzle game on my phone.

'Laila?'

I jump. 'Oh hi,' I say. Ellie slips into a chair next to me. 'How are you?'

'So-so.' She sighs. 'It's true what they say that grief comes in waves and hits you when you're least expecting it. It's quite the shock about Max, isn't it?'

I nod, unwilling to talk about him. There's an awkward pause before Ellie says, 'Hope you don't mind me asking, but are you pregnant?'

I glance at her with surprise. 'How do you know?'

She laughs. 'It's the pregnancy clinic this afternoon.'

'Oh,' I say, startled. Other than Jazmin, no one knows the truth. 'It's early days, and I haven't told anyone yet.'

'Don't mind me. My lips are sealed. Besides, I know what it's like in those early stages. You want to shout about it from the rooftops but are too scared to tempt fate. I don't know myself, of course, but being a childminder, I hear all of those things from my mums. And I lived it with Jackie too. Anyway, congratulations! You must be thrilled.'

'Yes, I am,' I say. 'Are you here for the clinic too?'

She laughs. 'No, I've got a regular doctor's appointment.' She doesn't elaborate further, but then my name is called. I get up, wave goodbye to Ellie and toddle through to the nurse's room. My examination goes fine although the nurse does reiterate that I need to rest. As I'm exiting the medical centre a few minutes later, Ellie is standing outside, leaning against the wall.

'Wondered if you'd like to go for a coffee?' she asks. I don't feel like I can say no; besides, perhaps I'll learn more about the Walkers. Ellie was very open the last time we spoke.

We stroll to a little coffee shop on the high street and take a seat near the back.

'When your babe is born, if you need any child-minding, I'm your girl,' she says. So that's why she wanted to meet up. 'Whoops! That wasn't very subtle, was it?' She laughs. 'Sorry! I don't normally hang around the pregnancy clinic to pick up clients. I genuinely had a doctor's appointment.'

'It's fine. And yes, it's great to know that you're available. Are you still looking after little Melanie?'

A cloud passes over her face. 'Yes, Finn is struggling. But I really don't mind caring for Mel. I stay over whenever I can, and it means that Finn can catch up on his sleep. He's got insomnia. No surprise, really. He's a broken man. There's no guidebook on how to recover from the shock of your wife's murder, is there?'

I shake my head.

'You're on the village fete committee, aren't you?' Ellie asks.

'Yes, why?'

'It's such a relief that it's been cancelled. You can't celebrate a village that's had two murders, can you, and with the murderer on the committee and all?'

I recall seeing an email in my inbox from the fete committee, but I didn't get around to reading it. Of course, it was the right thing to cancel, but Ellie saying out loud that 'the murderer was on the committee' jars. Instinctively I put my hand over my stomach.

'I know he was your boyfriend, but I never liked Max,' Ellie says. 'There's something about men like him, the ones that are too good-looking and overly confident. They're too pleased with themselves. It's good that he's out of your life, Laila. I'm sure you see that now. Anyway, I must get going. If you need anything, anything at all, don't hesitate to call me.' She hands me a business card with her phone number, and I watch as she hurries away. I wonder what she really knows about Max because, for sure, there's something that she's not telling me.

CHAPTER TWENTY-FIVE

As soon as I'm home, I search for the cameras that Max says he installed. It takes me a few minutes to find them because they really are tiny, concealed in little patches of broken grouting between flint stones at the front of the house and bricks over the lintel at the back. He did an excellent job of hiding them. The only way someone will notice either camera is if the sunlight catches the black lens, but I don't think that's very likely.

Back inside, I download the app WatchZnZ and log in using the cringe-making password that Max has chosen. He's absolutely right. There is footage neatly backed up and filed for each twenty-four-hour period since he installed the cameras. I choose a day at random and look at the footage. The camera above my front door captures both my doorstep, but also the portion of Violet Lane directly in front of my house and beyond to Phyllis' front door.

I swallow hard as it hits me. This camera has footage of Phyllis' front door, and it just captures the side of Finn's house too. With trembling fingers, I scroll to the day poor Phyllis died, the very first day that Max installed the cameras. I fast-forward to the middle of the afternoon. Violet Lane is empty. And then there's movement. Lots of movement. I pause as Max races across the street, except – hold on. There was movement before that. I rewind and reduce the playback speed to the minimum.

Finn emerges onto Violet Lane. He looks backwards and forwards, his movements furtive and nervous, his head bouncing from side to side. He's wearing all black. Black jeans, a black long-sleeve T-shirt and black trainers. And then he strides up to Phyllis' front door, again glancing around furtively. He presses the doorbell, and a few moments later, the door swings open. I catch a quick glimpse of Phyllis' grey hair, and then the door closes as Finn steps inside. My heart is hammering as I watch.

All is still until just four minutes later. Finn emerges from Phyllis' front door, slamming it shut behind him, and he literally runs towards his van. He tugs open the driver's door, puts the van into reverse, and although I can't hear any sound, I can imagine that he pulls away with squealing tyres. In a second, he's gone.

I press pause on the camera playback. What have I just seen? Surely this changes everything? I'm trembling from head to toe now as I press play again. Nothing happens for three minutes, five minutes. I speed up the playback. And then.

Max.

Max is sprinting across the road. He bangs on Phyllis' front door with his fists. He also glances around, and as he does so, he opens his mouth as if he's shouting. Then he turns the doorknob, and he's inside. I can't see him now, as the light is shining the wrong way, and the open doorway is shrouded in darkness. I feel sick as I realise at some point during this video, Phyllis will have been stabbed. And it looks distinctly like the police might have got things completely wrong. Finn went into her house first.

I lean back in my chair and run my fingers through my hair. Is Max telling the truth? But why aren't Finn's prints on the knife? I rewind the video until I see him entering Phyllis' house again. I pause the video and look at his hands. It's hard to tell if he's wearing gloves. If his hands are encased in gloves, then they're light or pale flesh-coloured. I watch the whole sequence several times, but nothing else leaps out at me. I need to show this footage to the police.

It's 6 p.m., and if there's no one at the local police station, I'll head down to Hove and go to the main station. There's no point in trying to explain this over the phone. I swallow a glass of water, grab my coat and handbag and head out of the house. As I walk down my steps, Finn is striding along the pavement, heading towards his home.

'Laila,' he says, a warm smile on his face, 'how are you?'

'Yes, fine.' I freeze, tongue-tied.

'I was wondering if you'd be free to pop over for a drink?'

'What, now?' I can't disguise my surprise.

'Well, if you're free. I'm not doing anything, and I'd like to say thank you for all your support.'

My head is spinning. All my support? If he knew what is on my phone, he might not be saying that. What should I do? I could make up an excuse and say I'm on my way out to meet with friends, or alternatively, I could accept his offer. Maybe this is the perfect opportunity to find out if he's guilty. I realise he's looking at me strangely, the length of time between his question and me replying is stretching awkwardly.

'Um, sorry,' I say at the same time as he speaks.

'Ellie will be joining us shortly. She's on her way back from the creche with Melanie.'

That changes things. If Ellie and little Melanie will be there, then surely I'll be safe. It's the thought of being alone with Finn that makes me nervous, especially as Max's words are still ringing in my head. And the fact that I know categorically that he entered Phyllis' house shortly before she was killed.

'Alright. I'll join you for a quick one,' I say. But as soon as the words are out of my mouth, I doubt myself. No one is going to rescue me if Finn decides to take a hammer to my head or a knife to my heart. My intuition is screaming at me. Turn around. Get in your car. Drive to the police station. Except my feet are following Finn as he walks up to his front door and inserts a key.

'Please excuse the mess,' he says. 'Ellie has been amazing, but Jackie was the neat freak. God, it's hard without her.'

It's my first time in the Walkers' house, and it seems significantly smaller than the others I've been inside. The ceilings are dark and low, and we have to push through coats and shoes that are stacked up on the side of the hallway, making the entrance even narrower. The kitchen, however, is delightful. The units are all handmade and painted a chalky white, the countertops a warm oak. It's tidy in here, with just a couple of mugs stacked in the sink.

'Ellie, bless her.' Finn sighs, waving his arms around. 'This was a mess when I left for work this morning.'

'It's a beautiful kitchen.'

Finn puffs out his chest a little. 'I made it myself. I'm a carpenter by trade.'

'Very impressive.'

I look at the row of pans hanging from a beam and the plates positioned sideways in an ornately carved plate rack. There's a small shiny black Aga and a Smeg fridge also in black. This is really a designer kitchen.

'What can I get you?' He opens the fridge. 'There's an opened bottle of white wine or a beer?'

'Thanks, but I'm alcohol-free at the moment.'

'Orange juice or water, then?'

As he's pouring me an orange juice, he squints towards me. 'You pregnant, then?'

I'm startled that he's worked that out, but then recall that Ellie might have told him, except we only had that conversation a few hours ago. 'Yes,' I admit. He hands me the glass and nods his head to the circular kitchen table.

'Is it Max's?'

I'm taken aback by both his directness and his insightfulness, but of course, he must know about Max and me. God, this is awkward.

'Yes,' I say. 'But he doesn't know.'

'Guess it's a bit hard to have that conversation with him in the clanger,' Finn says as he sits down. He takes a swig from a beer can and then stares at me. 'I'm sorry for you. It must be seriously crap to know you're carrying the child of a murderer. How do you even get your head around that?'

'He's innocent until proven guilty,' I add quietly.

'Yeah, I know. But forgive me if I say it makes me feel better to know someone is banged up for the murder of my wife. And he was having an affair with Jackie. We're in a right mess, you and me, aren't we?' He lets out a bitter laugh, and I realise he's right. This is the strangest of situations.

We're both silent for a while, but there's a voice screaming in my head. *You need to find out why he went to see Phyllis. What was he doing? Did he kill her?* But how do I ask that question? I glance around the kitchen and see a large knife block, one of those wooden and magnetic types where the sharp knives sit on the outside of the block. I realise with some horror that the largest knife is missing. Is that the one Finn used? Should I be dialling the emergency services right now?

'You alright?' he asks, and I realise I've frozen.

'Yes, fine. I was just thinking about poor Phyllis. I still can't work out why Max would have wanted to kill her.'

'Well, it's pretty obvious why he wanted to kill Jackie. He must have been distraught that she chose me over him.'

I don't say anything and take another sip of orange juice, although my hand is trembling. I hope he doesn't notice.

'But Phyllis,' I say again. 'I can't even remember the last time I saw her before she died. And she was so lovely to me, welcoming me into the neighbourhood. I wish I'd been a better friend to her. She invited me in for a sherry, but I didn't hang around long. When did you last see her?' I really hope that my words sound natural, that Finn doesn't realise that I'm probing for information.

'Yeah, she was a good woman. Nosey and all that, but a good woman.'

'When did you last see her?'

Finn looks off into the distance. 'I dunno. The day before she died or maybe the day before that.' Except Finn is not a good liar. He touches his nose and blinks several times, and then he glances at me, and I catch his gaze.

I know he's lying.

And he knows that I know.

He narrows his eyes and purses his lips, carefully placing the beer can on the table. 'What made you ask?' he says.

Once again, my heart is hammering.

'Um, I just hope that she knew we all liked her. That she had a good last few days.' The silence between us is vibrating with distrust, and I've got an overwhelming need to get out of this house.

'Right, I really must get back,' I say hurriedly. 'I've got a mountain of paperwork to catch up on.' My glass is only half drunk, but I push my chair back and stand up quickly.

Finn is equally nimble on his feet, and he's standing up too.

'Thank you, I need to–'

He doesn't let me finish my sentence. Instead he reaches out and grabs my wrist.

'Wait, Laila. I can explain.'

I knew I shouldn't have come here. Why the hell did I ignore my gut? Finn looks so evil now, his blue eyes glinting, his lips narrow and his shoulders tensed up. And no one knows I'm here.

'Let me go!' I say, tugging my wrist away. I glance around the kitchen wildly. I'd like to reach for a knife, but the knife block is on the other side of Finn. His grip is tight, and I feel the strength in him, realising that I don't stand a chance against a young, fit man like him. I step backwards, and to my surprise, Finn releases his grip. I swivel around and grab the nearest saucepan, its hook flying off the wall.

He looks at me, his eyes wide. Then he steps towards me, and I know that in the next instant he's going to have his strong hands around my neck, and he'll be squeezing the lifeblood out of me, just like he killed his wife and Phyllis. I swing the saucepan with all of my strength, practically toppling over as the back of it hits Finn's head.

He wobbles for a second, and then his legs concertina from under him, and he falls as if in slow motion to the floor, his head hitting the side of a chair, before his whole body slumps lifeless onto the ground.

CHAPTER TWENTY-SIX

Oh my God! What have I done? I freeze. The blood rushes to my head as I let the saucepan slip with a clatter onto the countertop. I've never hurt another person. Never. And I'm a lawyer. I'm meant to be upholding the law, not killing people. Panic grips my chest, my heart hammering in my ears. I'm staring at Finn, who is lying motionless on the floor. It's as if I'm paralysed. I'm unable to move, unable to even breathe, unable to pull my gaze away from the man, whose eyes are closed as if he's sleeping. But he might be dead.

It's Mum's voice that I hear in my head. 'Pull yourself together, Laila,' I imagine her saying. 'Go and check on him.' I let out a whimper as I take a step forwards and then bend down to my knees. I don't want to touch Finn, so I ease the back of my hand in front of his face, under his nose.

Thank heavens. He's still breathing. Minuscule puffs of warm air moisten my hand, and I can see that his chest is gently rising and falling. I knocked him out, but I haven't killed him. Not yet, anyway.

I need to call the emergency services, but what am I going to say? It was self-defence, wasn't it?

And then I hear something. The sound of a key in a lock, the opening of a door. A female voice. I jump backwards, away from Finn's body, just as the footsteps get louder.

'Hey!'

I swivel around to see Ellie standing in the kitchen doorway, her jacket half unzipped. Her eyes widen.

'What the hell?' She rushes forwards and bends down to Finn. 'What's happened?' she snaps at me. 'Have you called an ambulance?' She's got more first aid skills than me, because she gently manoeuvres Finn into the recovery position.

My voice sounds raw and croaky. 'Finn killed Phyllis.'

Ellie glances up at me, a frown on her face. 'What?'

'He killed Phyllis, and I can prove it. We need to call the police.'

Ellie stands up. She's gone very pale, the whites of her eyes shining, her mouth slightly open. She cocks her head to one side. 'What?'

It's as if she can't compute what I'm saying, and it panics me. 'We need to call the police. If he wakes up, we both might be in danger. In fact, we will. He grabbed me, wouldn't let go of my wrist, and I know he was the last person to see Phyllis alive.' I'm gabbling now, but the sheer panic of this situation is in danger of making me incoherent.

'One step at a time. You need to calm down, Laila. You look awful. Are you going to pass out?' She drags a chair away from the table. 'Sit down and take a deep breath. It's bad for your baby to be this uptight.' She's probably right. Adrenaline is rushing through me in massive waves, and I can't think straight.

'I need my phone,' I say, fumbling in my pockets and not finding it. 'It's in my bag.'

'Sit down.' Ellie is forceful now. 'I'll get your phone.'

I step over Finn and sit on the chair Ellie pulled out.

'Where's your phone?'

'In my handbag. I left it by the front door.' Why did I do that? I should have brought my phone into the kitchen with me, had it stuffed into my pocket.

She bends down to check on Finn, and I can see that her head is shaking slightly on her neck. It's no surprise. Perhaps she thinks I might come after her as well. 'Alright,' Ellie says. 'Finn's unconscious but breathing normally, and his heart rate is okay. I'm going to call the emergency services and take Melanie to her room. She's asleep in the buggy in the hallway. You need to stay here. I can't do with two sick people.'

God. How can she be so calm? Finn is unconscious on the floor, I'm hysterical, and she's completely holding it all together. It strikes me that she must be a very good childminder. She strides out of the kitchen and shouts to me from the hall, 'I'll call the emergency services.'

I hear her on the phone. 'Police and ambulance. It's urgent. Yes, 43 Violet Lane. Finn Walker. No, he's unconscious, but yes, he's breathing. I'm not sure what happened. I think he hit his head. He's dangerous. Yes, you need to come quickly.'

I hear fumbling, but my eyes are still on Finn, who is motionless. Ellie walks back into the room, holding Melanie's car seat. The infant is fast asleep, thank goodness.

'I'm going to boil the kettle to make you a cup of tea, and whilst it's boiling, I'll put Melanie in her cot upstairs. You stay sitting in that chair. I don't want you fainting on me.'

'But what if Finn wakes up?' I ask; my voice is shrill.

Ellie looks down at him, a strange gaze on her face, as if she's examining a specimen in a jar. I suppose knowing he's a murderer fundamentally changes how she feels about him. 'He's unconscious. He's not going anywhere. I know what I'm talking about. I've done several advanced first aid courses. We're safe for the next few minutes, at least until the police get here,' she reassures me.

I'm trembling from head to toe. How did he manufacture his alibi? I wonder. Is the North Wales client actually a friend, or did he pay him off? And why did he kill Phyllis?

Ellie is back quickly. 'You okay?' she asks, with her back to me as she takes a mug from the cupboard. I hear her pour boiling water into a mug. 'I'm giving you milk and sugar,' she says. 'You need it. I'll add some cold water to the boiling water from the kettle so you can get this inside you quickly. The sugar will calm your nerves.'

I'm in awe that she's so poised, but grateful at the same time. She hands me the mug of hot tea and then bends over Finn again. I take a sip. It's the perfect temperature, and she's right. I do need this. Ellie sits back on her haunches.

'Not much we can do until the ambulance arrives,' she says.

We wait in silence for long minutes. I sip at my tea, grateful for the warmth. 'How long do you think it'll take for them to come?' I ask, glancing at my watch. But weirdly the hands on the face of my watch seem to swim slightly, and I can't focus. I squeeze my eyes together and try to look again. Have I got dangerously high blood pressure from the shock?

Another couple of minutes pass, and the room seems to spin and tilt. I'm feeling increasingly disoriented and dizzy. Sleepy too. And then I manage to focus on Ellie, and she's looking at me with such a strange expression.

Suddenly it hits me. She's put something in my tea. Ellie has drugged me. What about my baby? She knows that I'm pregnant. Will this drug harm my unborn child? Is that what Ellie wants? My phone. I need to find my phone. Except it's not here. It's still in my handbag in the hall. I try to stand up, but the dizziness is too great, and I sink back onto the chair.

'What have you done?' I ask as her face morphs in and out of focus.

'What I had to do,' she replies curtly.

'I don't understand,' I say. I grip the edge of the table, trying to hold on to reality, to concentrate on staying alert.

'You're just a meddler. Of course you don't understand. Finn and I are meant to be together, and Melanie loves me as if I'm her mother. In fact, I am her mother now, and frankly, I'm better at it than Jackie was even before. Things were bad between Finn and Jackie for ages, so it's no surprise that Finn turned to me. There was Jackie, nag, nag, nagging; bickering all the time; complaining about everything. Finn and I fell into each other's arms. It was meant to be.

'And then Jackie, the little slut she was, had an affair with Max Critchley. I honestly thought that was the answer to my prayers. She could go off with Max, and I could have Finn. It would be happy ever after. Except no, she changed her mind, didn't she? All remorseful she was, running back to Finn and asking if they could give their marriage another go. I bet she got pregnant on purpose, to force Finn to go back to her. He dropped me like a hot brick, the bastard. I couldn't have that. Finn and Jackie were never good together, and I knew that she'd hurt Finn over and over again. I got rid of Jackie for him.'

What? Did Ellie just admit to killing Jackie? I'm finding it increasingly hard to concentrate, and all I can think about is how will I protect my unborn child? But my mind is fuzzy. It's as if clouds are coating my brain, pulling me away from reality. I dig my fingernails deep into the palms of my hands, eager to feel something, even if it's pain. If I let myself disappear into this fog, I know that I'm going to be next. That Ellie will kill me too.

'What about Phyllis?' I ask. For a moment I wonder if I actually spoke, whether that was just a thought. Except then Ellie lets out a huffing noise.

'She was a nosey old cow who realised that Finn and I were together. She started asking questions. So many questions. Finn tried to get her not to talk, not to say anything to the police, except Finn is weak. It's up to me to take action, and I knew I had to do something. Bye-bye, Phyllis. She's no great loss anyway.'

'And Max?' I manage to say. I have to concentrate on my breathing, to stop the dizziness and exhaustion from pulling me into unconsciousness. I count my breaths. One. Two. Three.

'We got lucky with your creepy Max. He was the perfect scapegoat. All I had to do was send him an anonymous tip-off to say that Phyllis was having a heart attack, and I knew he'd rush over to help. He was found with her blood all over him, exactly as I'd hoped. He even left his prints on the knife. Hilarious, really. I couldn't have planned it better.'

'And me?' I murmur. 'The fire?' It's so hard to articulate words.

Ellie laughs. She actually laughs. 'I tried to warn you off. I didn't want you to come to any harm, but you needed to keep your nose out of things. Except you didn't, did you? And now you're going to pay the ultimate price.' Her face is really close to mine, and it swims in and out of focus. 'No police are coming. You're going to die too.' This woman is pure evil, and I cannot let her kill my baby.

'No.'

We're both startled. There's movement on the floor, and Finn is hauling himself up into a sitting position. He turns to stare at Ellie. 'I can't believe you killed my beautiful Jackie and Phyllis! For what, Ellie? You disgust me!'

She's crouching down next to him now. 'Oh, babe! I did it for us, so we can be together. The three of us. You, me and Melanie. You know that's what you want.'

'What are you talking about?' Finn cries. 'I never wanted to be with you. It was a mistake. I love Jackie. I've always loved her.' Finn is standing up now, but Ellie is quicker than him, and she swipes him around the face with the back of her hand. Finn wobbles but rights himself, and then they're fighting. Physically fighting. Blows being thrown in every direction, and they move out of the kitchen and into the hallway.

I know that this is my chance. My only chance, quite probably. I haul myself up, the room spinning as I do so. My knees feel so weak, as if my legs can't support my weight. I grab the edge of the oak worktop and slide my hands along it until I reach the sink. And then I do what I've never done before and stick my finger deep inside my throat until I gag. I force myself to retch into the sink, and I throw up once, then twice. Switching on the tap, I drink cold water and immediately feel a bit better. But what now?

I can hear grunts and cracking and thumps coming from the hall, and then the terrifying sound of a man screaming. And I realise that I have to save not only myself, but Finn too. I grab the saucepan that I used to knock out Finn and tiptoe out of the kitchen into the hall.

Ellie has her back to me. Blood is pouring from Finn's face. I'm sure under normal circumstances he would be able to overpower Ellie, but he's only just regained consciousness from when I hit him, and now he seems like the weaker of the two. I don't think. I slam the saucepan down on Ellie's head as hard as I possibly can. She stumbles forwards, catching the side of her head on Melanie's empty pram. I bring down the pan again, slamming it into her head.

'Enough!' Finn says as I lift the pan back into the air for the third or perhaps fourth time. 'Enough, Laila. It's over.'

Finn's voice is muffled, and his face is a bloodied mess.

'Have I killed her?' I ask.

He's crouching down next to her. 'No, I don't think so. But I'm going to tie her up just in case. Call the police and ambulance.'

I find my bag on the floor in the hallway and rifle around for my phone. But it's gone. Ellie must have removed it and hidden it somewhere to stop me from calling the emergency services. It takes me a long minute of searching before I see the phone. It's half protruding from the back pocket of her jeans. Carefully, I extract it and call 999.

'I'll get a tea towel to clean up your face,' I say as Finn lowers himself to sit on the bottom step of the stairs.

'No, don't. I want the police to see what she did to me.'

I nod and sit myself down next to him.

'She's delusional,' he says. 'Completely crazy. I honestly thought she loved Jackie as much as I did. God, Laila. How can we get things so wrong? I'm so sorry that you were caught up in this nightmare. Max too. I was convinced it was Max's doing.'

'It's okay,' I say, squeezing his hand. He winces.

And then we hear the distant sound of sirens.

CHAPTER TWENTY-SEVEN

It's all over the news. Ellie has been charged with the murders of Jackie and Phyllis, along with grievous bodily harm towards me and Finn, and arson, for attempting to set my house on fire. Unsurprisingly, she hasn't been granted bail, and the thinking is she'll be in prison for the rest of her life. The papers have branded her evil, but the shock waves will take a long time to dissipate in South Gridgley. After all, numerous local families entrusted their infants to her. The general consensus is that she didn't harm any babies or children; she just saved her evil to murder adults.

Of course, this means that Max is innocent. He was released from prison this morning and sent me a long message, asking to meet up tonight. I owe him a huge apology for even considering that he might be capable of murder, but on the other hand, he has lied to me. I know we need to be honest with each other, but I'm nervous about telling him that I'm pregnant. In fact, I'm generally filled with trepidation about seeing him.

I LEAVE WORK EARLY, buy some flowers and prepare a roast chicken, laying the table and lighting a candle.

The doorbell rings at 7 p.m., and Max is standing there, freshly shaven and looking like the old Max. A little thinner maybe, and with dark rings under his eyes, but he's a different man to the one I last saw in prison.

'Hello.' He smiles broadly. He hands me a bouquet of flowers in multiple shades of violet and blue. We both talk at the same time and laugh uneasily.

'Come in,' I say, and he leans down to give me a kiss, except I find myself turning my face so that his lips land on my cheek. I wasn't expecting this tension between us, as if we're both tiptoeing around, not quite sure where we stand. I suppose I thought he'd be flinging his arms around me and I'd be the one keeping him at arm's length.

Max follows me into the kitchen. 'Beer or wine?' I ask.

'A beer would be great. How have you been?'

'It's been a tough time, but worse for you,' I say. My hand trembles slightly as I pass him a glass and a can of beer.

'I've missed you, Laila,' he says, but his words lack the confidence that I previously associated with him. 'I wasn't sure where we stood. Whether you still want–' He lets his words peter out, and he gestures between me and him. He sighs. 'I'd really like to pick up where we left off, but I completely understand if you don't want to.'

I'm still for a moment. I've missed Max terribly, the way our bodies fit together, how secure I feel in his arms, how my insides burn with desire when I'm around him.

'We have to talk,' I say, bending down to get the chicken out of the oven. 'The food is ready. Take a seat.'

WE'RE at the kitchen table, about to start the meal, and Max is gazing at me. 'You know, being banged up for a crime I didn't commit made me really consider the important things in life. I want to be with you, Laila. I want to marry you, and I don't want to wait. Do you feel the same way?'

In some respects, this is what I want to hear, except a warning sounds in my head. Was it the sentiment or the way he phrased it? He just said it's what *I* want. He didn't mention me. And what about the untruths he's told me? Besides, do I really want to commit to marriage all over again?

'There's stuff we need to talk about,' I say. My mouth feels parched, and I take a large sip of water. 'You've been lying to me. Who's the woman you've been visiting in Hove when you said you were seeing your mother?'

Max looks startled. 'How do you know?'

'It doesn't matter. Just tell me the truth.'

He lays his hands on the table. 'She's my therapist.'

'Your therapist?' I ask. Now it's my turn to be surprised. 'And the little boy?'

'Little boy? I don't know any little boy. My therapist has two children, I think. A girl and a boy.'

Could I have got this so wrong? That little child who I thought looked like a mini-Max, is he in fact a stranger to Max? And is the dark-hair, blue-eye thing simply a coincidence? Perhaps he chose that therapist because on some deep subconscious level, he finds her attractive.

'Why are you seeing a therapist?' I ask.

He sighs loudly and places his cutlery on his plate. 'Being a paramedic is physically and emotionally demanding. About three years ago, I was lifting someone, and I did something to my back. The doctors couldn't work out what was going on, but I was prescribed strong painkillers. My back cleared up, at least I think it did, but I got addicted to the drugs. They took the edge off all the pain associated with my work.'

He snorts. 'You'd think I should know better. And then there was a horrible road traffic accident two years ago. I was meant to save the young woman except I wasn't as sharp as I should have been because of the Oxy. She died. She shouldn't have died, and it was my fault.'

'How awful,' I mutter, wondering if that was the accident where Max had to give evidence at the inquiry.

'The thing is, I covered it up, botched a bit of paperwork, pretended that it wasn't my fault. I wasn't fired for it because no one knew the truth. I even managed to keep it all from my paramedic partner, but it got to me. I felt terrible about it, so I quit work. I realised I was in deep, so I took myself to rehab. Then I got the new job in Sussex and moved down here. But once an addict, always an addict, and I couldn't afford to screw up like that again. I'm responsible for people's lives. So I go to private therapy every week.' There's a long pause. 'I didn't want to tell you.'

'Oh,' I say, because I'm dumbfounded. I was not expecting an answer like this. 'And your mother?'

'I see Mum regularly. She's in a care home, but she has dementia, and most of the time she doesn't recognise me. There's little point in me introducing her to you. To be honest, she gets very anxious around new people.' He leans forwards and places a hand over mine. 'I'm sorry for not telling you the truth, but I thought it might scare you off, and I couldn't risk that.'

I suppose it explains his situation at his previous work and why his boss gave him a lukewarm reference.

'But what about Tara? Why wouldn't she talk to me about you?'

He rolls his eyes. 'It was genuinely a bad breakup. She knew I was addicted to painkillers, and she couldn't deal with it. We agreed to part ways. That's that.'

'And Jackie? Did you have a relationship with her?'

Max looks bashful. 'Yes. But it really was a one-night stand. There was no intention from either side for it to be anything more. It was such a shock that I got her pregnant. I genuinely didn't know. Of course I feel dreadful about all of that too. I behaved terribly towards Finn, but I suppose it takes two to tango.'

'You really have a type, don't you?' I look at him deadpan because the type thing doesn't make me feel good. Am I just another one of his dark-haired, blue-eyed conquests?

He shrugs his shoulders. 'I do like women with dark hair and blue eyes, but that doesn't make me a bad person, does it?'

'Of course not,' I say, because many people have preferred types.

'And you're by far the most beautiful of all the dark-haired, blue-eyed women in the world,' he says a little too earnestly.

That's rubbish, of course, but I'm not going to fish for further compliments.

'What about the DNA that the police found on the handkerchief in Jackie's coat?'

Max reddens. It's obvious that he doesn't want to tell me, but I need complete transparency if we're going to move forwards together. 'We were drunk, it was a one-off, as I said, and it should never have happened.' He puts his hand in front of his eyes. 'The condom broke, and I put it in the handkerchief.'

Gross, I think to myself. 'You've got form with broken condoms, haven't you?'

Max winces. 'I wonder if it was a dud pack.'

We're both silent for a while, and I start eating my chicken supper, which is getting cold. I know I need to tell him, yet something is making me hold back. But then Max frowns at me. 'Why aren't you drinking?'

'I'm, um...'

'Are you sick?' He looks really concerned.

'No, nothing like that.' I pause before saying, 'I'm pregnant.'

Max's mouth falls open, and his eyes flicker over my face as if he's searching for the right thing to say. I put him out of his misery.

'Yes, it's yours.' I'm tempted to make some sarcastic retort about being faithful and not sleeping around, but I manage to hold my tongue. I can't work out why I'm not feeling as ecstatic as Max evidently is. Despite everything he's told me, all of the explanations and how I've obviously jumped to erroneous conclusions, there's still a niggle at the back of my head.

The air is completely still. 'And are you happy about us having a baby together?' he asks.

'Yes, I think I am.' I smile.

'Me too,' he says, grinning broadly. 'In fact, it's the best news ever. Can I be involved? Can we be together?'

I nod, because I do want this baby to have a father, and despite everything, I feel something strongly for Max. Whether it's love at this time, probably not, but perhaps it will grow into love.

We smile at each other, and the next thing I know, Max has jumped up from his chair, and he's lifting me up and swinging me around the kitchen.

'Careful!' I yell, half laughing.

He puts me down and flings his arms around me. 'I am the happiest man in the world. I can't believe it! This really might be the best day of my life.' He moves to kiss me, but I push my hands against his chest.

'The food will get cold,' I say, peeling myself away from him and sitting back down. He stills for a second.

'I know I said there's no point in you meeting Mum, but this changes everything. I've got to tell her that she's going to be a grandmother, even if she doesn't understand. Shall we go to the care home now?'

'No, Max. I'm really tired. Another time.'

'Of course. I'm just overexcited.' He's like a bouncing puppy, and it's rather cute.

As we're clearing up the plates from supper, Max begins pawing me again, kissing my neck, hands tugging at the top of my tight waistband, and I'm just not feeling it. Is it because I'm tired, or is it because I've got the ick? Have I actually gone off Max? I can't stop thinking about him having vigorous sex with Jackie, and I wonder if he pushed down too hard on her throat too. Is this man too much for me, with his vigorous sexual appetite?

'I really need to sleep tonight, Max. I'm exhausted, and I've had a couple of scares with the pregnancy. My doctor and midwife have told me I need to take it easy and not have any stress. Would you mind if we take a rain check?'

Max's face tightens for a moment, and if I didn't know him better, I would find it hard to differentiate between anger and disappointment. But after swallowing hard, he softens and gently cups my cheek with his hand. 'Of course, darling. We need to do what's best for baby. Perhaps we can meet up tomorrow night?'

LATER ON, I lie in bed, ruminating over everything Max has told me. It all makes sense, yet I can't banish that frustrating worry, unable to pinpoint what it is that's niggling me. Is it because Max is prone to love-bombing? Or is it because he talks about how he feels, how we need to look after the baby, but never actually asks about me? Or am I overthinking things? Despite the late hour, I send Jazmin a message.

> Can we talk when you have a mo?

A second later, my phone rings. 'Yves is snoring next to me.' Jazmin speaks in a lower whisper. 'And I'm not even slightly sleepy. What's up?'

'I told Max about being pregnant, and he's cleared up a lot of things that I was worried about. I definitely jumped to conclusions when I shouldn't have done. Except I'm just not feeling it as I used to.'

'Hardly surprising. You thought the father of your unborn child was a murderer. That's a lot to step back from. Take it slowly, Laila. You don't need to jump back into bed with him. I mean, you haven't, have you?'

I chortle. 'No. I didn't feel like it.'

'Do you still fancy him?'

'Yes, absolutely,' I say almost too quickly.

'Then dial things back. Start the friendship all over again and just feel your way. And remember, just because he's the father doesn't mean you owe him anything. You should only be in a relationship with him if that's what you really want.'

'You're right,' I say. 'What would I do without you?'

'Ha ha. You know I'm always here for you.'

'And me for you,' I say. 'Feeling tired now?'

'Exhausted. Sleep tight.'

I feel a sense of ease as I lie back down on my soft pillow. Jazmin is right. Max and I need to feel our way gently. We had such a passionate affair, and then so much happened to undermine my trust. This time around, I want to get to know him better, to take my time.

CHAPTER TWENTY-EIGHT

A YEAR LATER

It's a beautiful day, and just as well, because today Max is moving into my house. He's roped in two of his paramedic mates to help him carry over the boxes and the limited furniture that we're incorporating into my house. He's rented out his house fully furnished, and the tenants arrive next week. It's going to be weird having strangers living next door.

The extension at the back of my living room is finally finished, and this morning, the specialist piano removals team dismantled his piano and carried it into my house. It took four men to manoeuvre it into place, but I have to say it looks lovely in its new home. The extension is bright, with plenty of glass set into the oak frame, and I can't wait to listen to Max playing the piano every evening.

Bea's face lights up when she hears her daddy play. He's been teaching me to play as well, and I'm grappling with some of Bea's favourite nursery rhymes. Max gets impatient with me, and considering how caring he is as a paramedic, teaching is not his forte. We laugh about it though.

Bea was born six months ago, and we got married a

month after her birth. It was a quiet affair, in the local registry office, followed by a reception at the local hotel for forty of our family and friends. It didn't seem right to have a big white wedding, especially because it's my second time around.

I vacillated for a long time as to whether to commit to Max or not, but he really was relentless in pursuing me. In the end I had to tell him to stop suffocating me; otherwise I'd walk away from him forever. It's strange how he didn't comprehend the boundaries. But ultimately, we love each other, and we have a child together. Bea needs a father, and I'm happy.

Our relationship has changed, and that overwhelming sexual passion has faded. Probably just as well, as Max's desire for vigorous sex was incompatible with late pregnancy and post Bea's birth. He seems fine about it, and we've settled into a steady, more gentle relationship. In a way, I'm almost relieved that there's less passion, and as Jazmin says, it's to be expected. I suppose because I never had any great passion with Jacob, I didn't know what I was missing. Perhaps we'll rekindle it when Bea is a little older and sleeping through the night.

'Okay, we're done,' Max says, wiping his hands on his jeans. 'I'm officially in.'

'Welcome to number 30!' I say, standing on tiptoes and kissing Max on the lips. 'Fancy a drink?'

'I sure do. I'm completely knackered.' Max has worked night shifts the last couple of nights and now has spent the day moving boxes and furniture. It's not surprising he's exhausted.

'Put your legs up in the living room, and I'll come and join you.'

A few moments later, I'm back with two glasses and a bottle of wine. Bea is lying on her play mat, gurgling contentedly as she bashes the little soft toy animals that hang above her head. Max is stretched out on the sofa, and he's switched the television on with the sound turned down quite low.

'Welcome to your new home,' I say. We clink our glasses together.

'Perhaps we should be having a welcome drinks like Phyllis did for you?' he suggests.

I pause for a moment, remembering our neighbour, recalling that initial barbecue, which feels like such a long time ago but really wasn't. Her house has been sold, and new owners are expected to move in shortly. I wonder what type of person is prepared to live in a house where a murder took place.

Finn is still living on Violet Lane, but his mum has moved in with them, and she's little Melanie's main carer. Poor Finn looks permanently exhausted, and I worry about him. He's away from home a lot, building bespoke garden rooms up and down the country. I think he does well financially from it, but I'm not sure he's allowed himself time to grieve.

And then there's the trial. It's crazy how long it's taking for Ellie's case to reach the courts, but the justice system is almost at breaking point. Incredibly she's pleading not guilty, so we're going to have to face a trial sometime in the next year. If Max and I are dreading it, I can't bear to think how much it must be weighing on Finn's mind.

I'm looking at the television, almost mindlessly, luxuriating in my family and my contentment. The presenter is talking about an attempted rape of a young woman in a park in Hove. It's the second in as many months, and people are getting scared. Max switches the TV off, and I'm glad. I want to enjoy living in my little rose-coloured bubble. I yawn.

'I'm going to unpack those two boxes,' Max says, pointing at a couple of boxes piled up by the door. He climbs off the sofa and slices through the tape on the box with a pair of scissors. 'It's just some books and piano music,' he says.

'Don't you want to play your piano?' I ask. 'Test out the acoustics in its new home.'

'Nope. It needs to settle first, and I'll have to get it tuned in the next week or so. Pianos don't like to be disturbed.' He's bent down and has a pile of books in his arms. 'Can I put my stuff on the bookshelf?'

'Of course you can,' I say. I've spent the last few days going through each room, clearing out belongings I no longer need, and making space for Max to put his things.

My stomach growls. 'Do you mind if we get a takeaway tonight?' I ask. I've become lazy about cooking, and that's the advantage of living in a small town. Everything is on our doorstep.

'I'll finish this box, and then I'll go and get us some food. Fish and chips or Chinese?' he asks.

'Chinese, please.'

When Max has gone out, I roll off the sofa and walk over to the bookshelf. He's placed a photograph of his mother on the left of the shelf. She was a beautiful woman in her youth, and my finger outlines her dark hair and azure eyes. She was so young in this photo, and now there's barely any life left in her. A wave of sadness passes through me, particularly that I never got to know her before the dementia set in. I've visited her a few times with Max, and she just stares at me blankly.

Bea starts grumbling. I check that she doesn't need a

nappy change, and she isn't due for a feed for a while, so I decide to play one of the nursery rhymes on the piano that Max tried to teach me. I lift up the lid to the keyboard and attempt to play 'Twinkle, Twinkle, Little Star'. But there's a weird rattle, as if something has come loose on the inside of the piano. I hope that the removal guys haven't caused any damage.

I lift the main lid up, as I've seen Max do on so many occasions, but I'm not sure what I'm looking for. The strings stretch over the large wooden frame, and I see a sticker marked with the words Bluthner and its serial number. Assuming that I'll have to wait for Max to check it out, I start playing again, but this time, with the lid up, it sounds more like something flapping than a rattle.

Bending down so I can see better under the strings, the light catches on what looks like paper, but paper in the same colour as the wood. I walk to the far end of the piano and hook my fingers underneath the strings. As I swipe them underneath, I realise that it's an envelope that has become dislodged, an A5 pale brown envelope. I wonder how that got inside the instrument, and I think of a news story I heard years ago, about a man finding some highly valuable coins stashed in an ancient piano. Perhaps I've discovered something old and precious.

I find a ruler, and pushing the envelope to one side, I manage to ease it out. It doesn't look old though. The envelope is lightly sealed, so I open it up and tip out the contents onto the sofa.

It takes me a few long moments to realise what I'm looking at. There are several newspaper clippings, and at the top of each is a lock of black hair that has been sellotaped to the paper. A sickening sensation clenches my stomach.

Every article is about the same topic. The victims of rape. The victims of rape in the south of England. Most of the clippings don't show photographs of the women, except there's one at the back. A woman commended for her bravery who came forwards and explained how she was raped. The lock of shiny black hair is attached to the photo of her head.

It's as if my brain has stopped working. I know what I'm looking at, but I can't process it. I shake the envelope onto the sofa again, and yet another lock of hair falls out, but this one isn't attached to any press cutting.

A terrible sense of dread settles on me.

What has Max done?

Is there any good reason for him to have these clippings and locks of hair, and why have they been hidden in an envelope in the piano? And then I think of the news report just half an hour ago about a woman in Hove who was nearly raped last night.

I let out a screech. Bea looks at me with startled eyes.

Where was Max last night? He said he was on a night shift.

My stomach clenches and heaves. I race to the kitchen, making it to the sink just in time before I throw up.

CHAPTER TWENTY-NINE

After rinsing away the contents of my stomach down the drain of the sink, I hurry back into the living room, where Bea is crying. It's as if she's sensed that our world has just collapsed. My darling little girl. I sweep her into my arms and rub her back, but I'm sure she can feel my trembling. I am literally shaking from head to toe.

With Bea in one arm, I grab my mobile phone and with shaking fingers find Saffron's number, Max's lovely paramedic friend who used to have blue hair but recently dyed it pink. She attended our wedding and has become a good friend. Saffron answers on the second ring.

'Hiya, Laila. How's married life?'

'Yes, great,' I say hurriedly. 'Just wanted to check something. Max has lost his debit card. Could it have fallen out into the ambulance last night?'

'Last night? Max didn't work last night. I thought he said he was taking twenty-four hours off to focus on the move. Did I get that wrong?'

'Oh, silly me,' I say as tears prick my eyes. 'I've clearly got the wrong end of the stick. Sorry for bothering you.' I hang up, cutting Saffron off mid-sentence.

AND THEN I hear a key in the front door, and I let out a little whimper.

'Hi, darling. I'm back. I'll put the food on the table,' Max shouts.

I stare at Bea, as if my little baby can tell me what to do. And then my eyes fall on the brown envelope and the newspaper articles and locks of hair lying on the sofa. I place Bea on the floor and shove everything back into the envelope, swallowing bile as I do so. Bea starts wailing, and I haven't got time to slide the envelope back under the piano strings, to hide it so that it's no longer obvious.

'Shush,' I say, knowing that my begging our baby to be silent will have no effect. There's an open box on the floor marked Piano Music. I grab the envelope, barely able to bring myself to touch it, and holding it gingerly between two fingers, shove it down the side of the box.

I don't hear Max walk into the room. 'Hey!' he says, creeping up behind me and making me jump. 'How are my two girls? Hungry?'

He steps away, glances at the piano and frowns. 'You've been playing?'

'I hope you don't mind, but Bea has been really grizzly, haven't you, sweetheart?' I bend down and tickle her tummy. She stops crying instantly, and she beams at her daddy. Her rapist daddy. 'Playing your piano very badly settled her down.'

I need to get out of here. It's as if that envelope is taunting me, and the contents are making my stomach roil again. 'Let's eat,' I say, even though it's the very last thing in the world that I feel like doing.

'Shall I take Bea?' Max asks.

Normally I wouldn't hesitate to hand her over to him, but now. Now, I don't want Max anywhere near my daughter. I wish he were on the other side of the world or locked up in jail for life. Except I know I'm going to have to conceal my true thoughts.

'Laila?' he asks again. His arms are extended, his fingers stretched out. Those fingers that have touched me all over and done other truly disgusting things. I have to repress a shiver.

'Sorry, miles away.' Reluctantly I hand him Bea, who continues to smile and gurgle at him. He won't do her any harm, not with me around. Besides, the women in that folder... No, I can't think about them. I just can't.

I follow Max and Bea into my kitchen, and already it no longer feels like my home. The place is tainted just having Max in it. What the hell am I going to do?

'Are you alright?' he asks as he slips Bea into her high chair. He's already spooned much of the contents of the containers onto serving dishes and has laid the table. He must have bought a bouquet of flowers because he's placed them in a ceramic jug on the table and has lit two candles. Pale blues, mauves and violets, his favourites. Under any other circumstances, it would be a lovely gesture. 'You look really pale,' he says. That's the trouble with Max. He's always too observant, overly loving.

'I'm feeling a bit under the weather all of a sudden,' I say.

'Oh.' Max looks crestfallen, and I realise that he wanted tonight, the first night that we are officially living together, to be perfect. Except now, everything is ruined.

I need to buy myself some time to think. 'You start eating,' I say. 'And I'll put Bea to bed. It's only a few minutes early, and she's probably overtired anyway.'

'If you're sure,' Max replies, giving me one of his dazzling smiles. 'I'll keep some food warming in the oven for you in case you change your mind later.'

I hurry out of the kitchen, Bea in my arms. I desperately need to get Bea and me away from the house, away from him. But how am I going to do that? I could try to sneak out in the middle of the night, but what if he follows me and realises I've discovered his despicable truth? If he becomes suspicious, I might not only be putting myself in danger but Bea too.

Perhaps I could creep up on him and knock him out the way I did with Finn and Ellie, but that is so risky. And with Bea in the house. What if he overpowers me and realises what I know? Even worse, he might kill me, and then Bea would be left motherless and would have to grow up with him as her only parent. What the hell am I going to do?

And then I have an idea. A horrific, mind-numbing, terrifying idea. It's so truly horrendous I don't know if I'll be able to pull it off, but it's likely my only chance.

BEA CAN DEFINITELY SENSE that something is wrong, as my normally excellent little sleeper takes what seems forever to settle. It gives me time to formulate my plan even though it's hard to think straight when I'm almost paralysed with fear. If Max finds out that I know his disgusting secret, what will he do to me? Will he rape me like he raped all of those women, or will he kill me? How could he possibly let me live? Surely he knows that I would go straight to the police. And if he kills me, what will happen to our little girl? I can't bear to think about that. Or does he think by marrying me, he'll have his very own legal counsel, and that somehow I'll protect him? I have to focus on the monster that I've married; I have to catch him out in such a way that there will be no repercussions towards me or Bea. It's not just my life that is in danger.

I pull open my wardrobe door. Max has already hung up his clothes, and I push them away from mine so they're not touching. Then I rifle through my clothes until I find the white lacy basque with suspenders that I wore underneath my simple cream sheath wedding dress. I remember how when we got back to our hotel room and Max slipped the dress off my shoulders, he gasped as he stared at me in the figure-hugging, sexy underwear. It might be a little too big for me now, as I wore it not long after giving birth, but I have to make it work. It's all I've got. I tug it on and tie it up as tightly as I can. I don't have time to study myself in the mirror, so I swipe on some bright red lipstick and put a silken gown over the top.

Before returning downstairs, I check on Bea. She's fast asleep, her limbs stretched out, a little smile playing on her rosebud lips. My beautiful baby. I shut her bedroom door. I know it's ridiculous, but I don't want her to hear what's going to happen, for however tonight plays out to somehow be seared into her subconsciousness.

My heart feels like it's going to hammer out of my chest as I walk downstairs, tottering ridiculously in a pair of stilettos. Max is still in the kitchen, and he has the television on, listening to the news again.

I push open the door. He looks up at me, and his jaw

drops open. 'Oh. My. God,' he drawls. 'You look absolutely stunning.'

I am going to have to put on the performance of my life. I force my lips to curl upwards, and I stick one leg in front of the other, letting the silk dressing gown fall apart and slip slightly off my shoulders. Am I looking sexy or ridiculous? Frankly, I feel like a whore.

'I thought we should christen our new home. What do you reckon?' I flutter my eyelids at him. 'Bea's fast asleep, and we have all the time in the world.'

'What do I think?' He jumps up from the table, spilling some rice, but he ignores that and paces towards me so quickly, it's like he's in a sprint. He wraps his arms around me and pulls me to his hard body, his lips on mine. How the hell am I going to do this? Gently, I lean backwards and push my hands on his chest.

'Upstairs,' I say, holding out a hand. Can I do this? No, it's not a matter of can I. I have to. There is no choice. This is life or death. I walk quickly, trying to keep upright in these heels, running on tiptoes up the stairs, Max taking the steps two at a time behind me. I career into the bedroom, and he's right there with me.

'Shut the door,' I say. For a horrible moment I think I've left the baby intercom downstairs, but no. It's on my bedside table. 'Hold fire,' I say. I have to switch it on.

Max seems desperate to get his hands on me, but I must take things slowly.

'We're going to do it my way,' I announce with a confidence I absolutely don't feel. 'My house, my rules. And as of tomorrow, our house. Our rules.' I make a silent prayer. There will not be an 'our'.

'Sit on the side of the bed,' I instruct him. Fortunately

Max does as I instruct, but I can see he's salivating, his trousers tenting with desire. Slowly I walk around the bed until I'm standing about two feet in front of him, just in front of the door. If only the bedroom were bigger.

'Have you unpacked your things?' I ask him. Of course I know he has.

Very slowly, I start undressing. Kicking off one shoe, then another. Letting the dressing gown fall to the carpet in a puddle of silk. Running my fingers from my chin, down my throat and in the crevasse of my breasts. Max lets out a groan.

'You know that box of sex toys,' I say, in as husky a voice as I can manage.

'Yes,' he replies, too quickly, too eagerly.

'Where is it?'

'In a box at the bottom of the wardrobe. Do you want–?'

'Yes, Max. I want.' My voice doesn't sound like mine, more like some porn star. I lick my lips in what I hope is a seductive manner. It feels disgusting.

He's off the bed in an instant, tugging open the wardrobe, down on his knees and rummaging around between the shoes. He pulls out the cardboard box.

'What would you like?' he asks.

'Put it on the bed. I want to take a look.'

I am shocked how the desire on his face, which only hours ago would have had me melting in his arms, now fills me with utter abhorrence. I shuffle to one side as I open the lid. I remove the items I'm looking for and dangle them off my index finger.

'The handcuffs?' he asks.

I nod. He reaches out for them, but I pull them away.

'No. Tonight I'm in control, and you're going to do what I want. I'm going to make love to you.'

His eyes moisten, and his lips fall apart. 'Put the box away,' I instruct him. He places it on the floor near the wardrobe.

'Now take off your clothes.' I force myself to watch, shifting my expression and softening my gaze. It's inconceivable how my feelings have changed in an instant. Yes, he may be well-toned, perfectly proportioned, strikingly good-looking, but my husband repulses me.

Max tears off his clothes, his excitement all too obvious.

'Get on the bed,' I instruct him.

As he climbs onto the bed, I reach behind me and grab a silk scarf from my chest of drawers. 'Lie down on your back.' He does as I tell him, and I walk slowly around to the side of the bed, sitting next to him.

'I'm going to tie this around your eyes,' I say, hoping my voice sounds tantalisingly husky. Max moans. He lifts his head up slightly, and I tie the scarf tightly over his eyes and around his head.

'Easy, tiger,' he says.

'Not too tight?' I ask. I hope it is, but I need to play it gently at first. He shakes his head. 'I'm going to give you a massage.'

He reaches his hands up, trying to feel for my body, but I edge away from him. 'No,' I say. 'You need to let me do all the work.' He relaxes his arms by his sides.

I take a deep breath and force myself to massage his neck and shoulders, letting my fingers dig deeply into his flesh, my fingernails scraping his skin. Then I lean over him and blow onto his neck, and he groans again.

'Hold your hands up above your head,' I instruct him. I

look at the handcuffs and hope that I can get them to work; otherwise my plan will be ruined. How many pairs are there? Four? I slip one over his left wrist and attach the other end to the bedpost; then I do the same with his right wrist. He is so excited now, his hips are bucking upwards.

'We're going to go slow,' I say.

I run my fingers down his chest, letting my nails scrape gently, and then down his stomach, skirting his throbbing erection, and then down the insides of his thighs. He pushes his legs apart exactly as I hoped, and I throw a cuff around his left ankle, attaching it to the bottom of the bed. I do the same with his right ankle.

'God, Laila. I didn't know you had it in you.'

'Shush,' I say. I slide off the bed.

'What are you doing?' he asks.

'No peeking.' I try to laugh, but it sounds distorted to me. Hopefully not to him. I pick up the bag where I shoved the clothes that I was wearing today and tiptoe towards the door.

'I just need to get something from the kitchen,' I say.

He smiles. I wonder what he thinks I'm going to get. A tin of whipped cream perhaps or a bottle of champagne. 'Don't be too long, darling.'

'I won't.'

I grab the intercom and tiptoe out of the room, closing the door behind me as quietly as possible. And then I race into Bea's room, scooping up my little girl, wrapping her in her blanket. I will her to stay silent, to stay asleep. Downstairs, I place her gently into her car seat and make sure she's well wrapped in the blanket. Hurriedly, I pull on my clothes, hiding the hideous underwear. My handbag is on the sideboard near the front door. Putting the strap over my head, I pick up Bea's car seat and open the front door. He may well hear the click of the door when I close it, but I will have to take the risk.

Outside, it's getting dark. I shut the door, my heart hammering in my chest, my breath jagged. I pace to my car and dig in my bag. Except no. The keys aren't there. Terror grips me. What if he realises that I've fled? Can I run away on foot, holding Bea in her car seat?

And then I nearly screech.

'Laila, are you okay?'

'Oh my God,' I say, doubling over when I see Finn. 'No, I'm not okay. Not okay at all. I need to get out of here.'

He doesn't question me. Finn puts his arm around my shoulders, and together we run towards his house. A few seconds later we're inside, and I burst into tears.

'What on earth's going on?' Finn's mum appears, and I can't tell them the truth, not in front of her.

'Please can you keep an eye on Bea for me?' I ask her. 'I've got to call the police. It's an emergency.'

'Of course, love. I'll pop her in Melanie's old crib. It's still in her room. Don't you worry, pet.' She walks heavily as she takes Bea upstairs.

'What's happened?' Finn asks, a look of alarm mirroring my own.

'Can I use your phone?'

When I tell the police that I know who the serial rapist is and that he's tied up in my house, I wonder if they will actually believe me. But when I tell them that I've found newspaper cuttings with locks of black hair attached, suddenly everything becomes serious. Finn looks as if he's going to pass out. The operator tells me to stay on the line whilst she dispatches emergency services, but I lose it and break down into desperate sobs.

CHAPTER THIRTY

A FEW MONTHS LATER

The police found Max in the compromising position I'd left him in. That gives me an iota of comfort. The humiliation of it all. It was never leaked to the press, and in my lowest moments, I considered doing so. But I didn't want to be a hero, I didn't want other women to think I was some avenger, I wanted, and still want, anonymity for Bea and me. I did what I had to do to survive.

The last few months have been terrible. The police went through all of Max's things with a fine-tooth comb. They found the evidence they needed in the box marked Piano Music. He had taken a beautiful old hardback book of sheet music and carved out the centre, using it to store a black balaclava and gloves, along with drugs that he'd stolen from work. Medicine that he used to drug women before raping them.

He's in prison now, awaiting trial. So that's two trials that Finn and I are going to have to deal with. Ellie's first, and Max's sometime next year. Max asked Jacob to be his solicitor, but Jacob refused.

My relationship with my ex is still lousy. He gloats over

my terrible mistakes every time he drops off Ludwig, but at least he refused to represent Max. He and Rose had a baby boy a few months before Bea was born. Despite everything, I hope that they're happy. And as for Ludwig, well, Rose decided that it was too much hard work to have a dog and a baby, so the custody arrangement has been swapped. Ludwig lives with us most of the time and visits the May household on alternate weekends. He and Bea adore each other.

Finn has been an amazing support. It was only a couple of weeks after Max's arrest and we were eating a Sunday roast at his house when DS Kolinsky turned up out of the blue.

'Would you like me to leave?' I asked, pushing my plate to one side.

'No,' Finn said. 'Whatever DS Kolinsky has to tell me, I want you to hear it too.'

'We have had a confession from Max Critchley,' DS Kolinsky said, looking nervously between Finn and me. 'And we have found the evidence to support it. Jackie was not unfaithful with Max; they did not have a fling. I'm sorry to tell you that Max raped Jackie. Sadly, your wife must have been too ashamed to tell anyone the truth.'

Finn wailed, and my heart broke all over again. At least Finn has closure knowing that his wife was faithful to him, knowing that she truly loved him. DS Kolinsky also confirmed what we already knew. That Ellie is a complete fantasist. She claims to have been in love with Finn for years and, in her crazy, sick world, imagined that she, Finn and Melanie might become a family.

Max has begged me to visit him in prison. I get letters from him, reversed calls from the prison, which I reject, and even a letter via his solicitor. He wants me to forgive him, to accept that he has an illness. Except I'm determined never to see him again. I know that I will have to face him in court, but until that day, I want to banish his memory.

TODAY, Finn and I are taking Bea and Melanie to the park. It's our regular Saturday outing, and it's going to be our last.

'I've started therapy,' Finn says.

I think of Max's therapist in Hove. I'd wondered if she really was his therapist and told the police about her, slightly ashamed to admit that I'd followed Max. Of course she wasn't. She was just another dark-haired, blue-eyed woman whom Max was courting. The lies that he spun... She will be one of many witnesses in court, sharing the humiliation of how Max tried to choke her during sex. At least her little boy isn't Max's.

'How's therapy going?' I ask.

'Good. We talked about how I ignored my gut instincts.'

'Me too,' I say. If only I'd listened to my gut. I knew for weeks that something wasn't right about my relationship with Max, but I ignored it. I ignored Jazmin's warnings, and I let physical desire and, most of all, my desperation for a family to blot out the warning signs. The fact that Max love-bombed me, that he spun me so many lies, that he had created a hero persona, all conspired to make me ignore my gut. Occasionally I think of the first time that Ludwig met Max, how he growled at him. Perhaps my darling dog sensed there was something bad about Max. If there's one thing I've learned, it's to listen more to my intuition. And Ludwig's.

'I never really liked Ellie,' Finn admits. 'Jackie had a soft spot for her, and Ellie just wormed her way into our lives, helping out more and more. And then after Jackie died, she was such a good support to me. I ignored my initial feelings towards her and let her infiltrate my life.'

'We were both conned,' I say, nudging him with my elbow. 'But it doesn't mean we're weak or feeble people.'

'You're right, but it makes you question yourself and your own judgement, doesn't it?'

I nod because he's right.

'How do you feel about leaving?' I ask. Finn is moving out of his house tomorrow, and I've just accepted an offer on mine.

It stuns me, but the notoriety Violet Lane gained from all the media coverage attracted buyers. Initially, I assumed the people who wanted to view our houses were voyeurs, eager to see inside Finn's and my lives, but I was proven wrong. Both Finn and I had competing bids on our properties and are selling for more than we bought for. I guess everyone is different, and perhaps some people like living on a street where bad things happened.

Finn is moving to the Scottish Highlands, where he's bought a beautiful stone cottage that he's renovating. His sister lives nearby, and his mum will be moving there too. As for me, I've put an offer on a house in the town where Mum lives. I'm looking for a new job as well, with William Parker's blessing.

'I want you to promise me one thing,' Finn says, looking at me earnestly. 'Don't give up on relationships. The vast, vast majority of men are good. You just happened to be ensnared by a baddie. If you had blonde hair and green eyes, none of this would have happened. And your bravery means that Max will never hurt another woman.'

'I know you're right,' I say, but the thought of dating fills me with horror. 'It's going to take both of us a long time to heal.'

'But we have to, for the sake of our girls,' Finn adds. He's right of course.

He stands up. 'It's time for me to go.' Finn opens his arms, and I step into them. He gives me a big hug, the first time I've been touched since Max. It takes a moment, but I let myself relax in his arms. Finn and I will always have a bond. 'Promise to stay in touch?' he asks as he steps away from me.

I smile. 'I promise.' I lean down and give little Melanie a kiss on her soft cheek.

I watch as he walks away, Finn wearing a brown anorak, his shoulders back as he pushes Melanie in her buggy. I'll miss him. But I'm hopeful for the future. I have Bea, I have Ludwig, I have Mum, I have Jazmin. I know I'll get a good job, and I've got my health. Bea and I will be just fine.

A LETTER FROM MIRANDA

Thank you so much for reading *Violets Are Blue.*

To celebrate writing my 25th psychological thriller with Inkubator Books, I wanted to try something I haven't done before – incorporate some steamy romance! Fortunately for me, my wonderful editor Jan used to write erotic fiction, so I knew I was in safe hands. I hope you didn't find the scenes too gratuitous.

It's been a while since I've written a book based on a romantic relationship and this time I wanted to explore the battle between the head and heart. My first romantic suspense book was *Roses Are Red,* so it seemed apropos to name this one *Violets Are Blue.* Of course the imaginary Violet Lane has rather a romantic ring to it too!

I give my newsletter subscribers and Facebook Group members the opportunity to name characters in my books. Thank you to the following people who suggested names.

Susan L Braverman, Jazmin Copeland, Phyllis Kaplan Fried, Debra Ann Kemmerley Brooks, Christine Myers, Clare Paton, Jill Sutheren, Cheang Wai Kuen. Thank you to Monique Orobona for choosing Ludwig, the dog's name. If I appropriated your name for a baddie, I hope you'll forgive me!

As I've mentioned in my previous books, I am so grateful to the book blogging community and the wonderful bloggers who take the time to review my psychological thrillers, share my cover reveals and talk about my books on social media. A special call out to Mark Jenkins who runs the Facebook Group, *Psychological Thrillers Book Club*.

I couldn't have written this, my 25th psychological thriller, without Inkubator Books. Thank you to Brian Lynch, Garret Ryan, Stephen Ryan, Jan Smith, Alice Latchford, Claire Milto, Elizabeth Bayliss, Shirley Khan and the rest of the team.

Most importantly, thank *you*. If you have a moment to leave a review on Amazon and Goodreads, this helps other people discover my novels and I'd be massively grateful.

If you would like a **FREE** copy of my novella, The Cheat, and the chance to name characters in my future books, please sign up to my newsletter at: **https://bit.ly/The-Cheat-Signup**

You'll also get exclusive access to new releases, giveaways and more!

My warmest wishes,

Miranda

PS – Here's that FREE thriller for you: https://bit.ly/The-Cheat-Signup

www.mirandarijks.com

DISCUSSION QUESTIONS

I have discussion questions available on my website for book clubs. You can find them here:

https://mirandarijks.com/book-club-questions/

Please note that there are SPOILERS in these questions, so if you haven't read the book yet, you might want to avoid reading the questions.

ALSO BY MIRANDA RIJKS

Inkubator Books Titles

Psychological Thrillers

THE VISITORS

THE ARRANGEMENT

THE INFLUENCER

WHAT SHE KNEW

THE ONLY CHILD

THE NEW NEIGHBOUR

THE SECOND WIFE

THE INSOMNIAC

FORGET ME NOT

THE CONCIERGE

THE OTHER MOTHER

THE LODGE

THE HOMEMAKER

MAKE HER PAY

THE GODCHILD

EVERY BREATH YOU TAKE

THE HOUSE SWAP

VIOLETS ARE BLUE

The Dr Pippa Durrant Mystery Series

FATAL FORTUNE

(Book 1)

FATAL FLOWERS

(Book 2)

FATAL FINALE

(Book 3)

FATAL SERIES BOX SET

Titles Published by the Author

GASPS

I WANT YOU GONE

DESERVE TO DIE

YOU ARE MINE

ROSES ARE RED

Printed in Dunstable, United Kingdom

67119774R00160